ALL OF US IN OUR OWN LIVES

ALL OF US IN OUR OWN LIVES

MANJUSHREE THAPA

Published with the generous assistance of the Canada Council for the Arts
and the Alberta Media Fund.

 Canada Council Conseil des Arts
for the Arts   du Canada   Government

Freehand Books
515 – 815 1st Street sw Calgary, Alberta T2P 1N3
www.freehand-books.com

Book orders: LitDistCo
8300 Lawson Road Milton, Ontario L9T 0A4
Telephone: 1-800-591-6250 Fax: 1-800-591-6251
orders@litdistco.ca www.litdistco.ca

Library and Archives Canada Cataloguing in Publication

Thapa, Manjushree, 1968–, author
All of us in our own lives / Manjushree Thapa.

Originally published: India: Aleph, 2016.
Issued in print and electronic formats.
ISBN 978-1-988298-34-4 (softcover).
ISBN 978-1-988298-35-1 (epub).
ISBN 978-1-988298-36-8 (pdf)

I. Title.

PS8639.H38A65 2018   C813'.6   C2018-902944-7   C2018-902945-5

Edited by Naomi K. Lewis
Book design by Natalie Olsen, Kisscut Design
Cover illustration by Sketchbook Designs/shutterstock.com
Author photo by Daniel Lak
Printed on FSC® recycled paper and bound in Canada by Marquis

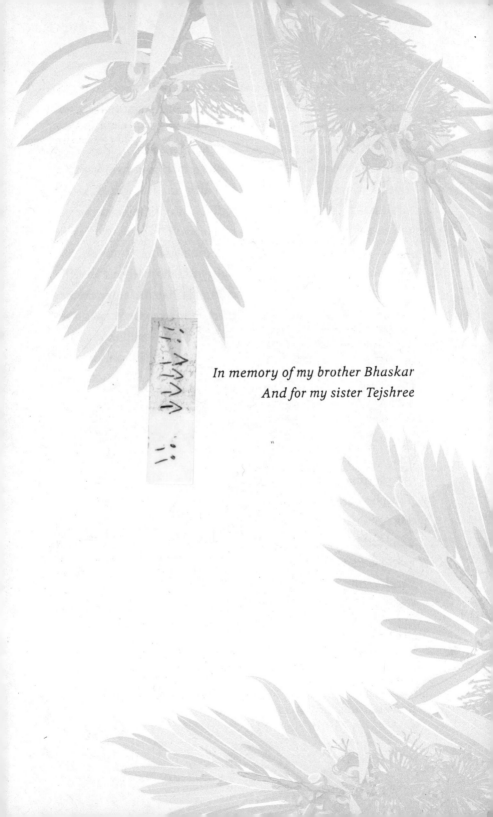

In memory of my brother Bhaskar
And for my sister Tejshree

I am part of a large family. And that's enough for me.

GREAT LAKE SWIMMERS
Ongiara

(What kind of place is this
not unknown to me, my own village
where in the bright light of midday
a whole life has vanished
Do you know where I might find it?)

BIMAL NIBHA
Cycle

But she said, sitting on the bus going up Shaftesbury
Avenue, she felt herself everywhere; not "here, here,
here;" and she tapped the back of the bus; but everywhere. She waved her hand, going up Shaftesbury
Avenue. She was all that. So that to know her, or any one,
one must seek out the people who completed them;
even the places. Odd affinities she had with people
she had never spoken to, some woman in the street,
some man behind a counter — even trees, or barns.

VIRGINIA WOOLF
Mrs. Dalloway

. . . everyone is really responsible to all men for all
men and for everything.

FYODOR DOSTOYEVSKY
The Brothers Karamazov

IF AVA COULD get back those ten lost days, she would swim to the whale rock at every chance, sunbathe on its surface and then plunge into the cool, sparkling water, losing herself in the depths, in the darkness, and staying underwater forever before coming up for a breath. Then she would plunge back down again. She wouldn't waste any time at the cottage talking — or trying to talk — with Gavin. She wouldn't miss a single chance to swim in the lake if she could get those ten days back.

She picked up a folder from her desk, put it down, and picked it up again. In front of her lay a hundred and seventy-one folders, stacked all the way from her attaché case to the crystal pyramid that she had received as a deal toy from her last big file, the Toralan file. Ava needed to locate the documents on some uncollected receivables for her current file, a small one generated from her own contacts. A large paper mill from Detroit was buying out a smaller one in Hamilton. The owner of the mill in Hamilton would retain an ongoing interest, including a seat on the board. Both parties had already signed a letter of intent and a confidentiality agreement.

Why hadn't Cory assigned her to another file? Ava knew she would need to work on much larger ones if she were going to become a partner. She had spent the past eight months under constant stress as the only associate assigned to Toralan from M&A. During that time, unhappiness had settled like a fog in her life, but when the deal had succeeded, the celebration at Harbour Club had been awash in champagne. Then Lester had left the firm, and Cory had become the head of the corporate department, and the fog in Ava's life had only thickened.

Fuck it. She tossed aside the file and stared out the window. At which point, on seeing that you've taken a wrong turn, do you change direction? At which point is it too late? From the forty-fifth floor of Canada Tower, Lake Ontario gleamed like an impossible dream. Lester had stranded her on Bay Street.

Ava had always wanted to go into the non-profit sector. Lester had convinced her to do otherwise: he had recruited her as an articling student, and after law school, he had invited her to join the firm as a junior associate in the corporate department, where he had persuaded her to focus on his own specialty, mergers and acquisitions. "Look, I used to be — I still am — a hippie," he had said in his compelling way, "but nothing has laid bare the framework of human civilization more clearly than the files I've worked on in M&A." For seven years, he had mentored Ava through increasingly complex transactions, taking her to the brink of partnership. And now he had left to provide bench strength to First Nations in their negotiations with the Crown, doing exactly the kind of work that Ava had once longed for. At his farewell dinner, he had said, "I believe that in our lifetime the First Nations are going to redefine what it means to be Canadian. We're innovating an entirely new configuration for citizenship and statehood. I'm tremendously hopeful. Miigwech and mahsi cho."

Get back to work, Ava told herself. Instead, she got up and went out to the kitchenette. The floor was quiet today. Half the M&A team were in New York on a large new file. Why hadn't Cory assigned her to it? In the kitchenette, she turned on the kettle, fished out her cell phone, and left a voicemail for Gavin, letting him know that she'd be home late. Then she remembered that he'd be out. For a function at the bank? For dinner? For drinks? "Av, I'll be at ..." What had he told her this morning?

Jesus. How had she become so dreary, how had she become so dull? She who had been born to the jagged world: she had always known that there were alternative lives out there that she could slip into. She and Luke used to talk about this all the time growing up. When their parents adopted Ava as an infant and brought her from Kathmandu to Overland, Ontario, they had set her off in one direction, but she could choose another direction at any time. She could even reverse course if she wanted.

The kettle reached a boil and popped off. Ava made herself a cup of green tea and waited for it to steep, regretting those ten lost days.

She had spent all her time at the cottage talking. "Remember, Gav, when we got out of law school — we were different. I wanted to really do something, remember? I didn't want to end up on Bay Street. You didn't want to work at a bank. We're in a rut, Gav."

"A pretty comfortable rut, Av."

Georgian Bay had glittered around them as they spent every day — not arguing, because they never argued, but — deliberating. They hadn't got around to having sex even once. Ava couldn't actually remember the last time they had ... was it after Gav's thirty-fifth at Oyster Boy? She had been busy on the Toralan file, and Gav had stopped initiating. Why had he stopped?

As she left the kitchenette with the cup of green tea, Ava saw Cory barrelling down the hall ahead of her. Her heart sank as she watched him barge into her office. When she came in, he was pacing back and forth like a caged animal.

Cory had a blunt manner that bordered on boorishness. "Ah-vah!" he said. He had told her, early on, that he found the pronunciation of her name pretentious. "What, were you taking a tea break, Ah-vah?" With a flick of a finger, he indicated that she should sit down.

Then he moved in closer to her desk, till his thighs were pressed up against the Toralan deal toy, and said, "Here's the thing, Ah-vah. Your evaluation's coming up, and, as you know, I'll be writing it this year."

A fog began to swirl in the office. Cory's voice floated in as if from far away:

"Now, we all know Lester was soft on his protegés, otherwise why would he have recommended you for partnership? But my view is? I'm not seeing a lot of motivation from your side, Ah-vah. I'm saying it as I see it, Ah-vah. You want a future at the firm? Then you and I, we need to talk."

Ava was already gone.

IN HIS NARROW room in Sharjah, they lay entwined in the sheets, wrapped up in each other's heat and contentment. Maleah was talking, Gyanu was caressing her hair. On their days off, he loved losing himself in her words, swimming in the swirl of the sea in her stories and drifting along with her voice. When Maleah stopped talking, he murmured, "Tell more, meri maya."

She smiled. "What more you want me to tell, mahal?"

"Tell me: the men who catch fish."

"You always want to listen about that," she said.

She nestled in closer and told him about her father and brothers going out on their nightly excursions from their village in the Philippines. Gyanu could see the lamps glinting off the water as the trawlers receded into the night. He could hear the roar of the sea in her voice, he could taste the salt water in his mouth. The trawlers returned at sunrise as lorries rumbled into the village, setting the day in motion. The tuna catch was transported to a cannery, from where it was shipped to towns all over the South China Sea.

Some of the leftovers ended up in the village homes. "Every day we eat fish, depends on the season," Maleah said. "There is rice and plantain, my mother cooks that first. My father and brothers come back, then she cooks" — her English fell away — "bilong-bilong, apahap, kabayo, lapu-lapu."

Maleah often cooked sea bass for Gyanu, infusing his room with the coconut, lemongrass, and lime leaf of her fishing village. They usually shared leftovers from Five Spices, though when there was time, Gyanu would also cook, flavouring his meals with fenugreek and mustard, turmeric and dried chives: the hard rock and soil of Nepal.

With Maleah, Gyanu escaped his past. He loved everything about her. He knew that Maleah had married young. At sixteen she had run away with a boy from town who kept bad company, though with her he was tender. She was happy till his body showed up in the cannery garbage dump. Their son Crisanto now lived with his grandparents. "My anak will never know his father," Maleah had said once, and her sadness had unleashed Gyanu's.

But Maleah was talking, now, of happiness: the meals her mother used to cook as she and her father and brothers sat around the kitchen, waiting to eat. "There was nothing," she said, and he felt the innocence of childhood: a feeling of plenty. She said, "There was no big house, no fancy furniture, no nice clothes, no money. But there was love, so there was everything." She turned to Gyanu. "Like when you were a boy, mahal?"

He nodded, thinking back to the day Ma brought him to the village by the blue hills, to the house of the stranger who would become his ba. Gyanu was fortunate. His stepfather was a kind man. After Sapana's birth, the scandal around Ma and Ba's marriage subsided, and their family was whole — till encephalitis took Ma. Now cancer was claiming Ba. The last time Gyanu called home, his sister had said their father was asking for him: "Ba needs a son to light the funeral pyre, Dai. And he wants to see you one last time."

Maleah noticed his silence and asked, "You talked to your sister, mahal?"

"My father will not live long, meri maya."

"You booked the ticket?"

"I booked it," he said. He hadn't, however, asked Shantanu Kumar for leave. The Indian manager of Five Spices was fond of Gyanu; he used to call him his Nepali beta, his Nepali son; but Gyanu knew that no one was indispensable in the desert. He had learned this well over his years as a busboy at the Al Majaz in Abu Dhabi, a kitchen hand at the Safeer Café in Sharjah, and a mess chef in the Ramla Restaurant in Burj Khalifa. Only when Shantanu Kumar hired him as a sous chef at Five Spices had Gyanu found stability. He would have to risk it to visit his father.

He didn't say more on the subject, and neither did Maleah. They were accustomed to living in uncertainty in a land they could never settle in permanently. Maleah had come here on a two-year contract. One of her roommates was looking for work as an au pair in Europe. Another was looking for alternatives in childcare. Maleah was enrolled in an English class and had convinced Gyanu to do the same. She sometimes talked about moving elsewhere. She wanted to live with Crisanto somewhere, anywhere, where she could give him the kind of full, free childhood that she'd had.

For now, she reserved all of her love for Gyanu. Their few hours together always raced by. It was already quiet next door: the Tamil construction crew had left for the day. The neon sign at the Al Faraby Hyper Express blinked on as the dusk deepened. Maleah would have to leave soon.

Gyanu propped himself up in bed to look at her. Maleah Balana. He had seen her one Sunday while accompanying his roommate Jairus to church: her head bowed, her face framed by lace. "Our Father who art in heaven, hallowed be thy name." He had heard her whispered incantations. "Thy kingdom come, thy will be done on earth as it is in heaven." How had he won her love, how was he going to keep her? Moving his hands over her shoulders, he felt the grace of her in his life. He removed the sheet and took in the sight of her pale body against his dark skin. They had been lovers for a year, and he couldn't envision a life without her.

"Mahal," she whispered.

"Meri maya," Gyanu said. My love. He leaned in to kiss her, and she arched her back, drawing her legs up to close him in to her.

OF ALL THE European cities Indira had travelled to for work —
London and Brussels, Helsinki and Cologne, Copenhagen and
of course Frankfurt, several times — Paris was definitely the
prettiest. Indira had been here before, eighteen-nineteen years
ago, for her first-ever international conference, a UNIFEM
summit on women: she remembered it warmly as a blur of
national costumes and inspirational speeches. The best part
was the city tour at the end. The delegates had been taken to
the famous boulevard, the Champs-Élysées, and from a stone
bridge Indira had taken photos of the Seine. Where were those
photos now? Lost in time. Awed by all she had seen, she had
vowed to return, and now here she was, back in Paris!

A fashionable lady in stilettos sashayed by. A boy drove his
scooter onto the sidewalk and stopped in front of an automated
teller. A tall man in a tailored suit cavorted down the sidewalk,
smoking a cigarette.

Indira shadowed the tall man so as not to be spotted by the
organizers of the Women's Empowerment Initiative. There were,
in her experience, two kinds of conferences in this world. The
first was organized by veterans from the developing world, who
understood that formal interactions were greatly enhanced
by informal activities such as sightseeing or gift shopping.
Indira had formed lasting bonds at such conferences. Years
later, she still kept in touch with Abena Kwasima from Accra,
Rudo Gamble from Cape Town, W. Werry from Jakarta, Mei
Wang from Shanghai, Juana Hernández from Lima, and the
formidable Kadri Pütsep from Tallinn. Together they formed a
sisterhood of global change-makers.

The Women's Empowerment Initiative was, however, the
other kind of conference, the kind organized by amateurs,
usually American, who tried to squeeze out too many outcomes

in too little time. From the very first Inspire! Breakfast on, Indira had had to pursue an asset-based approach using the principles of appreciative inquiry to discuss her work at WDS-Nepal. All day long, she had been trapped in lectures and workshops, and in the evenings, she had had to attend Solidarity! Dinners with earnest cultural shows: a one-woman play set in Ciudad Juárez, an all-woman Roma folk band. Tonight there would be a slide-show on female genital mutilation. And tomorrow morning she would leave.

Why organize a conference in Paris at all? Why not meet, as WDS-International had one dire, under-funded year, at an airport hotel in Frankfurt? Why not save money and teleconference, for that matter, or video chat, Skype-shype, Viber-shiber — all that?

The tall man turned abruptly into an alley. Spotting a stately stone bridge directly ahead, Indira hurried towards it. Having stolen out of a session on role playing, she had two hours, or maybe three, to buy a present for Aakriti, for having passed out of ninth class. Indira also had to pick up something for Muwa, though nothing would ever please her witch of a mother-in-law. Aakaash was easy: she would buy him a computer game at the airport duty-free; and two bottles of Johnnie Walker Black Label would suffice for Uday Sharma.

Indira reached the bridge, and her heart fluttered: was it — could it be — it was! It was the very same bridge she had been to nineteen years ago! She reached for the railing as she would for an old friend, and found the stone smooth and hard and warm to the touch. Oh! She had once been young here.

She walked the length of the bridge, overcome with nostalgia.

On the far side of the bridge, she came across a row of bou-tiques. A mannequin in a slinky dress stood in one boutique window. A dress would be perfect for Aakriti, she thought – not this one, the neckline was low, but a dress from Paris would be perfect for her daughter.

The next window contained an array of jars filled with fruits, vegetables, and nuts: dried, oiled, marinated, pickled, preserved. Yet another window was decorated with fine white lace panties. Another contained nothing but wine. Here, she lingered. The bottles – white, red, rosé – glinted like precious gems in the sunlight. She imagined Uday Sharma lifting a long-stemmed goblet and toasting, "To you, Indira Sharma. To our marriage of twenty years."

"To us."

"No, to you."

It wouldn't happen, not in this lifetime. Whenever Indira was in the developed world, she always rued the way she, as a Nepali, was obliged to blunder through life without grace, without refinement, merely getting the needful done. Emotionally it saddened her, though rationally she understood why it was so. There was no comparing and contrasting the life of a Kathmanduite with the life of a Parisian, because the developed world was the developed world, and Nepal was Nepal.

Next to the wine shop was a beauty parlour. On an impulse, she went in: she would buy a face cream for Muwa here. A bell tinkled. The interior smelled like roses. A redheaded saleslady came up to her, high heels clacking, and after babbling in French switched to English: "May I help you, Madame?"

"I need a face cream," Indira said, pointing at a jar on a shelf.

"Ah, oui, there is much desiccation." The saleslady whisked out a magnifying mirror and held it up to Indira's face, assaulting her with a vision of the furrows and grooves, dots and patches, stains and blotches on her middle-aged face. To Indira's horror, the lines under her eyes had deepened, and her complexion, once clear, looked mottled.

Briskly, the saleslady said, "I strongly recommend a treatment, for you it is urgent, Madame." She mentioned something called Eau Vitesse. "That will make the skin tight, but my advice is to go for microdermabrasion. It aids the revitalization of youth."

Indira noted that the saleslady herself had flawless complexion, even though she was — how old? Quite old. "How much?" she ventured to ask.

"Just one hour, Madame."

"No, no. How much money is it costing?"

It came to over twelve thousand, when converted into Nepali rupees!

Twelve thousand rupees for a beauty treatment! That was simply immoral! Though, of course, Indira's per diem could easily cover it, and it wasn't unreasonable when you converted the cost back into euros. Plus, a treatment, as the lady said, was urgent for her. A global change-maker ought to look good. Also, a beauty treatment in Paris: when would she ever get this chance again? But then again — twelve thousand rupees! Oof. Chances taken and opportunities missed, longings and qualms, desires and disappointments pulsated through Indira — yes, no, yes, no — till with profound regret she decided: "I will take one face cream only."

"Bof. Your choice, Madame."

High heels clacking, the saleslady took a jar to the cash register.

The bill came to nine thousand rupees.

Nine thousand rupees for a jar of face cream! A high-quality cream, to be sure, a cream from a beauty parlour in Paris. She shouldn't waste it on Muwa. It would be a gift to herself.

As Indira left, the saleslady called out, "Au revoir!"

"Bonjour," Indira replied grimly.

Outside, she felt just awful. What was she doing buying a nine-thousand-rupee face cream for herself? What did she think, that it would bring back her youth? That Uday Sharma would notice, and they would recover their marital happiness? What? Walking along the row of boutiques looking for a dress for Aakriti, she excoriated herself:

Look at yourself, Indira Sharma. Tchee! Look. Just look at what you've become.

A WATERY LIGHT filtered through the banana plants, dappling the lawn with crazy dancing shadows. Sapana was sitting with her back to Kakarvitta bazaar, looking out at a bridge. The land on this side of the bridge? This was Nepal. And the land on the other side was India.

"Can't we go?" Sapana asked, though she knew perfectly well that they couldn't. "Just for a minute," she said. "Just so we can tell everyone at home that we went abroad on this trip."

Around her, the women tittered. They were waiting around indolently for their midday meal on this, the final day of their study tour. They were completely worn out. Over the past five days they had visited a cooperative dairy, a pig farm, a carpet factory, a fish hatchery, and a tea estate. They had gone to a silk factory and seen silkworms feeding on mulberry leaves. They had met women who earned an income selling baskets, brooms, cardamom, vegetables, nuts, dried fruits, and just about everything else. Every day had been full of discovery, every evening had been full of fun.

If only Chandra had been on the tour, then it would have been perfect, Sapana thought. Sapana was hoarding her observations to share with Chandra when she got home. There should have been other girls of her age on the tour, really. Sapana had, herself, been included by favour of her uncle, Thulo-ba, only after the chairperson of the women's committee pulled out, saying her family couldn't spare her for a week. Ba couldn't spare Sapana either, but Chandra had insisted: "Ey, girl, aren't I here to care for your ba? Haven't I been here for you all these years? Don't miss this chance. Go."

As far as Sapana could tell, this study tour was the only thing her thulo-ba's sham CBO had ever done for the women's committee. The women's committee was itself a sham: half of its members couldn't even read or write! No one in the village knew why the CBO had even bothered to set it up. But then the CBO — which, Sapana had learned on the tour, stood for "community-based organization" in English — was just a means to fund Thulo-ba's politics. There was no point expecting much from it.

But this was no time to be negative: this was a moment to savour. The light, the lawn, the women. There, past the bridge: India. "Can't we go?" Sapana asked again.

Rama-bhauju, who was sitting beside her, called out to their minder, the widower Jeevan Bhatta: "Lau, Secretary-ji, you're going to have to turn this into an international tour, re!"

The other women tittered.

Jeevan Bhatta flashed them a loopy grin. He looked a fool, but was the secretary of the CBO, and Thulo-ba's most trusted political worker. "If I were to take you across the border," he said, leering, "the police would nab me."

"Why?" Rama-bhauju demanded. "Is it against the law to go to India?"

"They'd think I was going to sell you-all to a brothel!"

"Haaa!" Rama-bhauju's face soured.

Jeevan Bhatta guffawed.

Sapana grimaced. What a horrid joke! It immediately made her think of Chandra's sister, Surya-di. After failing out of tenth class, Surya-di had decided not to marry. She had decided to look for work instead. She had always been a different kind of girl, plucky and bold. A family friend knew a manpower agent in Kathmandu, and over the phone, the agent said that he would find Surya-di a salaried job in India's capital, Delhi. "I'll be the son you never had," Surya-di had told her muwa-buwa. "I'll send money home so that Chandra and little Tara can study."

The lodge owner began to serve the women dal-bhat-tarkaari — a simple dish of rice, lentils, and vegetables — steaming hot in aluminum thalis, but Sapana didn't feel like eating any more.

What excitement there had been on the day Surya-di left! Sapana and Chandra had escorted Surya-di all the way to the highway. "You girls, don't be like me," Surya-di had said sternly. "Study hard. Pass out of school. Make something of yourselves. Take care of Muwa-Buwa. Help raise little Tara. Always be good."

The agent was waiting at the highway with a van. He had a wiry moustache, and Sapana and Chandra kept looking at him and giggling. They found that moustache so funny. Two of Surya-di's friends from school were also going with her. After they arrived, the van drove away, and Sapana and Chandra raced all the way home.

A few days later, when Chandra's muwa-buwa phoned the agent, they found his line disconnected. Neither they nor the other families ever heard from their daughters again.

"Ey, girl!" Rama-bhauju nudged Sapana. "Your food's getting cold."

"I'm not hungry, Bhauju."

"It's a twenty-hour bus ride! Think about how hungry you'll be in six hours, and eat!" After saying this, Rama-bhauju burst into laughter. "That's why I'm fat — I'm always eating because I think I might get hungry in six hours!"

Sapana looked at her. Rama-bhauju was so good-natured. Just last year, Rama-bhauju's schoolmaster husband left her for a young new wife. Rama-bhauju was raising their four children all by herself, but looking at her you would never know she had any troubles.

The others on the tour — Jethi-didi, Laxmi-aama, Kanchan-bhauju, Naina-di, Hasta-ma — all had their own troubles too, as, of course, did Sapana. Sapana had lost Ma only a few years ago, and now she was going to lose Ba. But then all of us experience sorrow, she thought: and yet here we are, across the country, on a study tour, in an animated discussion about — what?

Yogurt. "The yogurt from here is famous," Jethi-didi was saying, prompting Naina-di to say, "Ssss! A bowl of fresh yogurt would be so refreshing at the end of this meal!"

"There's nothing in this world like fresh yogurt," Rama-bhauju declared.

"Ssss, now I really want some!"

"Sahu-ji!" Rama-bhauju called out to the lodge owner. "Give us some yogurt, will you?"

The lodge owner shrugged. "The batch I made this morning is finished."

"Buy some from another hotel, then!"

"Do that!" The others chimed in: "We came all the way across the country to try the yogurt."

"Lau na, Sahu-ji!"

"We won't leave till we have some world-famous yogurt!"

With another shrug, the lodge owner went to find them some yogurt.

A cheer went up at this small victory. Sapana had to smile. As much of a sham as this women's committee was, it was fun to be part of. The tour had given her a respite from the sadness around Ba's cancer. Sapana felt lucky to be here. She felt grateful — to the committee, to Thulo-ba, and even to Jeevan Bhatta, for if the old widower hadn't started the women's committee, this tour wouldn't have taken place at all. So what if he and Thulo-ba were profiting off the CBO? Whoever had given them the money for the tour had also enriched Sapana's life; and anyway, maybe there's no such thing as 'my life' or 'your life,' Sapana thought. Maybe everyone's life is part of a whole. It felt so to her, because when she thought about it, she felt that the actions of one person shape the lives of others, and ... don't all of us in our own lives shape the lives of others? We do. It's like a pattern, she thought. Not a pattern, but some kind of design, some kind of order. Chandra always said there's no God, and maybe she was right, but to Sapana it felt as though ...

"Ey, girl! Eat! Or you'll be hungry in six hours!"

Sapana smiled. She loved Rama-bhauju so much right now. She loved all the members of the women's committee; and actually, right now, she loved life.

She drew the dal-bhat-tarkaari towards her and began to eat.

"GYANU?"

"Hm?"

"Let's live in Nepal, all of us. Mount Everest and all — it's beautiful there, na?" Jairus said. "You and Maleah can raise her son as a mountain boy. I'll bring my wife and daughters from Karachi. We can start a tour business; there are big dollars in that, hey."

Gyanu knew his friend was only trying to soothe him.

Jairus patted him on the knee. "Don't be upset, Gyanu. These things happen. Nothing comes from dwelling on them. You have to forget."

"I know."

"I mean it, friend. Just — forget."

Earlier in the evening, Jairus had stopped by Five Spices to pick up kebabs, and had found Gyanu and the rest of the staff subdued. One of the servers, a young Nepali brother, had hanged himself the previous night.

"Come with me, come, come, come." Jairus had dragged Gyanu along for the first part of his tour to Ras-al-Khaimah. They were in the dunes outside Dubai, in a tent at the back of the tour company's compound. Jairus's clients, IT entrepreneurs from Tamil Nadu, were sitting in the main tent, where a belly dancer was gyrating indifferently to a Lebanese pop song. The clients looked bored. Serving them dinner, the tour company's staff looked bored. Even the dancer looked bored.

"Jairus," Gyanu said. Between them they spoke a mix of Hindi and Urdu. "He was a really nice boy. Always happy, always smiling."

Fucche: small boy. That was the server's nickname. Bright eyed and quick to laugh, he was one of nine siblings — disposable, he used to say. "A burden to our parents, that's all we are."

28

His gaiety must have masked a deeper desperation. He had got into debt and borrowed. Then he had got deeper in.

"He was happy on the outside," Jairus said, "but who knows how he was suffering inside? It does no good to dwell on it, friend. Look at the dancer, she's from Turkey, she has green eyes. See, how pretty she is."

But Gyanu couldn't take his mind off the boy. Fucche's body would have to be flown home. His roommates had notified the embassy in Abu Dhabi. Gyanu had already helped Shantanu Kumar call his parents in Kathmandu ... and Gyanu had other reasons to worry. He had asked Shantanu Kumar for leave, but wasn't sure the manager would grant it.

"Jairus," he said, "what if Shantanu says I can't go to visit my father?"

"Why would he say no to his Nepali beta?"

"Look after Maleah when I'm away?"

"You don't have to ask, hey."

"What will we do?" Gyanu said in a fit of despair. "Maleah and me." He meant: how were they going to forge a life together?

Jairus understood. In his calm way, he said, "You have to look at the world through a wide-angle lens, Gyanu. People like us, we've done all right by comparison to others. How many of your brothers and sisters in Nepal come into this world just to suffer — and how many of my brothers and sisters in Pakistan? In this world we're powerless, na. Everything is in God's hands. You and I, friend? We must have faith."

In the main tent, one pop song ended and another one screeched on. The belly dancer went on gyrating. After dinner, Jairus would drive on to Ras-al-Khaimah. Gyanu would catch the bus back to their shared rooms in Sharjah.

Jairus picked up a kebab and held it up to him. "You want?"

Gyanu shook his head no.

"It's good, hey, so tender. You should know, you made it!" Jairus laughed.

"You eat it, you'll need energy for the drive."

Gyanu got up and left his friend to his meal. Beyond the tent, the sky was glittering with stars. He walked out to the far edge of the tour company's compound, to a stall overlooking the dunes. A camel tethered there snorted as Gyanu approached. Its minder, a thin man in a dusty thobe, sat on a pallet smoking a cheroot. With a nod, he invited Gyanu to sit.

The screech of the pop songs was more muted here. The golden lights of Dubai glowed on the horizon. The dunes were velvety and dark. The smoke from the minder's cheroot wafted, sweet and heavy, in the air. A shadow darted through the scrub. Gyanu took a deep breath. He loved the desert: its starkness felt honest to him. Outside of Nepal, the desert — the Gulf — was the only home he had known. It was a difficult thing to love a land you could never call yours.

Jairus was right. He was fortunate. So many Nepali brothers and sisters suffered at home, and then came here and suffered even more. So many, like Fucche, perished here. Everyone who worked in the desert recognized the haunted expressions of the distressed. In the past month alone, six workers from Gyanu's home district had been cheated by a manpower agency. A Nepali sister had got pregnant from rape. One of the new servers at Five Spices kept breaking down in the middle of work, but wouldn't say why. The desert could be ruthless, Gyanu knew: but it had given him everything he had. His livelihood. A future. Love.

The camel shuffled in the stall. The smoke from the cheroot kept wafting by. Gyanu scanned the sky till he saw the familiar giant, Orion, and across from it, his birth sign, Gemini, its stars splayed in a pleasing symmetry. Early on, he had pointed it out to Maleah from the shores of the Sharjah canal, and she had shown him another constellation, higher up, Auriga: a herd of goats. "When I think how life brings us together, I think — like that, mahal. From so far, we come together," she had said.

Gyanu looked, now, for the goats, but couldn't pick them out in the sky. From the corner of his eye he caught a movement: a satellite. He followed it. It was gliding so fast, it was hurtling, it looked as though it might crash into a star, though of course it didn't. He followed it across the sky till it vanished into the golden lights of Dubai.

"**MUMMY, WILL I** ever be pretty?" Aakriti said, scowling at her reflection in the gilt-frame mirror.

"You are pretty, Chhori, you're the prettiest girl in the world," Indira said, wanting to add, you look exactly like I did at your age, but holding back, because — given the way she looked now — how was that helpful?

"But I'm not — it's not — I don't! I look like a skeleton in this!"

The dress was far too big for the girl. The sashes drooped, the bows sagged, the buttons hung limp from the holes.

"It's my fault," Indira said. "I bought it in a size you can wear next year." She cinched the dress at the waist. "The tailor will take it in, and it'll be perfect, although even without a dress from Paris, you're the prettiest girl in the world, Chhori."

Her daughter only scowled harder.

"Listen to me, Aakriti Sharma. All the boys will line up to marry you one day!"

"It doesn't matter because I'm going to be a doctor in America and who cares about boys anyway!" Aakriti stomped out of Indira's room, the dress billowing like a sheet behind her.

Oof. Indira followed her out.

The girl slammed into her room and bolted the door from inside.

"Aakriti?" Indira knocked on her door. "Listen to me, Chhori, you're very pretty, but you're right, it doesn't matter —"

From inside came a wail.

"Open the door, Chhori. Open the door. Open the door for just one minute."

Another wail.

What to do, what to do. Indira stood around, flummoxed.

Durga shuffled into the hall with a tray bearing hot kheer and milk. "Snacks, Hajoor." The servant girl looked frightful, like a beggar, a vagabond. She had stopped grooming herself after the vegetable vendor she had abruptly got engaged to had just as abruptly abandoned her.

"Kheer!" Indira said, eyeing the hot rice pudding. "Aakaash's favourite! Did you put cardamom in it?"

The girl nodded.

"And cashews?"

"Yes, Hajoor."

"Go and serve Aakaash."

The girl shuffled to Aakaash's door and knocked.

Indira jiggled the handle to Aakriti's door. "Snacks, Chhori, snacks, Durga's made snacks," she said, remembering that her daughter despised rice pudding. "Open the door, I say."

There was no reply.

There was no reply, either, from Aakaash. Durga muttered, "Babu never hears me knocking, he just stares at the computer, I knock and knock but he never hears."

He was playing one of those games Indira had bought for him at the duty-free shop. Indira went over to her son's door. "Open, ey, Aakaash. Durga's made your favourite kheer."

Silence.

"Open, I said!"

"He never hears me, Hajoor."

"Aakaash, open the door, open the door, open the door!"

Nothing.

Oof, that boy, he was useless, Aakaash was a useless, useless boy.

Indira took a bowl of kheer and a glass of milk from the tray. "Take the rest back to the kitchen," she said. "The children will eat when they're hungry. And Durga," she added, "wash your face. Comb your hair. Make an effort to look respectable, will you."

The girl shuffled away glumly.

What was the point, there was no point, it was all useless, her entire family was useless.

Kheer and milk in hand, Indira went down the hall to Muwa's room. Even from outside, the smell of incense was so dense as to be cloying. The old witch prayed constantly in her room, though her fevered piety never lessened her witchiness. Indira hated her mother-in-law. Nevertheless, a Nepali daughter-in-law had to do what a Nepali daughter-in-law had to do. With false cheer, she called out, "Snacks, Muwa," held her breath, and entered a miasma of myrrh.

A TROPICAL BREEZE tumbled in through the window, warm, fragrant, forgiving. The 112 was lined with billboards advertising cheap flights to Cuba, El Salvador, Jamaica. Past a palm grove, Ava turned off on the exit to the 195. She checked the speedometer: she was going twenty above the limit. The rental car swooped down to a causeway on Biscayne Bay.

There was something about America, Luke had said after moving here, that freed you. Being one of three hundred million: that scale. In Canada, even in a world-class city like Toronto, everyone was from a small place. Your past held you in somehow. "Man, I'm never coming back," Luke had said to her. "I'm out of there, Big Sis, I'm gone."

Following her brother's directions, Ava drove past the pastel art deco buildings and crowded high streets of Miami Beach. Luke lived in North Beach. She recognized his apartment complex from his Instagram postings. She parked on the street and took out the single suitcase that contained everything she hadn't stored in her parents' garage. She carried it and her attaché case into a sprawl of stucco and tile: her little brother's low-budget paradise.

She found the key to Unit 4 under the doormat. Luke's apartment was furnished just as perfunctorily as his old Kensington Market studio, with an unfinished table, an outrageous pink chandelier, and a few dented metal chairs. One of his paintings, a yellow monochrome, was drying on the wall. It made everything smell of linseed oil.

Luke had a class today. Ava had the afternoon to herself. There was a line of sunbeds in the lawn outside the apartment. She changed into a bathing suit, grabbed a towel, and went out to take in the sun. Lying back with her eyes closed, she listened to birds — thrushes? larks? — chirping exuberantly over the lawn. The heat of the sun melted in from her skin into the muscles, the sinews, the bones, easing away Cory and her last humiliating months at the firm. The fog had lifted, was still lifting, from her life. She turned over and let the sun warm her back, easing away the pain of Gavin and his confession, their confusion, her sharp decision to leave.

She was heading in, feeling light and limber, when Luke arrived.

"I see you found the sun," he said.

"Little Brother!" She hugged him fiercely. "What a place!"

"Don't you love it?" He grinned. He looked luminous. Back home, her brother used to be wan, but his platinum hair and grey eyes had found a corresponding light here. "Let's get you dressed," he said. "Hector Duarte from the sculpture department has an opening tonight. The party's going to be epic."

Before long, they were heading out in his battered red Mini. This was how it always went with Luke. Fuelled by impatience, he flitted from activity to activity, as though incapable of sitting still. "You caught some of this on your way in?" He gestured as they drove by the art deco buildings. "We'll come here tomorrow for a birthday bash. But first, tell me, what news of Mom and Dad?"

"Did Mom tell you about the Halloween parade?" Ava said.

"Her latest dust-up with Mayor Jenkins?" Luke pointed at a wrought-iron gate. "That, by the way, was where Versace was shot. So, listen. I've got to teach tomorrow, but a friend, Anthony, he's in the film department, he's offered to show you around."

"You got me a babysitter?"

"He's a sweetheart. Plus, he's local, he knows all the cool spots. I figured you might like a change of scenery." He glanced over. "You doing okay, Big Sis?"

Discussing the separation, Ava stuck to the facts. She and

Gavin had signed an agreement, and if they chose to file for divorce, they would do so jointly. "Of course, it's difficult," she said. "Six years, you know? Gavin's staying in the house till it's sold. The agent's saying we should be able to sell up."

"So, then everything's hunky-dory."

Ava ignored his ribbing tone. "You know, I'm really excited about this new job," she said.

"You'll be the director of women? At what — the forum to save the world?"

"The International Development Assistance Forum. It's called IDAF for short."

"And since when have you wanted to get in touch with your roots, Big Sis?"

Ava sighed. She could never get anything past Luke. Their parents had had him immediately after adopting her. The two of them had grown up like twins, closely, jealously attuned to one another.

Ava said, "Remember my friend Kim Armstone from Osgoode Hall? She's in Juba, in South Sudan, she does humanitarian work there. I got in touch with her on Facebook, and she put me in touch with a colleague, a guy from Quebec who works in Kathmandu. He gave me the lead for this job."

"But we hated Nepal when we went there, remember?"

"We were kids, Luke."

He arched an eyebrow. "Whatevs."

Their parents had raised them liberally, teaching them about Ava's 'birth country,' and taking them, one Christmas, on a family trip to Nepal. Ava and Luke were fourteen at the time. The trip had been a disaster from start to finish. The orphanage — "Oh, this is where we first met you, honey" — turned out to be a crumbling wreck out of a Charles Dickens novel. A group of children playing ball had stopped to stare at them, immediately grasping the story of a white family with one brown child. Ava had recoiled from their gaze. The family had walked through a warren of cold, empty rooms to reach a draughty office, where a dour official had translated the few notes on file: "Mother passed away in childbirth. Father is unknown. Name was given for official purposes." He had pronounced her name as it was spelled in the adoption papers, with an aspirated b. "Abha: it means early morning light." He had no information about Ava's biological parents. "Caste is unknown." He had looked her up and down and pronounced, "Skin is dark, but — only God can know."

For the rest of the trip, Ava had refused to leave the hotel, and back in Overwood she threw herself into her life — her real life, her Canadian life. Till adulthood, her rejection of Nepal had been vehement.

"You know how I feel about the whole roots thing," Luke said, returning to a conversation they had been having all their lives.

"I know I don't have to connect with my past, but the timing feels right," Ava said. "It's a, I don't know, an instinct." They were passing a strip mall with Spanish shop signs: Gigante, Tapito, Maya Market. "Remember my mentor Lester?" Ava said. "After he left the firm, I felt trapped in a career I didn't want. And with Gavin, too, there was this — fog."

"Well, here comes the sun." Luke turned into Wynwood, a neighbourhood of converted warehouses, and parked.

The sculpture exhibit, Masculinities: Plural, consisted of a room of glandular plastic protrusions. "It's conceptual, not retinal, it's not meant to please," Luke said breezily, walking Ava through it. At the front, the sculptor was making an incomprehensible speech about masculinities. When he was done, the crowd scattered around a cash bar.

Luke's friends were always bohemian, or perhaps feckless. Ava couldn't imagine living the way they did. That evening she met a painter who had shown at Art Basel — "Just jumping through the art market's hoops" — and found herself listening in on a debate between a journalist and a poet who refused, on principle, to publish:

"The world urgently needs more silence."

"But you gotta pay the rent, man!"

The poet turned vexedly to Ava. "What do you think?"

"I, um ..."

She was rescued by a heavily pierced woman: "Hey, I'm Revolution Mary, you want another drink, babes?"

"Oh. No, thanks. I'm good."

"Aw, come on. I'm a performance artist, it's my social practice to make dirty martinis."

The martini went straight to Ava's head. And so, late at night, when a man — tall, dark, and handsome — came up to her with a flirtatious "So, Masculinities: Plural. Yes or no?" she flirted right back:

"Well, my husband and I just split up, so I guess that's a yes."

"I'm extremely sorry to hear that," the man said, sounding not in the least bit sorry. "Hi there. I'm Anthony Watson."

"I'm Ava Berriden."

"Luke's sister, right? I'm hoping to show you around tomorrow — if you're up for it, that is."

The next morning, Anthony picked up Ava and drove to Coconut Grove, where his family had first settled. "Bahamian immigrants — though we're all mixed in now," he said as they walked under the big blue sky. They went to look at some murals. Then he took her to a taquería for lunch. "You ever had mahi-mahi?

And you've got to try the local microbrew, it's the best." The tacos were hot, and the beer was cold. Later, they sat in a park with elderly Cuban men playing chess.

"I can see why Luke loves it here," Ava said.

"Yeah, people think Miami's all art deco and beaches, but there's a lot of history here, a lot of African-American history. And now it's like the centre of South and Central America. Hey, Luke told me you're on your way to Nepal. I read a bit about it this morning — one of the poorest countries in the world, huh. So, you were born there?"

"Did you know that they're drafting a new constitution?" Ava said, deflecting.

"Is that why you're going there? To draft a constitution?"

"That would be well above my pay grade." Ava laughed, and asked about his films.

Anthony's last documentary was on the Maras of Guatemala. "They're not fooling around, our cameraman almost took a bullet," he said. "I'm dying to start a new project already. Anything going on in Nepal?" Then he shook his head. "Just my luck. I meet this gorgeous woman — and she moves across the world."

Ava shot him a look and he winked.

She blushed involuntarily, surprised, embarrassed, not displeased. This, she remembered, was what it was like to flirt. This was what it used to be like, once, with Gavin.

That night, Luke took her to a South Beach club for Revolution Mary's birthday bash. The music was deafening and the strobe lights blinding. The air was heavy with perfume, marijuana, sweat, and lust. There was no talking to anyone. Everyone drank dirty martinis and danced.

The following day was Ava's last one in Miami ahead of her flight to Kathmandu. She and Luke spent the day on the beach. He was kitted in a Hawaiian shirt and Bermuda shorts. She had picked up a new bikini on Lincoln Street. They lay on lounge chairs, sipping Campari tonics, gazing out at the moss green sea.

They were due for a talk. This was always how it went in their get-togethers. They spent the first few days studying each other, saving a heart-to-heart for the end.

Ava started it off: "So, Mom wanted me to find out if you've met anyone."

"You know Revolution Mary?" he said. "She and I are in an open relationship."

"Oh." A heavily pierced performance artist. Her brother had always had bad luck, or poor judgment, in relationships. "And how does an open relationship work?" Ava asked, careful to keep her tone studiously neutral.

"She sees other people, I see other people, but we have to pass it by each other." He shrugged. "There are all these rules."

"Don't you get jealous?"

Any hint of disapproval made Luke bristle. "I hate to be indelicate, Ava, but you're really not a great spokesperson for monogamy right now."

"But is it the kind of relationship you'd prefer to have?" Ava persisted. "Given a choice, is this what you'd want, Luke?"

"When have I ever done the right thing?" he said. " I like things fucked up, you know? I could never be like Mom and Dad — so upright and proper, so unbearably correct." He clinked the ice in his drink, then laughed. "Fucking do-gooders. Remember all those causes Mom and Dad went on? Mom's mission to end world hunger, or — oh God! Remember Dad's Black Power phase?"

"He was just trying to fill me with pride about my complexion." Ava smiled. "Remember Mom's solidarity potluck with the only gay man in Overwood?"

"Dad's environmental phase! All those trees he uprooted because they weren't native to Ontario!" Luke groaned. "I hated it! I still hate it. Mom and Dad, setting out to right all the world's wrongs: you know how it makes me feel? Like I can't just—exist. Like it's not worthwhile to just—be."

"You know they mean well."

"And now it's your turn to save the world," her brother said.

"That's not what I'm doing."

"I think it's worse," Luke said. He had obviously given this some thought. "I think, Big Sis, that you're going to Nepal because this rich Canadian dentist couple rescued you from a life of Third World poverty, and you think you don't deserve it, you think you have to repay the debt."

"That's not fair, Luke."

"Gavin's been calling me," he said.

"What?" Ava sat up, stung. "Why is Gavin calling you? What's he been saying?"

"He sounds really sad. He says the separation was your idea, he wanted to work things out, but—"

"He cheated on me, Luke—with an equity sales director! Did he tell you about Leez Anne Williker? Ask him about Leez Anne Williker! See what he says about that!"

"You want to throw away everything because of one indiscretion?"

"Our marriage wasn't an open relationship!"

"Touché." Luke got up and asked, "Want another Campari tonic?"

"No!"

"Oh, don't be mad at me, Big Sis." He sighed theatrically. "Okay, maybe I'm being selfish, maybe I want you to remain the stable, boring kid so that I can be the kid who's fucked up. Because if you get fucked up, I'll have to become stable and boring just to balance out the family dynamics."

"I've finally found a career I can believe in, Luke," Ava said. "Nepal relies heavily on aid, and do you know how bad things are for women there? I've been doing some background reading, women can't even confer citizenship to their children —"

"Just promise me you'll be okay."

"I'll be okay."

"And if slumming doesn't work out, you can always come back." Luke strolled off to order another drink.

Ava got up, rankled. Her brother could be so cutting, so barbed. It was just how he was: angry. He judged their parents so harshly — unfairly, in Ava's opinion. It wasn't as though they had transplanted him from one part of the world to another. It wasn't as though he ever had to wonder about his origins.

She walked out to the waterline. Two girls were playing with shells at the edge of the water. A couple was playing Frisbee nearby. A wave surged up to Ava's ankles. She followed it in, her feet sinking into the cold, wet sand.

She couldn't believe Gavin had been calling Luke. Gavin had also been calling Mom and Dad. Last week in Overwood, Mom had pleaded with her not to file for divorce. "We're not saying you shouldn't go to Nepal, honey, of course you should, but we just... I hope you understand. We love Gavin too."

The next wave surged up to her calves. Ava walked in till the waves lapped at her thighs. The water was cold, but she continued on, jumping the waves till they were waist deep. Then, taking a deep breath, she plunged in.

Through the shock of the cold, she swam into the churning waves and came back up. The ocean was swelling on a gentle roll there. She floated there awhile, observing the lightness of her body in salt water.

Last week, in Overwood, even Dad had said that it wasn't like her to be so rash. "You've always been cautious," he had said. But that had been exactly the problem, Ava thought. She had been cautious all her life. Too cautious. She was done with being cautious.

She swam out to the depths.

On her return, she encountered a current. It was mild, but she noticed, after fighting it awhile, that she was swimming in place. At first she tried to fight the current, then she stopped, letting it sweep her back out to the depths, where it released her with a wide, gentle spin.

That night, Luke took her for a farewell dinner to the bar where Revolution Mary worked, by a shipping channel. All of Luke's friends were there, including Anthony.

"Ms. Berriden."

"Mr. Watson."

"I was thinking, you should forget about Nepal and move to Miami instead."

"Oh, really?"

Anthony was impossible: smart, charming, and attentive. It pleased Ava that they sat together all evening. After dinner, they sat at the edge of the bar and watched cargo ships glide through the inky black channel. The air was lush. The stars were out. They talked easily about nothing much.

At one point, Anthony said, "So, are you upset about your split-up?"

What needs, what exigencies, make strangers feel as though they understand each other?

"I guess I'm going through a lot," Ava said.

"Yeah." He reached out for her hand. "You know I'd never do anything to make you uncomfortable, but if you want to talk or anything, I live just a few blocks away."

Ava thought of Gavin. Her caution. The fog. "I'd like that," she said. And after a quick whisper to Luke — "Don't wait up for me!" — she strolled out with Anthony into the tropical night. Daring herself to explore all that was there. To follow unknown paths and unexplored trails, to wander, to stray, to get lost and be found. To leave the life she had and start her alternative life.

THE VILLAGE WAS asleep, the house was silent. In her room, Sapana switched off the kerosene lamp and slipped in between the mean, frozen sheets. Her teeth chattered involuntarily, and she whimpered. Chandra had oiled her own hair earlier in the day, and she smelled sumptuously of coconut. Sapana snuggled up to her for warmth.

Chandra grunted.

"Move over," Sapana hissed. "Let me into the warm spot."

"How's Ba?"

"Move over, will you? I can't even talk, it's so cold."

As soon as Chandra shifted, Sapana burrowed into her side of the bed, taking in the warmth of her body. Chandra was bigger than Sapana, and stronger too, with sinewy arms and muscular legs, though her belly was nice and soft. If Sapana positioned herself just right, she could warm her entire back against Chandra. Curling into position, she felt Chandra's toenails poking into her. She would cut her nails for her tomorrow. She would cut her own nails too. Ba had required constant attention, and they had both been so busy with him that they had neglected themselves.

Sapana eventually warmed up, and stopped shivering. She could tell from Chandra's breathing that her friend was still awake. She said, "Ba's aware of everything that's going on, Chandra. He can hear us. I told him, just now, that Gyanu-dai's coming, and — it wasn't a smile, but a peaceful expression came over his face."

"When will Gyanu-dai get here?"

"You know what he's like, I've stopped asking, but I'm sure he'll come. Or — you don't think he'd stay in the desert, do you?"

"I'll go to my muwa-buwa's house while he's here," Chandra said.

47

"No! You have to stay, Chandra, remember, we're going to live together after …" Sapana couldn't get herself to talk about Ba's passing.

Chandra shifted in bed. "Just for a few days. How long will Gyanu-dai stay? I'll move back then."

"Maybe he won't leave, though," Sapana said, battling away her sadness. She had been sad for so long with Ma, and now with Ba: she was tired of being sad. "Maybe Gyanu-dai won't leave again, Chandra. Maybe we'll all live here together," she said, and the thought cheered her momentarily. Then the sadness returned. She said, "The other day I was thinking: after Ba goes, no one will ever call me Chhori."

"What kind of talk is that."

"I won't be anyone's daughter anymore." Sapana hated crying, but couldn't help it.

"Tch, tch, tch." Chandra turned over and put her arms around her. "I'll be here for you, won't I? I'll be here for you, and you'll be here for me. And yes, maybe Gyanu-dai will stay on, and we'll all live here as a family."

"Maybe, hai?" Sapana wiped away her tears.

"Talk about something else," Chandra said. "Tell me more about the study tour. You were telling me about the pig farm earlier. Tell me more about that."

"I don't feel like it."

"Then tell me again about the silkworms, tell me again what they looked like."

"I don't want to talk about that. I don't want to talk about anything right now."

"Then go to sleep."

"Hold me till I fall asleep?"

"Come." She drew Sapana closer in.

48

Sapana could hear Chandra's heartbeat, slow and steady, in her chest. It felt good to be held, to be touched. After Ma left, Sapana had longed to be able to touch her one more time. The sudden absence had been bewildering. With Ba, now, she spent all day holding his hands, wiping his face, cleaning him, rearranging him on the bed, because soon he would be gone and all she would be left with was his absence. Listening to Chandra's heartbeat, she thought: hold me always. Be here, right here, where I can always feel you.

"Chandra?" she said.

Chandra grunted.

"I can't sleep."

"Close your eyes and think about something nice," Chandra said.

"Like what, Chandra?"

"The study tour. Think about something on the study tour."

"La, I'll try, hai. Keep holding me?"

"Of course."

"La, I'll sleep now."

"Try."

"I'm sleeping now."

"You're obviously not sleeping if you're talking."

Sapana smiled in the dark. "I'm sleeping, I'm actually asleep."

"Idiot."

"Honestly, believe me, I'm talking to you in my sleep, ah-ha-ha."

"Go to sleep!"

"I'm asleep, ah-ha-ha-ha-ha, I'm really asleep!"

MALEAH, MALEAH. If she could see this land, would she love him more, would she love him less? She of saltwater waves and drifting tides: what would she make of these backbreaking hills? From the water tap, Gyanu looked out at the ancient, familiar village: the stand of bottlebrush trees, the mud huts and concrete houses and the terraced fields, thick, in this season, with corn. The mist was light this morning. The mad river was visible in the distance, as were the low blue hills where he and his friends used to pick wild berries as boys. The greenery made everything look deceptively abundant. From his first glimpse out of the airplane window through the long drive from Kathmandu, he had been struck by the fecundity of the land. How accustomed he had grown to the desert.

The cold tap water quickened his pulse, ridding him of the stiffness of the thirteen days of austerities and awakening him to the world.

Gyanu had got to the village in time for Ba's last breath. Then he had shorn his hair, put on white clothes, and lit the funeral pyre, as he had for Ma. For thirteen days, he had received the company of mourners from all over the village. At meal times he had eaten unsalted food, and at night he had slept fitfully under thin, unstitched sheets. With the completion of the Shraadha ceremony yesterday, his filial duties were done.

As he washed, his sister called out: "Aren't you finished, Dai?"

Sapana was in the front porch standing exactly the way Ma used to, with her hands on her hips. Since Gyanu's last visit to the village, her sharp eyes and dark lips had become more defined. She was fine boned like Ma, with the same agreeable manners that disguised a more willful depth. She called out, "Hurry up, Dai, I've made all your favourite dishes!"

"I'll be right there, Bahini."

When he went in, Sapana sat him down at the old laminate table, which had sat in the same corner since the day Gyanu had come into the house as a boy. It had been a novelty then: Gyanu had never seen laminate. Now the surface was scratched and chipped, and the table was rickety.

His sister placed a plate of food in front of him on the table. "It's good to see you back in your own clothes, Dai. All these ragged old rituals — I hated seeing you in white. Will you have hot water with your food?"

"Cold is fine."

"It's been so long since I cooked for you."

Sapana had made his favourite kind of dal-bhat-tarkaari: rice, black dal with dried chives, and cauliflower with potatoes. After she served herself, they sat and ate together for the first time since Gyanu's return.

They didn't talk about anything pressing — How long will you stay, Dai? What will you do now, Bahini? — but lingered, instead, over diversions. Gyanu asked after his boyhood friends: "How's Ram? Did Bisnu come back? Is Kisne around nowadays?"

Sapana asked about his life in the desert.

He told her that most of the staff at Five Spices were Nepali. "We live together in the same building. We speak Nepali, we eat dal-bhat-tarkaari. If it weren't for the heat, we'd think we were in Kathmandu."

"How hot does it get there, Dai?"

"In the summertime?" he said. "It's unimaginable."

A vision of Maleah came to Gyanu: Maleah lit up by the neon sign of the Al Faraby Hyper Express on their last night together. Earlier that day, Gyanu had bought a coin from Suleiman-bhai, a Nepali jeweller in Deira. Four grams: enough for a ring. When he gave it to Maleah, she had looked at him with questions in her eyes.

Gyanu waited for the vision to pass, then said, "How are you doing, Bahini? It's been hard for you, all these years, taking care of Ba."

Sapana didn't want to dwell on her sadness. She talked, instead, about a study tour she had gone on a few months ago. "They took us out east," she said, lighting up at the memory. "Out there, it's not like here, it's completely different. They don't farm for food the way we do. They think of the market and plant cash crops like fruit trees and cardamom and broom." Gyanu noticed that she said *market* and *cash crops* in English. Thulo-ba's CBO had organized the tour. "In the beginning, everyone kept calling it seebeeyo, seebeeyo," Sapana said, "I didn't understand." She laughed: "They were saying CBO in English, for community-based organization." Then she grew earnest. "The CBO has a women's committee, Dai. I wouldn't have been asked on the tour, but old Laptanni Budhi, she's the committee's chairperson, she dropped out. It was me and nine other women — we had such fun!"

How memorable this tour had been for her, Gyanu observed with a pang. How small, how sheltered his sister's life had been.

Sapana got up to serve seconds. "Have more, Dai."

"I've already eaten too much."

"You didn't like the food. It's not as good as the food you make," she said.

"It's the best meal in the world, Bahini."

Gyanu got up to help clear away the dishes, but Sapana snatched away his plate. "Leave it, I'll do it."

"Ey, Bahini," he laughed, "in the desert I wash my own dishes, and the dishes of others —"

"But you're at home now," she said, suddenly grave. "You know, with Ma and Ba gone, it's just you and me now. We're all that's left of our family."

She turned away, her eyes glistening with tears, and began to clatter about the kitchen to fend off her sadness. Whenever Gyanu tried to help, she protested: "Put that down, Dai! Do you want tea? I'll make tea. Don't do anything, just sit there and drink your tea."

At the end, she was back to her usual self. "Dai, what are you going to do today?" she asked. "Are you going to visit Thulo-ba? He'll be expecting you." She hesitated, then said, "It's been so long since I've left the house, I'll go out too, all right?"

"You don't have to ask for my permission."

"Rama-bhauju, she's the secretary of the women's committee, she wants to talk to me. I think she's going to ask me to join the committee. Do you think I should join it?"

"Do you want to?"

"I really do!" she said. "Tchee, look, there's an oil stain on my kurta, I'll have to change first."

She left in a flurry of excitement.

Alone in the house, Gyanu walked from room to room, re-acquainting himself with its cramped dimensions. Ba had broken away from the ancestral home that he and Thulo-ba had inherited to set up a new life with Ma here. The house was small, but it used to be proud. It had fallen into disrepair over the years. The kitchen table and chairs needed mending. Everything needed repainting: where the doors and windows used to be a deep sea-green, they were a muddy brown. When Gyanu came for Ma's funeral, he had had the house wired, but neither Ba nor Sapana had been able to connect it to the power line after that. They still used kerosene lamps at night.

Gyanu checked the larder and saw that it was stocked with last year's potatoes and corn, lentils and rice. There were tomatoes, onions, garlic bulbs, and ginger roots, and the usual spices — cumin and coriander, sesame, fenugreek, turmeric, dried chillies. But there were none of the finer spices: clove or nutmeg or saffron, certainly no nuts or dates or raisins or lemon grass, lime leaves, galangal. Back in the kitchen, he noticed that the pots and pans were rusty, and all the knives were dull. There were no shelves; everything was stacked — tidily, but without any system — on the countertop.

He had realized, over the last thirteen days, that he was Sapana's guardian now. He needed to set her up: but how?

"Thirty days, Beta," Shantanu Kumar had said when granting him leave. "Not one day more."

Gyanu had only two weeks of leave left.

The morning mist had burned away by the time he set out for Thulo-ba's house. Down the way, by the bottlebrush trees, blind Gharti-buwa was sitting on a straw mat, sunning himself. Gyanu greeted him:

"You're looking well, Buwa."

"It's already been thirteen days, Babu?" Gharti-buwa turned his face up.

"The days pass by so fast."

"Your ba was a very wise man."

They talked awhile about family: Sapana on Gyanu's side, and Gharti-muwa, Chandra, and little Tara on Gharti-buwa's side. Then Gyanu took leave and walked on, passing Gharti-buwa's modest hut. Gharti-buwa's family had always been poor, but a pall had fallen over the family after their eldest daughter, Surya, disappeared. This entire stretch of the village felt blighted to Gyanu. Next to Gharti-buwa's hut was an empty house, abandoned by the family after their only son died in a bus accident. Beside the empty house, a brick house had been divided in two after the sons launched a court case for their inheritance. By the time the sons won the case, their parents had died, and the sons had, themselves, emigrated. Both halves of the house lay rotting by the path now.

The rest of the village wasn't as desolate. Further down were concrete houses that had been built from the earnings of family members in the cities, or abroad. From there, the path dipped past the terraced fields to the large feudal estates. Gyanu passed the bungalow of the Amatya clan, whose son was a doctor in Kathmandu. Nearby were the spread-out mustard fields of the Sah clan. Then came Thulo-ba's vast plot, marked off by stone walls.

Ba's plot abutted Thulo-ba's. It was large enough to have sustained the family once. After Ba's cancer diagnosis, Thulo-ba's family had taken to farming it in return for half the yields. That arrangement would have to continue, though it had occurred to Gyanu, over the thirteen days, that he ought to transfer the land deed to Sapana.

Thulo-ba had had the old ancestral house painted pink, as though to flaunt the prosperity of its owners. Gyanu found his uncle in the courtyard, surrounded by his usual coterie of party cadres, favour seekers, hangers-on, and lackeys: the eternal unemployed of the land. Dressed in a traditional labeda sural, Thulo-ba looked every bit the patriarch. Governments had fallen, regimes had changed, a Maoist insurgency had started and ended, the monarchy had been abolished. Allying with every new power in Kathmandu, Thulo-ba had remained ascendant throughout. Gyanu had often had to supplicate himself before Thulo-ba. He could not have even obtained citizenship papers had his uncle not helped forge a birth certificate. Though Thulo-ba held no official position at the moment, everyone called him the chairman.

Gyanu bowed to him.

The old man proffered his blessings. "You've changed out of white, already, Gyanu-babu?"

"Just this morning, Thulo-ba."

"Well, no one expects you to observe a whole year's mourning," his uncle said.

Old hurts — the wounds of family life — winced through Gyanu. He said, "Ba was the only father I knew, Thulo-ba."

"And you've been a true son to him. Sit, Babu." The old man turned to his lackeys. "Make room, ey, boys, make room for Gyanu-babu. Move."

"Actually, Thulo-ba," Gyanu said, "I was hoping to talk to you alone, if possible."

His uncle nodded, and dismissed everyone with a flick of hand.

When the last of his coterie had straggled away, Gyanu said, "I need some advice, Thulo-ba. It's about Sapana."

The old man's eyes glazed over in boredom. He had anticipated this talk. "Yes, I tried to bring up the subject of Sapana-nani's future with my brother," he said, "but ... ey, I don't have to tell you, he was a dreamer. He always told me: that girl's got fire, she'll look after herself. But you and I know it's not easy, Gyanu-babu. Did Sapana-nani tell you, I sent her on a study tour? The CBO had no budget, mind you. I sent her at my own expense."

"She benefited," Gyanu said. "We're grateful."

"It's our dharma to look after our own," his uncle said. Then his tone hardened. "We'll continue to look after your ba's land — unless you'd rather take responsibility yourself, Babu. Though how could you, if you're going back to the desert?"

"I'll have to go back."

"And how can Sapana-nani manage it all by herself?" his uncle said. "Also, Gyanu-babu, she shouldn't live in that house any more. A lone girl. She can move in with us, we've got plenty of room here. We'll cover her expenses from your family's share of the yields."

Thrown by this turn, Gyanu tried to steer the conversation back. He said, "I was thinking that we should put the land in her name, Thulo-ba."

The old man fixed him with a cold gaze. "That's not a big concern, Sapana-nani would just have to sign a few documents. Ey, don't worry about small matters like that, there are bigger concerns ahead of you. You know, Sapana-nani takes after your mother," he said, "and as a man, you understand: that kind of beauty attracts bad men. The wickedness of the world only increases," he said. "Even here, in the village, we hear: this family was tricked, that girl was sold, that girl died of AIDS in a brothel in Mumbai. As her guardian, you must talk to her, Babu. What your sister needs is a groom."

Gyanu could find no response. He wanted more for his sister than an early marriage — though what other life could Sapana possibly have in this village? Even if she were to move to Kathmandu, she was only a high school graduate: and he wouldn't be there to look after her. She had missed the deadline for enrolling in the Plus Two in Butwal Bazaar. Should he take her with him to the desert? Unsure, he said, "There's so much to think about, Thulo-ba."

"It's true. Your entire family structure has changed, and it's too early to think about worldly matters. There's the prayer on the forty-fifth day. You'll stay for that, won't you?"

"I should." Gyanu was immediately stabbed by remorse. He couldn't stay that long: he had to leave.

"We'll talk about everything in time, Babu."

"I look to you for guidance, Thulo-ba." Gyanu got up, and bowed again. For form's sake, he went to seek out his aunt before leaving. She was in the yard behind the house, picking stones out of a basketful of rice.

"You won't stay awhile, Gyanu-babu?"

"Another day, Thuli-ma."

"You and Sapana-nani come for a meal soon."

"We will."

Gyanu left, feeling miserable. He was going to be trapped here. Of course he was. He should have expected obstructions, he should have expected delays: it took wherewithal, and patience, to undo the knots of obligation, debt, need — and power — in the village. Thulo-ba hadn't come to be known as the chairman for nothing. He wanted control over everything, even his dead brother's assets.

On his way home, Gyanu stopped on a ridge to survey Ba's plot. As a boy, Gyanu had helped Ba till the plot, plant crops, repair the irrigation canal, and harvest the yields. On hot days, he and Ba used to rest beneath an aged willow tree. The tree had been chopped down long ago, but its stump remained. Gyanu wondered how much this plot would fetch if they were to sell it.

Any such decision would be Sapana's to make. This was her inheritance. Gyanu had more than exceeded his claim when Ba sent him to Kathmandu to enroll in a hospitality course, and to find his way into the world.

Sapana was still out when he got home. The house felt deserted. Gyanu felt restless being alone. He checked his mobile phone. Maleah would be at the gift shop right now. There were no phone signals in the village. He would have to go to Butwal Bazaar to call her. He would do so tomorrow.

For now, he decided to prepare the evening meal, to make something special for Sapana. He went out to the backyard, and after poking around, found a head of cauliflower, some mustard greens, two carrots. There were chives in the yard, there was basil. Further out, tender young shoots were sprouting in the bamboo grove. By the grove was a lime tree. He plucked a few of its soft, tender leaves.

By the time Sapana returned, he had finished cooking the meal.

"Ey, Dai, what are you doing?" she cried, seeing him at the stove.

"Tonight, Bahini, I'll feed you a five-star meal."

He sat her down at the table, placed a napkin on her lap, and served rice with toasted sesame, crispy mustard greens, stir-fried cauliflower, and fragrant lime tea.

Sapana delighted over everything. "What's in this, Dai? I've never tasted anything so ... how much do your customers pay for a meal like this?"

"For a dinner for two? About ten thousand rupees in our currency."

"Tch, when will Nepalis ever be able to afford a meal like that, hai? Ey, Dai," Sapana said. "Rama-bhauju asked me to join the women's committee, not just as a member — as the treasurer!" She laughed. "I didn't realize the committee members have been paying a hundred rupees' due every month. They've been giving out interest-free loans with that money. I thought the

60

committee was a sham — and it is, Thulo-ba and Jeevan Bhatta are profiting from it, but today, listening to Rama-bhauju, I was thinking about what Ba always said: that there's nothing you can't do. Even in this village, if you try, there's nothing you can't do, Dai."

She sounded every bit as lofty as their father.

"Bahini," Gyanu said, "do you want to move in with Thulo-ba?"

Sapana looked startled.

"I went to see him," Gyanu explained. "He suggested it."

"Do I have to?" Sapana said. "I don't want to, I really don't want to, Dai. Chandra and I made a pact," she said. "When the doctor said Ba would go, we decided to live in this house together. I've been meaning to ask, Dai: Chandra's miserable in her muwa-buwa's house. Would it be all right for her to move back here?"

"Of course."

"I'll tell her you said so!" Sapana beamed.

Gyanu tried to return to talking about her future: "Are you going to enroll in the Plus Two next year, Bahini?"

"I guess I should," she said. She hesitated. "Chandra and I talk about it sometimes. She can't afford the fees."

"That shouldn't stop you."

"I know." Sapana went silent for a while, and then began to talk, again, about the women's committee. "I can't believe I'm going to be the treasurer, Dai. These old women, they need help even to do simple addition and subtraction. They should bring other girls in, girls like Chandra and Ritu and Namrata. We've studied, we're young and energetic, we can really get things done..."

Gyanu listened to his sister, wondering whether this — her life in the village — would be enough for her. Perhaps it would be for now. As for the future, well, it was chance that propelled people forward, wasn't it? Maleah had started off in a small fishing village in the Philippines, and was now in Dubai. Who knew where she would end up? Who knew where he would, himself, end up? He, who didn't even know where he had been born: for Ma's life before Ba had never been acknowledged in their family. Only at the very end, on her deathbed, had Ma alluded to it. "You had to give up your past so I could live," she had said to Gyanu, placing her hand in his. "I couldn't even give you your own identity."

Could a man who didn't even know where he had started ever know where he would end up? Everyone, everyone followed chance, Gyanu thought. This would be true for Sapana, too: who knew where she would end up? He would try to enroll her in the Plus Two. This would be a start. He would transfer the land deed to her name.

And then, and then: he could leave.

IDAF'S OFFICE FELT like a fortress, ringed as it was by a
high stone wall — a rampart — topped with sharp metal spikes.
At the front gate, a flank of former Gurkha soldiers whisked
visitors through a metal detector, scanning bags and examining all incoming vehicles for bombs. The office had apparently
received threats during the Maoist insurgency. The insurgency
had ended, and the threat had passed, but the security meas-
ures remained. Ava had learned from a risk assessment report
that the office building had also been retrofitted to minimize
the risks posed by earthquakes, as Kathmandu fell in a seismic-
ally active zone. The building walls had been reinforced and the
windows had been fitted with shatterproof glass. The office was
hermetically sealed, as though to keep Nepal out. Entering the
conference hall for a senior staff meeting, Ava noted that but
for the country map on the wall, there was no indication as to
which part of the world she was in.

She found this unexpectedly soothing. The hotel she was
staying in was part of an international chain, and it bore only
a few decorative traces of Nepal, though her room did look directly out onto a crooked brick house. At night, Ava would stare
out the window, both attracted and repulsed by the house's
flimsy structure, its moss-covered tile roof, its dirty windows.
The people of the house huddled together on the floor in a tiny
room, their faces lit up by the flickering blue light of a television screen. Being in Nepal was more upsetting than Ava
had anticipated. The drive from the airport to the hotel alone
had revived memories, and she had recoiled like a wounded
child at the shabby streets, the pell-mell crowds, the ugly concrete-block houses. There was garbage festering openly on the
street leading up to her hotel. Fortunately, her daily commute
to the office was short. She knew she would have to immerse

herself in Nepal eventually, but for now she was grateful for the barriers that existed. She wasn't ready to breach them just yet.

"It's donor shopping, plain and simple!" Andrew Scheiffer from Employment Generation strode into the conference hall with a woman Ava couldn't recall from the staff chart in her orientation package. "These NGOs beg us for funding," Andrew said, his voice booming. "But if we demand accountability, they go to another donor. I'll bring this up at the next donor harmonization meeting. In fact..." He whipped out a cell phone. "Hello, Greg? It's Andrew Scheiffer from IDAF. Andrew Scheiffer. Andrew Scheiffer. I said it's..." He turned around and strode back out of the hall. "Can you hear me now?"

Without as much as acknowledging Ava, the woman sat at the far side of the hall.

Her unfriendliness seemed to be in keeping with the institutional culture at IDAF. No one at the office smiled or said hello to each other, or at least none of the international staff did. The secretaries — all Nepali women — talked constantly among themselves, gathering in groups in the halls, in the offices, in the women's washrooms. Their names were Geeta, Sharmila, Indu, Prativa, Meera — Ava couldn't yet match the names to the faces. They always greeted Ava with a punchy, "Namaste, Ava-madam!" pronouncing her name in the Nepali way: Abha. Early on, one of them had said, "You are so pretty, Madam, a black beauty, like our own girls from the Tarai-Madhes, in the south," and another had chimed in, "I was thinking that also!" Worried that they would ask about her background, Ava had since avoided the secretaries. Not that they seemed to mind, or indeed to notice. There was an unspoken, if rigorous, hierarchy at IDAF separating the support staff from the program staff, only two of whom were Nepali. They were both paid considerably less than the internationals — in keeping with local rates, apparently — and they were also placed below the internationals in the chart. They were tasked, essentially, with assisting the internationals.

One of the Nepali program staff, Vishwa Bista, came into the hall. "Is this chair free?" He sat down beside Ava. He had brought a paper that Ava had drafted in her first days of work, a paper on Gender Responsive Budgeting, a subject that Ava had had to learn about overnight. He began to pore over the paper. Ava would be presenting it at a stakeholders' meeting with senior government officials later in the week.

Ava watched Vishwa pull out a Mont Blanc and mark up a passage, and asked, "How is it?"

"Mmm. One or two small things, nothing major." Vishwa had studied in the US, at Ohio State University, and had a marked American accent. "I'll come by your office later to discuss it."

"Thanks."

"Sure." He made a note on the margin.

Vishwa was responsible for guiding Ava during her six-month probation period. He was helpful, and did more for her than called for by duty. He picked her up at the hotel in the morning and dropped her off at the end of the day. He ate lunch with her at the canteen, and every afternoon brought her a cup of the sweet, milky Nepali tea that he brewed in his office. He had debriefed Ava on safety, helped her buy an earthquake kit, and even found her a real estate agent so that she could move to a place of her own at the end of the month.

Jared Lukkinson from Peace Building entered the conference hall with Shova Simkhada, the other Nepali program staff. Shova worked with Andrew Scheiffer on ... something. Ava hadn't quite grasped what when she had gone to Shova's office to introduce herself.

Everyone knew Herman Banke from Social Inclusion wouldn't be coming to the briefing. He had dispatched a circular this morning—I OBJECT IN THE STRONGEST POSSIBLE TERMS!!!—protesting IDAF headquarters' directive to downgrade his program to a short-term project on resilience. He had appealed to headquarters to reconsider the directive. Meanwhile he was refusing to work, spending his workdays sending furious circulars: SOCIAL INCLUSION IS THE MOST PRESSING ISSUE BEFORE NEPAL!!!

The deputy country director Claire Ross-Jones arrived with a slam of the door. "Good morning, everyone." She was direct and commanding. "We're waiting for William, he had a meeting at the Home Ministry, he's been held up, the student unions have blocked the roads." She scanned the room. "Jared, I wanted to make sure you've spoken to Dana Spinkof at Save the Children?"

Jared shot her a surprised look. "But of course. We're cooperating on a joint strategy on non-compliance."

"Will it touch on governance?"

"Naturally."

"Super. Now, has everyone set up their sectoral briefings with our new director of Women's Empowerment Program, Ava Berriden?" Claire turned to Ava. "Ava, I ran into the Secretary of Health yesterday, and it occurred to me—how did Nepal do on MDG Six?"

MDG Six. Ava had brushed up on the millennium development goals, but couldn't recall what the sixth one pertained to.

Vishwa helped her out: "I'm still briefing Ava on the MDGs, so let me answer. Nepal was a little behind on MDG Six, Claire. At first, we saw significant progress on HIV-AIDS, but there was a reversal. The indicators on malaria, tuberculosis, and other preventable diseases were also mixed. The key problem, Claire, has been resource gaps."

Claire nodded. "And will the paper on Gender Responsive Budgeting address these resource gaps going forward?"

This time, Ava was able to reply. "It will. It'll also highlight Post-Priority Themes," she said.

"And don't forget, you'll need to double your budget for the Five Year Outlook."

The country representative William Tomlinson came in at last, trailed closely by Andrew Scheiffer, who was booming: "It's donor shopping!"

"Yes, yes." William Tomlinson was rumpled and unfocused in the eye, like someone who had just woken up from a nap. "My apologies, everyone." He sat heavily at the head of the table. "These goddamn student unions, always screwing around. I don't know what they think they're doing. All right, let's begin."

Claire took charge of the proceedings. "We're here," she said, "to hear from Daphne Muirwood." She nodded at the woman at the far end of the hall. "Daphne has been deputed from headquarters to help us integrate the Paris Declaration on Aid Effectiveness into the Five Year Outlook. Daphne, please."

"Thank you." Daphne Muirwood gave the room a thin smile. "I'm in Nepal on a limited mandate for six months. My brief is to innovate an internal implementation strategy in low-performance country offices in the Asia-Pacific Region as we draft the Five Year Outlook."

Ava paid close attention, trying to follow her.

"The implementation strategy is envisioned as being two-pronged," Daphne went on. "The implementation strategy addresses the latest updates on the Paris Principles. There'll be a modular component as well, which I'll apprise you of later. But first let me begin with an overview of the updates of Accra and Busan."

Ava soon learned that her predecessor, Catherine Christy, had left IDAF after receiving a poor review for under-budgeting. Claire Ross-Jones was keen that Ava not repeat this mistake. She had given Ava four months to draft the women's empowerment component of the Five Year Outlook, telling her more than once, "I can't stress this enough: I need the budget doubled, Ava."

Proposals for next year were also pouring in. It was part of Ava's brief, as the director of the Women's Empowerment Program, to assess each one for funding. She began to spend all of her office hours, as well as her evenings and weekends, studying reports, policy papers, assessments, briefs, circulars, and memos as stacks of documents piled up, half-read, in her office and hotel room.

And yet she had to scramble to keep up. A few days after the weekly briefing, at a briefing of the Employment Generation Program — Paradigm Shift on Schemes for Employment Generation — Ava couldn't even understand what Shova Simkhada was saying, in part because Shova's voice was so soft as to be inaudible. "The application of cash transfers from transitional societies in sub-Saharan Africa to transitional societies in South Asia remains practically untested," Shova said before a cough from Jared Lukkinson drowned out her words. For a while her lips appeared to move soundlessly. Then Ava heard, "Preliminary baseline study carried out by our partner shows that microfinance still has a higher point estimate," before Shova's voice faded again, till these words drifted across to Ava: "Nevertheless this paradigm shift must be acknowledged.

Therefore, it is our recommendation that the Five Year Outlook allocate resources for cash transfers to our clients..."

"Stakeholders," Andrew Scheiffer cut in.

"Stakeholders. Sorry. Yes." Shova closed her eyes. "Sorry, Andrew. I mean allocate transfers to our stakeholders, not clients. Stakeholders, stakeholders," she said. "Stakeholders. In conclusion, what I am saying is that in the Five Year Outlook we must allocate additional resources for cash transfers to our stakeholders."

Was she recommending that IDAF hand out cash? Was this a common practice in aid?

Ava never got a chance to ask, though she did stop by Shova's office several times in the following days. Shova was either in meetings or on the phone or out of the office. Everyone at IDAF was extraordinarily busy, or if not busy, then preoccupied — so much so that Ava couldn't help but wonder if there were something wrong here. It didn't feel normal to her.

She felt so especially on the day of her briefing with William Tomlinson. As she headed to his office, she rounded a corner and came across Herman Banke and Jared Lukkinson arguing in the hallway. Herman was shouting: "Without social inclusion, what peacebuilding can there be, Jared? Inclusion is key to peacebuilding in this country! There are more than a hundred identity groups here, we cannot support their systematic exclusion by the PEON, the PEON, the Permanent Establishment of Nepal!"

Jared had put his hands up as if in surrender.

Unable to get around the two men, Ava stood by as Herman went on shouting: "The government of Nepal tells us to write 'poor and marginalized,' instead of 'socially excluded,' and you comply! I demand that you put the term *excluded* back in your report, Jared!"

"Naturally —"

"If you don't reinstate the term *excluded*, I'll fight all your work, Jared! I'll undermine everything you do! I'll destroy you! There'll be no more peacebuilding for you!"

Jared stepped aside and walked away, hands still up.

Herman turned furiously towards Ava, his face blotched with fury.

"Sorry, I'll just —" Ava passed by.

What had she stepped into?

The country representative's office complex occupied the sunny top floor of the fort. His secretary was seated outside the door. Was she Geeta? No, Geeta was Claire's secretary, who had a soft, full face. This woman had more angular features. This was — Sharmila? Indu? Prativa? Or maybe Meera?

"Good morning, Abha-madam!" The secretary smiled. "Please go in, William-sir is waiting for you only."

"Thank you." Ava stepped in.

William Tomlinson was on the phone, fulminating. "The fucking minister, how many times do I have to tell him, how do I get it through his thick skull — oh, hello." He sat up when he noticed her. "Ava Berry. Were we supposed to meet today?"

"Berriden. We're scheduled for a briefing. I can wait outside if you're busy."

"Ah, I see." He took a long gulp from a glass of — tea? It glinted like aged Scotch. "Just a sec," he said into the phone, and turned back to her. "Look, I'm sorry, Ava, but the Minister of Youth and Sports has thrown us for a loop, he's demanding that we allocate extra funds for a stadium if we want his support on youth leadership programs. Can we reschedule for next week? Oh, wait, I'll be in London next week, and then I've got family time in Luang Prabang — have you ever been?"

"To Luang Prabang?"

"It's out of this world. We'll have to postpone the briefing till after I come back, I'm afraid."

"Oh. All right."

"Thanks for understanding, Ava. And on your way out, will you tell Sharmila I've run out of ice?"

IDAF *was* a major aid organization. It had a fine reputation internationally. Back in her office, Ava scoured the web to reconfirm this and reassure herself. In Nepal, IDAF funded not just the government, but also some of the country's largest international and national non-government organizations. The problem was with her: she hadn't yet adapted to this new line of work. It surprised her, in retrospect, that her application to IDAF had been accepted at all. What did she know, after all, about women's empowerment? Her annual program budget was upwards of two million pounds. What qualified her to oversee it?

She did a quick scroll of her personal emails. Kim Armstone had emailed from Juba asking how things were going.

Ava sent a peppy reply: *I'm learning a lot!*

Did you meet Tomás Barba? Kim had written. *I told him you're originally from Nepal. I hope that's all right?*

It wasn't quite. Ava didn't want anyone here to know that she had been adopted from here. It felt too private somehow. She hadn't put up family photos in her office, and when Vishwa Bista had asked about her background, she had lied: "We have mixed ancestry — it's complicated."

Now Kim's friend Tomás Barba knew. Ava had exchanged emails and cell phone numbers with him, but didn't want to meet him, now that he knew.

Every night, she ordered room service and looked out the window at the crooked brick house. Kathmandu was going through twelve-hour power cuts, and on some nights the house was entirely dark. She watched the family moving in the shadows, and imagined their lives. She felt so far removed from Nepal. Several weeks into IDAF, she couldn't really tell what impact her work had on the lives of Nepalis. Outside of work, she didn't even know any Nepalis.

For now, Vishwa Bista was her sole source of companionship. He helped her prepare for the stakeholders' meeting, and, on the day, picked her up early in one of the more ostentatious office SUVs, the kind that only program staff were authorized to requisition. Vishwa had taught Ava how to requisition them for her own use, but she hadn't had reason to do so till now. The meeting was at a resort outside Kathmandu. Ava had dressed in a formal suit and armed with her attaché case. She wanted to look confident to disguise her nervousness.

The driver — one of many at IDAF, they seemed interchangeable, no one ever introduced them — steered away from the usual turn to the office, through a row of tumbledown buildings.

Vishwa was in a garrulous mood. "We'll be taking a — what do they call it?" He smiled. "When I was at Ohio State, a group of us — foreign students — drove from Columbus to Detroit once along a — that's it — a scenic route. We'll be taking a scenic route today."

The tumbledown buildings gave way to a stretch of concrete block houses. Much of Kathmandu was ugly, there was no sugarcoating it. The modern city was drab at best, and at worst squalid. There was something personal about Ava's disappointment in this. As they drove on, she found herself picking out fragments of beauty — a flowering cherry tree, carved woodwork on an old house, a shrine strewn with marigolds — in the fug of mist, dust, and exhaust.

After weaving through traffic, the driver turned onto a four-lane highway. Vishwa pointed out points of interest as they drove on. "You see there? That's the government department for herbs and herbal products. And that's the TB hospital, Ava, you know, tuberculosis. When we were growing up, this area felt so far away, in the countryside. Now ... Kathmandu has really grown."

"Has it?"

"You can't imagine. Now if we were to turn right here, we'd get to Bhaktapur. Have you been there yet? I can take you. It's one of the three ancient kingdoms of Kathmandu Valley."

He began to tell her about the valley's history, fragments of which were familiar to her. Her parents had made her and Luke read guidebooks before their Christmas trip, and after accepting this job, she had sought out books on history, politics, and sociology. But she was happy to learn more, and Vishwa was happy to talk. "And so the lake was drained, you see, by the sword of the Bodhisattva..." He became eloquent, even flowery, describing Kathmandu's origin myths.

The air cleared as they left the city behind. The sky shifted from grey to white to blue. They drove past terraced fields and small, scattered villages as the road meandered up into the hills. This was the Nepal of the guidebooks Ava had read at age fourteen: beautiful and utterly alien.

On a high ridge, the driver turned off the main road, into a swank resort. Getting out of the car, Ava had to stop to take in the sweep of undulating green hills and steep black mountains, and beyond, the Himalayas: sharp, spiky, white, shimmering like a hallucination.

"Nice, huh?" Vishwa said,

"I've never seen anything like it," Ava said. Nothing in

Kathmandu had prepared her for the sight of the Himalayas. This, she thought, was what she had barricaded herself against that Christmas. It was what she still was, consciously and subconsciously, barricading herself against: the risk of developing an affinity for this land.

Nepal was beautiful.

The stakeholders' meeting took place in a musty hall with absolutely no view. There were about a hundred people in the hall. Ava and Vishwa sat together at the front, but just as the meeting started, Vishwa excused himself and went to talk to a man in a traditional trouser-and-tunic costume and colourful cap. The official at the orphanage had worn the same costume, Ava remembered. There was a name for it: she used to know it. It was the national costume.

The presentations, when they began, took place in Nepali. This took Ava aback. Was she supposed to have known about this? She glanced around nervously, noting that she was the only foreigner present. Surely she wasn't expected to understand, or speak, Nepali? The language gushed and bubbled and lilted and popped. She wondered if it was difficult to learn. At one point, she looked at Vishwa to see if he could possibly translate for her, but he was absorbed in conversation with the costumed man. So she sat, discomfited, and increasingly bored, as one after another speaker — all men — came up to the podium. Even the PowerPoints — the charts, graphs, captions — were in Nepali.

By the time her turn came, she was rattled. She hated public speaking, and right now she couldn't even tell whether the audience understood English: though surely they did? She stood at the podium, trying to project authority: "Good morning. Namaste. Thank you for having me here."

The audience was mostly unresponsive, but a woman in the back was smiling at her and nodding, as though encouraging a child at a school performance.

Ava went ahead and made her presentation.

Everyone clapped at the end, but there was no telling whether anything she had said — about Gender Responsive Budgeting, about the MDGs, about the Post-Priority Themes — had made any impression.

The meeting concluded with a buffet lunch in another windowless hall. In the food queue, Vishwa introduced her to the costumed man. "Ava, please meet the labour secretary." He turned to the man, "Sir, our new director of WEP, Ava Berriden, is from Canada."

"Oho!" the labour secretary exclaimed. "My daughter is also living in Canada, in Ottawa! She is having a job as software designer in a company. Very good salary!"

"Oh," Ava said. "That's wonderful."

"My son-in-law is also having a very good office job! They are living in Blackburn Hamlet. You know Blackburn Hamlet?"

"No,"

"They bought one house there, in Blackburn Hamlet! They are saying to me to visit. Where I should apply for a ten-year super-visa, Miss, in Delhi, or in Kathmandu itself?"

"Oh. I don't really know," Ava said. An awkward silence followed. To break it, she said, "You know, I have a question, and you'd probably be the right person to ask it to. I've been following the news a little, but can't tell — when is the new constitution going to be promulgated?"

"Constitution, ha ha." The labour secretary turned away towards the buffet table.

As they picked over the greasy Indian-Chinese lunch, the woman who had smiled and nodded during Ava's presentation came and introduced herself. She was the deputy co-director of an international NGO called World Development Systems-Nepal. She didn't mention her name. "I am working on a proposal to submit to IDAF," she said. "WDS-Nepal is a long-time partner, as you know. Catherine Christy, she was my good friend. You are free on Friday, Ava? You come to my house for a nice Nepali dal-bhat: you and Vishwa-ji."

Dinner at the house of a Nepali woman. Ava felt she ought to extend herself. "If Vishwa's free," she said, unsurely. "I'd love to."

"Sure, sure," Vishwa said. "Ava, you should know that Indira Sharma-ji here is one of the senior-most Nepali women in the aid sector."

"That is true." The woman — Indira — beamed. "I am senior-most!" Then she said something under her breath, in Nepali, to Vishwa.

He replied in English, "But we can discuss this at your house, Indira-ji."

"Most definitely! Most definitely! It is confirmed, then: Friday at seven!" The woman shook hands with Ava. "Looking forward to it very much!" she said.

"Me too," Ava said.

By the time they left the resort, a haze had settled over the sky, and the Himalayas were no longer visible. Ava stared, nevertheless, at the undulating hills and steep mountains, which were beautiful. There were houses scattered about in small clusters — villages. One or two houses stood alone, sep-arated from the rest. They looked so fragile, and unprotected, against the vastness. It was impossible for Ava to avoid the thought: I could have been born in one of those houses.

On the drive back, Vishwa praised Ava's presentation. "We got a great response from the stakeholders, now we'll have to build on that, Ava. Ah, look." He pointed at a row of sheets drying beside the road. "See that? That's handmade paper made from hemp, it's part of the handicrafts industry of Nepal."

Vishwa talked about handicrafts as they drove out of the hills, into the grey fug of Kathmandu. He talked about papermaking, basket weaving, woodcarving, stonemasonry, metalwork, jewelry design. He told her about the special repousse technique used to cast bronze statues of Hindu and Buddhist deities. Then he began to explain the deities.

By the time they returned to IDAF — the fort — Ava was exhausted.

In the washroom, she splashed water on her face, and this revived her a little. But then, drying off, she suddenly felt intensely alone. She wished she could talk to someone, someone from her world. Not Gavin. And not Anthony either, though Anthony had emailed a couple of times: she owed him a reply. She wished she could talk to someone who knew her, who also knew Nepal.

Luke. She missed Luke.

On the washroom wall, by the dryer, was a cancer self-testing aid: a replica of a woman's breast, made of rubber. It stuck out of the wall like a gristly trophy. Ava gave it a poke and felt a lump on the sticky underside. Had she made a mistake coming to Nepal?

She took a cell phone photo of the breast and attached it to an email to her brother: *Help, there's a Nepali woman trapped in the wall, I don't know how to empower her. Talk soon? I need to vent! xoxoA*

OLD LAPTANNI BUDHI'S house stood at the foot of the hills on the far shore of the mad river. Sapana ducked in through a side door, shivering underneath her thick brown shawl. The mist was so dense this morning that it seeped into the veins, chilling the blood. The members of the women's committee were all huddled by the hearth. Kanchan-bhauju patted a cushion next to her, and Sapana sat down cross-legged on it. Jethididi and Naina-di shifted to make room when Hasta-ma and Laxmi-aama came in. One of Laptanni Budhi's countless daughters-in-law served everyone glasses of hot, steaming tea.

Laptanni Budhi looked around. "Where's the secretary gone? Ey, where's Rama? She was here just a moment ago."

"I'm here, I'm here!" Rama-bhauju hurried in and sat in the centre of the room. "Something's wrong, I need to pee all the time, I really should go to the medical shop in the bazaar." Rama-bhauju took a cup of tea from the daughter-in-law and said, "Lau, let's start the meeting." Then she grew officious. "The agenda of today's meeting is: accounts. Now that Sapana-bahini is the treasurer," she said, "she'll have to do the accounts for us."

"Lord Shulinbaba sent us a treasurer just in time!" Laptanni Budhi said. "My nephew Jeevan told me we have to do the additions and subtractions in writing."

"In writing?" Rama-bhauju gasped. "He wants it all in writing?"

"That's what he told me," Laptanni Budhi said. "He told me the CBO's asking for money from foreigners. We have to tell them how much money we collected, how many loans we gave, and what profits and losses everyone made."

"And we have to do all that in writing!"

This piece of information stumped everyone. The entire room fell silent.

Then Laptanni Budhi said, "If the foreigners give them money, my nephew will take us on another study tour next year. That's what he told me."

This reanimated the room:

"Another tour would be fun!"

"We had such a time!"

"They talk funny out there, remember how hard it was to understand the woman at the pig farm?"

"Quiet, everyone!" Rama-bhauju said, turning to Sapana. "Lau, Bahini, that means you'll have to do the accounts for us — in writing."

Sapana wanted to laugh out loud, but held back. These old women were shameless about making her do all their work. She didn't mind it, actually; in fact, it felt good to be needed. She had brought an old copybook from school. She slipped it out from under her shawl, opened it up to an empty page, and said, "You'll have to give me all the information about the committee."

But it turned out that no one knew very much. Laptanni Budhi claimed that there were seventeen members in the committee, but then listed twenty-two names. Sapana hadn't realized that Chandra's muwa was also in the committee. No one could remember who had joined when, or for how long they had paid their monthly dues. There was no record of the loans the committee had offered, or of repayments received. And worse, when Sapana asked how much money the committee had, Laptanni Budhi held up a battered tin box and a stack of loose hundred-rupee notes:

"I lost the key to the padlock, we haven't been able to open it for more than six months, Nani."

"You store your money in a box?" Sapana was aghast. "You should put it in the bank, it'll earn an interest there."

"We discussed that once," Rama-bhauju said. She turned to the rest. "Didn't we discuss that once?"

"We did, that was that time we met at my house," Hasta-ma said. "The time you made that anarasa roti! Ssss! That was so good, I can still taste the toasted sesame seeds."

"That's right, we had it with tomato achaar."

"Ssss! That was the best!"

Laptanni Budhi hushed them. "Sapana-nani's right. We should put the money in the bank. So do it for us, Nani. You know how to do it. So, do it."

But as soon as Sapana mentioned that the bank would require the chairperson, secretary, and treasurer to open the account, Laptanni Budhi and Rama-bhauju began to fuss.

"Who has the time to go to the bazaar?"

"I don't have the time."

"We don't have the time. Do the accounts first, Nani. Then we'll see."

They were just so lazy. Sapana agreed, of course, to do the committee's accounts. "I'll have to meet all the members, so it'll take a few days, but I'll do the accounts for you — in writing," she said.

"Jaya Shulinbaba!" Laptanni Budhi handed over the tin box and loose notes.

Everyone immediately got up, relieved that the meeting had ended.

"Our work's done, isn't it?"

"I have so much to do, I have to go."

"Me too, I can't sit around, my mother-in-law will kill me!"

The room quickly emptied out.

Laptanni Budhi asked Sapana to stay on. "My daughters-in-law are cooking fresh corn, have some, Nani."

But Sapana wanted to go to Chandra. "How can I be the only one with nothing to do?" she shot back. "I'm also busy, I also have to go."

The mist was still dense outside, and would likely remain so all day. Every winter, there was a cold spell when the sun never came out, and then it would rain, and the seasons would turn.

Sapana crossed over the mad river and went up the hill, to Chandra's house.

Chandra's buwa was sitting, as he did every day, by the bottlebrush trees. When he heard her, he turned towards her. "Is that you, Nani?"

"I don't think the sun will come out today, Buwa. Shall I bring you a blanket?"

"I'm fine as I am, Nani. Go in. The other girls are also there."

Chandra's muwa was in the courtyard, bottling a batch of fresh radish pickles. Sapana could remember a time when Muwa wasn't so pinched and emaciated, before Surya-di disappeared.

"Muwa," she called out, "I didn't realize you were in the women's committee!"

Chandra's muwa smiled wanly. "I joined last year to see if I could sell pickles." She looked exhausted, as always. "You know." Her brows furrowed. "If you girls didn't visit, Chandra wouldn't do anything. Was she like this at your house, Nani? All she does is lie in bed, reading."

"She reads too much, that girl."

"She hardly even speaks to us. She acts as though we've harmed her, Nani."

Sapana felt sorry for her. She said, "It's not that, Muwa. It's, well, you know what Chandra's like."

Obstinate: that's what she's like, Sapana thought, going into the house. She knew Chandra blamed her parents for what had happened to Surya-di. It was unreasonable, but Chandra felt that if they weren't so poor, Surya-di wouldn't have had to go to India, and nothing bad would have happened to her. Even little Tara protested, "That's not fair, Di!" But Chandra just couldn't forgive her muwa-buwa.

The house was dark, with a sour air. Surya-di's old room was used, now, for storing pickles, and the stench of fermentation wafted out of it. As Sapana passed by the door, she saw someone in the shadows, and stopped.

All three sisters — Surya-di, Chandra, little Tara — had smooth hair that cascaded down in black sheets. All three had flashing eyes and a mannish build. Among them, Surya-di was the tallest. Her eyes were dull as she gazed at Sapana.

For the longest time, Sapana couldn't move or think or even breathe. Finally, she stammered: "What — what happened to you, Di?"

I died, of course.

The world convulsed. Sapana reeled, losing her balance. She reached for the wall for support. There was no one there, of course, the hall was empty: it was just a shadow in the shape of a person.

Heart pounding, Sapana burst into Chandra's room, and found, to her great relief, that everything was normal there. Little Tara was bent over in a corner, mending a torn shirt. Ritu and Namrata were sitting on the floor, talking, and Chandra was lying in bed above them, leafing through a book. Sapana flopped down beside her friend, trying to stay calm.

Chandra turned to her and eyed the tin box. "What's that?"

Sapana forced a smile. "I robbed the women's committee! I grabbed all their money and ran over here!"

"Ey, Sapana," Ritu said, grinning slyly. "Is it true that Jeevan Bhatta begged you to join the committee?"

Ritu was a gossip: you had to be careful what you said around her. "I joined it for you," Sapana said. "I did it to arrange your marriage to him."

"Tchee! Who'd marry that old widower?" Ritu made a face. "Besides, he's already got his eyes on you. Tch, Sapana, it would make him so happy if you were to marry him!"

"I'd never marry that old man!"

"Well, I'll never marry anyone," Chandra declared.

"Me, neither," Tara chimed in from the corner. "I'll never marry!"

Ritu pouted. "Me, I want to get married, otherwise how will I ever leave my parents' home? But I need a husband who's young and handsome, and rich too. Ey, Sapana, isn't your brother looking for a wife?"

"You want me to talk to him for you?"

"Not for me. For her." She pointed at Namrata.

Poor Namrata, she was so proper, and so easy to tease. "I'll kill you, Ritu!" she hissed, turning red.

Ritu cackled wickedly. Then she asked, "Gyanu-dai must earn a lot, working in a five-star hotel. Is that so, Sapana?"

Chandra scoffed. "Can't you talk about anything but boys?"

"Look, Namrata and I aren't like you two," Ritu shot back. "We're not smart, we didn't pass out of school, and we're no beauties either, so we can't be picky, we'll have to marry the first boy who'll have us, right, Namrata?"

"Be quiet!"

"Tell me if I'm wrong!"

"Shut up."

As they bickered, Sapana turned to Chandra. "Ey, girl. What are you reading now?"

"Why should I tell you?" Chandra pouted. "You won't read it anyway."

"I don't understand all those big words you like to use." Sapana laughed. "Progress and materialism and — what? Historical necessity."

"So, then?" Chandra turned the book away from her. "You don't need to see what I'm reading."

Ritu glanced over. "Is it a dirty book? Remember that book you were reading once, about the girl who loved two boys at the same time? Is it like that?"

"Yes, it's exactly like that," Chandra said. She opened the book and read from it. "He entered her like a hot knife in butter."

"Tchee!" Namrata cried, scandalized.

"Gasping, she submitted," Chandra went on. "She gave up her most cherished womanhood." As she read, Chandra rolled over in bed to face Sapana, and lowered her voice seductively. "He looked into her eyes and said, 'I love you, darling. Do you love me too?' 'Yes, I love you,' she said. He cupped her breasts with his hands, and, thrusting harder, said, 'Do you truly love me, darling?' In ecstasy, she moaned, 'I truly love you, darling, I love you, I love you, I love you!'"

With this, Chandra drew in and kissed Sapana on the mouth.

Chandra's lips were soft, and she tasted of milk.

"Tchee!" Namrata cried again.

Ritu cackled.

Little Tara squealed.

"You're crazy!" Sapana cried, extricating herself from Chandra.

"Ah-ha-ha!" Chandra sputtered. "I love you, darling, I truly love you!" She kissed Sapana on the mouth again, and collapsed back on the bed, laughing.

"Let me see that book." Sapana lunged for it, wresting it out

of her friend's hands. Then she saw that it wasn't a dirty book —
it was someone's life story. "Idiot!" She tossed it back.

"Ah-ha-ha!" Chandra laughed. "You wanted to read a filthy
book, didn't you? You wanted to read about hot knives and
butter, ah-ha-ha!"

"Be quiet!"

"You want a hot knife in your butter, ah-ha-ha!"

"Be quiet, will you?" Sapana said, though in truth, she loved
to see Chandra laughing like this.

It took forever for Chandra to stop laughing. When she did
so at last, she wiped away her tears and explained that the book
was the life story of a Maoist woman soldier. "She ran away
from home at fourteen and joined the revolution. She learned
how to use guns, she raised money for arms, she even went to
battle." Chandra hooked her arms through Sapana's. "Come,
let's run away, you and I. Let's run away and become revolu-
tionaries, Sapana."

"Lau, we'll do that, but first, move back with me," Sapana said.

Chandra looked at her.

"I asked Gyanu-dai, and he said you should move back,"
Sapana said.

The others were watching her, waiting for an answer. They
knew how much Chandra hated being in this house.

Even little Tara knew that. "If you go," she said, "I'll have this
whole room to myself again, Di."

Ritu joked, "You can move back, ey, Chandra, but Gyanu-
dai's booked for Namrata."

"I'll kill you, Ritu! I'll really kill you!" Namrata hissed.

Chandra kept looking at Sapana, and then asked, "Really?"

"Really," Sapana said. "Come back. The house feels empty
without you."

NOWADAYS IT WAS impossible to buy a simple kurta that wasn't marred by beads, embroideries, sequins, or mirror-work. Indira covered up the gaudiness with a plain black pashmina shawl and checked the mirror. She felt, and looked, fatigued: her monthlies had started, though she had kept this from Uday Sharma, because how could she possibly supervise a dinner party if she were barred from the kitchen for being impure? She leaned forward and scrutinized her face. Every morning she daubed on the beauty cream from Paris, but the furrows and grooves, dots and patches, stains and blotches remained.

"Durga!" she cried, stepping out to see to the evening's duties. The servant girl had aired out the house, but a trace of myrrh clung stubbornly to the air. In the sitting room, Indira plumped up the sofa and ran a finger along the shelves to see if Durga had wiped off the dust. She had. The girl had stuffed too many dahlias into the cut-glass vase. Indira loosened up the bouquet and placed the vase at the centre of the new oval marble-top coffee table from Luxury Home Decor.

"Durga!" she cried again, going to check on the children. Aakaash was playing computer games, as always, and Aakriti was hunched over a book. The door to Muwa's room was closed. Good. May it remain so all evening. The old witch was growing crankier by the day, convinced as she was that Durga was whoring. Just this morning, she had asked Indira, "How else can she afford to buy red lali for her lips?"

"I gave her one of my old lipsticks, Muwa."

"That girl has very bad character," the old witch had said.

"Durga!" Indira cried again.

The girl finally showed up, loping into the sitting room, her clothes torn and her hair a rat's nest. "Hajoor," she mumbled.

"Is the food ready, Durga?"

"The chicken's still cooking, Hajoor."

"And the snacks? Are they done? Let's go and inspect, shall we?" Indira led the girl to the kitchen, where, sure enough, the crystal bowl was heaped with walnuts. "How many times must I tell you, Durga: don't fill the bowl to the top!" Indira cried. "People don't eat nuts by the handful; they take one or two at a time. Put half the nuts back — and seal the bag so they don't become soggy!"

The girl slouched miserably over her task.

Now Indira felt bad. "Look, Durga, this party isn't for fun, it's part of my office work," she said. "Now, don't forget: first, bring the nuts, then the dried meat, then the pakodas, then the momos. Only then serve the meal. But first: change into something nice, will you. The guests will think I don't pay you. The red kurta I gave you last month? Wear that."

"It tore."

"You've torn it already?" Indira had to stop herself from shouting at the girl again. "Then find something else, Durga. When I go to the office, I don't wear rags, do I? This house is your office. Of course, you live here, it's your home too, but it's important for us working women to look our best."

Oof, what was the point.

Indira went back to the sitting room, and found her husband at the bar, pouring whisky into a tumbler. It made her blood pressure rise. "What kind of a host?" she cried. "You're not even waiting for the guests!"

Uday Sharma gave her a drunkard's smile. "Indira Sharma, you worry too much," he said.

"And you, Uday Sharma, worry too little!"

"Relax," he said. "I got your man a Black Label — not a Chinese knock-off: the genuine thing." He took a gulp from the tumbler.

"Ho, that's smooth, all right." He lowered himself onto the soft black leather recliner and grinned at Indira. "And there's brandy for afterwards. VSOP. Everything will be all right."

Indira looked at him sprawled there, so cocky, so confident. "How do you know that?" she wondered out loud. "You don't actually know that, do you? You don't know, Uday Sharma. You have no idea what it's like to be a Nepali woman."

"I'm telling you."

"You really think?"

"A hundred percent."

Why was this at all reassuring?

The doorbell rang. Indira shot towards the door as her husband gulped down his whisky.

She opened the door, and there he was, IDAF's senior program officer, Vishwa Bista, with his smug face, floppy hair, his pricey name-brand clothes, and his America-educated sheen of privilege. Behind him was the dark, twiggy woman who had replaced the American Catherine Christy as IDAF's new director of WEP.

The woman was wearing a mini dress and looked exactly twenty years old. "I hope you like wine." She held out a bottle. "It's an Argentinian cabernet sauvignon, the best one at my hotel."

Indira stepped aside so that her husband could handle the alcohol, and made the introductions: "Ava, this is my ..." Hindu decorum prevented her from uttering her husband's name out loud. "He is under-secretary at the Ministry of Works and Physical Planning," she explained. To her husband, she said, "Ms. Ava Berriden has replaced Catherine Christy at IDAF."

Uday Sharma leered at Ava. "You are from Argentina, Miss?"

"Canada, actually."

"You please call me Mr. Indira," he said, repeating a line he used on all of Indira's colleagues. "We men should take second place, isn't that so? Today, I am on bartender duty. Can I serve you beer-wine-fruit-juice-soft-drinks?" For Vishwa Bista's benefit, he added, "We also have Black Label."

"I'll have that." Vishwa Bista said.

"And for you, Miss?"

"I'd love a glass of wine, please."

Uday Sharma busied himself at the bar while the others sat down.

The Canadian turned to Indira with a smile. "You won't have wine?"

"No, I never — at home." What would foreigners know of the restrictions on a Nepali daughter-in-law? "Actually, I will have apple juice," Indira said. Then she went to the kitchen to fetch it herself.

She found the chicken bubbling furiously on the stove. Durga was nowhere to be seen. Indira turned down the flame, poured herself a glass of juice and returned to the sitting room, where her husband had served the drinks, and was already decrying the latest scandal — the home minister had released an underworld don from jail.

"In all my years as a public servant I've never seen something like this!" he said, already slurring his words.

"You're right, it's shameless," Vishwa Bista said, and the men were soon trading laments:

"In all my years!"

"Utterly shameless."

"I've never seen!"

The Canadian listened on, polite but uncomprehending. Indira wondered why she was so dark. Was she of African descent? Were there people of African descent in Canada? During a lull in the men's conversation, Indira asked her, "You are from Ottawa, Ava?"

"No, I'm from a small town — you wouldn't have heard of it, it's called Overwood, it's in Ontario. But I've lived in Toronto since my college years."

"I see." Indira searched for something else to say about Canada, but nothing came to mind. She knew nothing about that country — just as the Canadian, likely, knew nothing about this one. This was invariably the case with IDAF's international staff. They wielded immense power over their local counterparts such as Indira, whose careers, and even lives, depended on them. Yet they knew nothing whatsoever. And by the time their counterparts educated them, they were ready to leave the country, climbing the next rung of the career ladder after their stint in Nepal.

Nevertheless, networking with donors was a crucial component of Indira's job, so in the next lull in the men's conversation, Indira turned back to the Canadian. "You have ever had our Nepali dal-bhat, Ava?"

"When I move into my new place, my didi will make it for me," she said.

Her didi. She had just arrived, and already had servants. "You are living where?" Indira asked.

"Do you know where Catherine Christy used to live?"

"The house with the fountain."

"It's too big for me, I don't have a family like she did, but, well, it's earthquake-proof, and when the agent showed me the garden, I couldn't resist."

No family. How old was this Canadian? "You must please keep in mind," Indira said, repeating the old platitude, "that

Kathmandu is not the real Nepal. Isn't that so, Vishwa-ji?"

"Absolutely, Indira-ji. To see the real Nepal, you have to go to the villages," Vishwa Bista said.

"Yes, I'm hoping to fit in a field trip," the Canadian said. "Maybe next month, though there's a divisional meeting, and then there's a workshop on ... is it best practices?" She smiled apologetically. "I have to confess that my background is in corporate law, and it's taking me a while to get up to speed on IDAF's work." She asked Indira, "I was reading WDS-Nepal's report from last year, and I noticed that you work in areas which are high risk for trafficking."

"Oh, trafficking is a big problem in Nepal."

"I'd love to see that work. Maybe we could go together to one of your project sites?"

"To the field?" Indira said. She shuddered at the memory of her last field trip. Even going to the toilet was indelicate when you were the only woman. And the evenings were especially intolerable: the men would go to a bar, fostering the kind of boozy camaraderie that gave them such a huge professional advantage over women, while she, to maintain her respectability, would eat alone in her hotel room, as though she were untouchable. "I will check my schedule," Indira said, though she had no intention of doing so.

At this point, Durga — changed, washed, combed, if sullen-faced — shuffled into the sitting room with the walnuts.

"Snacks!" Indira steered her towards the Canadian. "Have."

The Canadian took one walnut.

Indira steered the girl towards Vishwa Bista. "Vishwa-ji, have."

"After you, Indira-ji."

"Have, have." Indira saw that his tumbler was empty, already.

She glared at her husband till he noticed as well, and got up for refills.

The snacks phase of the evening passed smoothly, in this manner. After the nuts, Durga brought dried meat, then pakodas, and then momos, as instructed. Whenever the men stopped lamenting — "I've really never seen anything so shameful" — Indira exchanged pleasantries with the Canadian:

"You like the momos, Ava? You have eaten goat before?"

"Oh, was that goat meat? I've had it — there was a Greek restaurant that I and my, um, that I used to go to near our — my — house."

"Have some more, then."

"Oh, it's delicious, but I'm stuffed."

"Just one more momo."

"Really, no. Thank you, Indira. That was a lovely meal."

"No, no, no!" Indira laughed. "This is snacks only! Dal-bhat is still coming!"

"Oh, my goodness."

Through these surface pleasantries, Indira remained closely attuned to Vishwa Bista. She was waiting for a signal from him, a sign, the merest hint. Would he —?

He did. The hint came over dinner. They were seated at the dining table. The power had gone off, but the inverter switched on automatically, and the Belgian chandelier cast a soft, sophisticated glow over the room. Durga had served them and had gone off to serve Muwa and the children in their rooms. The conversation had drifted to work. Vishwa Bista was going on, as he was wont to, about IDAF-this and IDAF-that, when Indira noticed a certain tightening of his voice.

"The main challenge for an organization like WDS-Nepal," he was saying, still lucid on his fifth Black Label, "is that you fail to

prioritize the customization of the results log frame, Indira-ji."
To the Canadian, he explained, "You see, Ava, many of our
partners don't realize that with us donors, the management
response corresponds directly to the integration of a proper
alignment agenda." He flicked his floppy hair and struck a
pensive pose. "Especially with our ongoing commitment to
donor harmonization, Indira-ji, it isn't enough to incorporate
the MDGs or the PRSP or even the CSP and CAP. It's also critical
to match our policy priorities, wouldn't you agree? Otherwise" —
and here his voice tightened again — "how can we monitor and
evaluate the reported outputs?"

Indira sat forward, clenched and prepared. She was ready
for this. She was, in fact, more than ready. This was the scenario that she had been anticipating, in a way, for all of her life.

"Vishwa-ji," she began, "in the process of donor harmonization," and her voice unexpectedly quavered. "Capacity
enhancement for WDS-Nepal is the utmost priority." Her
pulse quickened. Her breath shortened. "For example." She
coughed. "Excuse me. For example, last year." A liquid heat
swirled inside her. "All of WDS-Nepal's sectoral strategies were
implemented successfully, though of course some operational
approaches had to be modified due to local conditions," she
said. Trying to sound as sure as possible, she explained to
the Canadian, "You see, in this transitional period there are
many conflict-exacerbating factors at the ground level, Ava.
WDS-Nepal has adopted the Do No Harm principles, and
accordingly, we have to continually adjust our operational
approaches."

The Canadian looked lost.

"Nevertheless." Indira soldiered on. "WDS-Nepal has successfully met all the target outcomes and outputs. But Vishwa-ji, it

may be the case that we must further emphasize monitoring of our partners, who lack capacity."

"Sure, sure," Vishwa Bista said. He took a long, thoughtful sip of Black Label, as though to signal that he wasn't going to make this easy for her. "And yet, Indira-ji, all we have to go by is WDS-Nepal's results log frame," he said, shaking his head like a disappointed parent. "We donors see this all the time. All the time." He turned to the Canadian. "Our partners may be doing good — excellent — work, Ava, but there's no transparency in their reporting, which makes us worry about the delivery of tangible results to beneficiaries, especially when the size of the grant is very large. That's why we, as donors, support organizations such as National Network Nepal, who emphasize the customization of the results log frame."

Pleading with him now, Indira said, "It is just a small problem of capacity enhancement, Vishwa-ji. At the grassroots level, all the target outcomes and outputs have been met. As you understand, our partners are unable to follow the format. We need to help them with customization. Reporting is not our partners' strong point. Vishwa-ji, they need additional help with capacity enhancement."

"You may be correct," he conceded.

Indira looked at him beseechingly.

"It may be that you're correct," Vishwa Bista said. "It may indeed be a matter of greater capacity enhancement."

"I really think so, Vishwa-ji."

"You're right," he said. "The problem isn't with WDS-Nepal, Indira-ji, it's with your partners: the CBOs at the village level. They urgently need capacity enhancement, I think."

"Yes, and National Network Nepal is an excellent organization for this," she said.

"I'm glad you agree, Indira-ji."

"I agree very much with you, Vishwa-ji, I completely agree, thank you, thank you. Thank you so much."

"You're welcome," he said.

How she loathed him.

But with this, they had reached an understanding, and an important one for Indira's career: Indira would increase the budget for capacity enhancement in her proposal to IDAF, and, on the condition that the funds be routed through National Network Nepal — Vishwa Bista's cousin-sister-in-law's NGO — he would ensure that IDAF would approve it. Indira would thus secure WDS-Nepal's largest grant ever.

Throughout their exchange, Uday Sharma had stared at his tumbler like one of those monkeys who saw, heard, and spoke no evil.

A stunned silence followed.

The Canadian eased it away with a question: "Have you been in this line of work for a long time, Indira?"

The question brought back memories from when Indira had started off, full of dreams, at Help. It brought back all the development agendas she had worked on: poverty alleviation, income generation, women and development, women in development, awareness raising, mainstreaming, rights-based development, sustainability, advocacy, empowerment… All the cynicism she had eschewed. What's a DINGO? A development NGO. What's a WINGO? A women's NGO. What's a FINGO? A five-star NGO. All the reports, proposals, budgets, papers, summaries, evaluations that had passed through her desk… All the training, self-improvement, and professional development she had suffered through… Battling her natural womanly shyness, she had learned to speak up at meetings, workshops, seminars, conferences. For decades, Indira had worked tirelessly, truly tirelessly, but only when the development agenda had come around to "social inclusion" had she been promoted to WDS-Nepal's deputy co-director, alongside a man, of course, her number one rival, Chandi Shrestha.

Indira replied, "Yes, Ava, I have been in this line of work for a long time."

"So, you'd be familiar with the entire range of non-government organizations, from the village-based CBOs all the way up to NGOs at the district and national levels."

"Local, district, regional, national, international: everything I know, Ava."

"I've been familiarizing myself with them." The Canadian frowned. "And I guess I'm accustomed to more structure, or to more of a legal infrastructure around organizations. Do you know what I mean? Some of these NGOs and CBOs seem, I don't know — quite flimsy."

Indira looked at the Canadian and wondered whether she would be an ally to her, as Catherine Christy had been. *You mustn't stop at deputy co-director,* Catherine Christy had always said: *you must become the first Nepali woman director of WDS-Nepal.* Which was true. WDS-Nepal's present director, an Australian hippie with the horror name of Rick Peede, was retiring soon, and WDS-International had announced that it would prioritize in-house applications for his replacement. The director's job came with a dollar salary that was more than quadruple what Indira currently earned, which was part of the reason why she had had to bribe Vishwa Bista, because only if IDAF approved her proposal would she edge out her rival Chandi Shrestha for the job.

"Ava," she said, "I am happy to share my experiences. You call me with any and all questions."

"Same here," Vishwa Bista said. "If there's anything, Ava, just call me — at night, during the day, Saturday, Sunday, holidays, it doesn't matter."

"Thank you, you're both so kind."

Durga shuffled in to serve seconds. Indira steered her towards the Canadian.

"Oh, I'll explode if I have one more bite!" the Canadian said. "Actually, I do have a question for all three of you," she added. "How hopeful are you about the prospect of getting a new constitution soon?"

Only then did Uday Sharma deign to rejoin the conversation. "Nothing will happen, Miss!" he cried. "Constitution will never come!"

Vishwa Bista said, "One of our consultants wrote a report, I'll give it to you, Ava."

"Nothing will happen!" Uday Sharma cried.

"I'll give you the report on Monday," Vishwa Bista said. His tumbler was empty again.

The men had one more Black Label with the ice cream dessert, and then back in the sitting room, Uday Sharma insisted: "One peg of VSOP, Vishwa-ji!"

"A small peg, sure."

"Also for you, Miss!"

"No, thank you. Actually, I should get going," the Canadian said. "Maybe the driver could drop me off and come back for you, Vishwa?"

"No, Miss, you have one peg VSOP!" Uday Sharma cried, sloshing out three snifters of brandy.

The Canadian hardly touched her drink as the men gulped down theirs and returned to lamenting:

"Shameful."

"This country is run by underworld dons."

"In all my years!"

When they were done, the Canadian got up in obvious relief. "That was lovely," she gushed. "Thank you so much, Indira and, um, Mr. Indira. I had a wonderful time."

"You like our Nepali dal-bhat, Miss?" Uday Sharma leered.

Elbowing him aside, Indira said, "Come back for a proper dinner, Ava. You didn't have enough dal-bhat this time." To Vishwa Bista she said in Nepali, "The proposal..."

"Submit it directly to me," he replied.

When the guests were gone at last, Indira was overcome with revulsion — for Vishwa Bista, and also for herself.

Remember? How innocent she had been in her youth, how pure? On her first field trip for Help, in impoverished Jumla District, she had cried upon seeing flies on the mouth of a malnourished child. She had vowed to dedicate her life to helping the poor — and today she had offered a bribe.

She was corrupt. She was excrement. She was filth.

Her husband was pouring more brandy into his snifter. "It went well, Indira Sharma, now relax, have a peg, I won't tell Muwa."

"I won't have any brandy and you shouldn't have any more either!" Indira snapped, though she knew there was no stopping her husband now. He would have his fill and stumble gracelessly into bed, reeking of booze from every pore.

For Indira, sleep wouldn't come easily tonight. She went to check in on the children. Aakaash was still playing computer games, and Aakriti was still studying. "Go to bed," she said, knowing that they wouldn't listen to her. She stopped at the door to Muwa's room, took in the scent of myrrh. All was silent inside.

As a final chore, she went to the kitchen to make sure that Durga had cleaned up. As she entered, she saw the girl hunched over the sink, heaving and sobbing.

"Ey, what's this?" Indira rushed to Durga's side. She tried to draw the girl up, but the girl kept heaving and sobbing. Indira put an arm around her. "Tch, tch, tch. Don't cry," she said.

Poor Durga. Poor, poor Durga. It was her fault, Indira thought: overwhelmed by work-travel-family she had neglected the girl; and Durga had no one in the world. She had come into this house wild-eyed at age twelve, the eldest of six unwanted daughters. Her father had been taking her from house to house in Kathmandu, begging for work. The days of keeping a child servant were over, but who could reason with Muwa? The old witch had insisted on taking the girl in, saying, "Village girls are honest and hard-working."

"Raise her, look after her, she's yours now," the girl's father had said to Indira. To Durga, he had said, "Do as your masters bid, they're your gods now." He had never come back for her.

Indira had enrolled the girl in school, but Durga dropped out after class three, settling into the life of a servant girl. She was sanguine by temperament, and seemed content with her lot — till her disastrous engagement with the vegetable vendor. Now he had abandoned her, and her life was ruined. She was only seventeen.

The girl was disconsolate: she kept heaving and sobbing over the sink, as though the world were ending.

"What's wrong, tell me what's wrong," Indira said, though she knew perfectly well what was wrong. "Tch. Durga, don't cry," Indira said. "I know it's been hard for you, but it'll be all right, I'll always take care of you, girl, you're like my own daughter. Durga? Tell me. Tell me, girl. Tell me what's wrong."

THE ROAD TO the house was steeper than Ava remembered from the time she had come to see it with the real estate agent. When the cab driver honked at the gate, a dog began to howl in the compound next door, its baying filling the air. The cab driver had to honk again before the gate finally opened and a skinny guard waved them in.

The landlady was at the front door, dressed in a blood red sari, as she had been for the showing. She was tiny — four-and-a-half feet at most — with jet black hair pulled back in a tight, oily bun. The contract listed her name as Mrs. Thapa.

Ava stepped out of the cab carrying a box of office documents and her attaché case, which was stuffed with a gargantuan proposal from WDS-Nepal. Mrs. Thapa shouted in Nepali, prompting the skinny guard to scuttle over to help. He unloaded Ava's suitcase from the trunk, along with the earthquake kit that Vishwa had helped her buy.

After the cab left, the landlady held up a bunch of keys and jangled them. "It is saancho," she said, indicating, through mime, that Ava unlock the front door.

The main hall stretched through the house, to the back door. A woman of indeterminate age was standing there, smiling shyly.

"Oh, hello," Ava said, surprised.

The woman said, "Namaste, Madam."

"It is Luna," the landlady declared, launching into a babble of English and Nepali. "Luna cooking, cleaning, ghar safa garne, pakaune, Luna making dal-bhat, tapain ke khane, food, you give money, Luna cooking cleaning shopping making dal-bhat."

"Okay."

The skinny guard toiled behind them, carrying everything into the house.

Mrs. Thapa prodded Ava. "You coming!" She pointed to a stack of electronics near the back door. "Battery back-up inverter Wi-Fi, you no touch, light going, battery power automatic, you no touch!" She produced a chit of paper from her blouse. "Wi-Fi password."

"Okay, thank you."

"Coming." She marched Ava out the back door, into the garden. The fountain at the centre of the garden had been on when Ava had come to see the house, but was off now. "No water," Mrs. Thapa declared, waving her hands at the sky for emphasis. "Monsoon, then rain, then water, now no water, no water, no water." She pointed to an old man pruning a hedge with rusty scissors. "It is Jaleswor garden, he kaan sundaina, no eai, dherai kura gardaina, no talk. Here it is three servants: Harihar guard, Luna maid, Jaleswor garden. Salary you give to me, I give to servants, twenty thousand rupees, you give tomorrow."

"Oh." The contract mentioned the staff, but Ava had assumed that their salaries were included in the rent. Twenty thousand rupees: two hundred dollars — for a staff of three? "Okay," she said, discomfited.

"I go, you stay," the landlady said. "If problem, you coming to my house." She pointed at a modern brick house across the garden. Then she marched across the garden, climbed a set of stairs carved into the compound wall, and disappeared, only to reappear on the balcony of the house next door after some time. From there she waved at Ava.

Ava waved back.

The garden was an oasis, a tropical idyll, lushly, extravagantly beautiful in the midst of modern, ugly Kathmandu. The agent had identified the flowering trees for Ava — jacaranda, acacia, crepe myrtle — though she couldn't remember, anymore, which were which. She walked through them, feeling their barks, running her hands through their leaves. Green shoots were sprouting on some branches. There were fruit trees here too: pomelo and guava and kumquat and plum. Cane garden chairs sat at the edge, by a hedge — a jasmine hedge — on the verge of budding. She stopped beside it and looked out at Kathmandu: the dinge, the sprawl, the concrete maze hemmed in by hills. The agent had said that the Himalayas would be visible on clear days. All she could see was the usual grey fug.

When she turned back, Mrs. Thapa was still on her balcony, staring at her.

Feeling slightly claustrophobic, Ava went into the house through the back door. She could hear Luna in the kitchen. Luna maid, she thought. Luna maid, Harihar guard, Jaleswor garden. The guard had deposited the earthquake kit in the main hall. She found her suitcase in the largest of the bedrooms upstairs. There were two more bedrooms upstairs, both, like this, with en suite bathrooms. The house was absurdly large. On the ground floor were a study, a living room, a dining room, a kitchen, and a guest bathroom. She had once lived in an orphanage in Kathmandu, Ava thought: and now here she was, living in a mansion.

She unpacked and went down to the study. She would have to wade through WDS-Nepal's proposal ahead of a meeting with Claire Ross-Jones next week. For now, she set it aside and opened her laptop. The Wi-Fi password worked, but the connection was slow. She had fallen behind on personal emails. She fired off a note to Luke first:

Moved into the new place! I'm living in style, with household staff, three of them! My landlady introduced them as Luna maid, Harihar guard, and Jaleswor garden. Yikes! Talk soon? xoxoA

Then she turned to the emails she had been avoiding. Gavin had sent two last week. She opened the first. Its tone was mercifully neutral. The real estate agent had received offers on their house, but felt they would do better if they held out for an auction. *The market's booming,* Gavin had written. *The agent's very confident.*

His second email was a mess:

How's Nepal treating you, Av? Is your job everything you hoped for? Have you found what you were looking for? Are you happy there? Ava could hardly read this email; Gavin's words seared. *I miss us, I miss being Av and Gav. I keep thinking about it and don't really understand why I did what I did. You seem hell bent on leaving me, and if you want a divorce, the decision is yours, but I want to tell you I love you, Av.* At the end, he had added: *I thought we'd be Av and Gav forever.*

She didn't have it in her to reply to him.

Anthony had also emailed. His message sat disconcertingly next to Gavin's in the inbox.

The connection we had that night was magical, he had written, and this made Ava cringe a little, though it was true. That night in Miami, she had crossed an important threshold, and Anthony had given her company through that crossing. *I'm seriously thinking of visiting you in Nepal,* Anthony had written. *Let's have a FaceTime date sometime? Lots of love, Ax.*

Ax, she thought. Ax.

She couldn't reply to him either.

Her mother had sent her a long, chatty email a few days ago, and she turned her attention to it. *Dearest darling Ava.* Mom's voice instantly heartened Ava. She was her usual self, prattling on about her latest cause, the lowered water levels of the Great Lakes: *Mayor Jenkins, of course, will hear nothing of it, it's his friends in the military-industrial complex across the border who are causing the water level to drop, after all. I saw him at the Christmas fundraiser. He was sitting next to Tom Boretta from Detroit!!! Do you remember Tom Boretta, honey? His son Jamie's out of rehab and back home now, working for his father's company...* She went on to gossip about all of Overwood.

Ava enjoyed the predictable arc of Mom's communications. All of her emails read like this. Only at the end did she veer to the personal: *Are you settled into your new job, honey? We're so proud of you for being there — but of course we worry. We want you to be happy with your decision.* Then she had written: *Gavin came by for dinner last weekend. He seems to be coping, though sometimes it's hard. After he left, your Dad and I were talking. You've never asked us about it, but in case you want to know where the orphanage is, here's the address.*

Ava stared at the address in dismay. She didn't want to go to the orphanage yet — or maybe ever. Not all adoptees needed to learn about their origins, after all. She didn't; she needn't; there was no imperative to do so.

She closed the email, left the laptop, and paced about the study in a pique. Mom knew perfectly well how she felt about this. Ava had talked to both of her parents about it endlessly, growing up. Or — did they think that's why she had come to Nepal? Was that, in fact, why she had come here? Did she want to go to the orphanage?

She suddenly felt very thirsty. She remembered that there was a water filter in the kitchen, and went there.

Luna, Harihar, and Jaleswor were sitting cross-legged on the floor, eating with their hands from large aluminum plates. They scrambled to their feet in alarm as she came in. Their hands were smeared with dal-bhat.

"I'm sorry, I — please don't let me interrupt your meal," Ava said. "I'll just get some water."

"Water, Madam!" Luna lunged to the sink, washed her hands, lunged to the cupboard, took out a glass, and lunged again to a water filter to fill it. She placed the glass on a tray before presenting it to Ava.

"Oh. Thank you. There was no need. I could have —" Ava took the glass and backed out of the kitchen. "Please — please finish your meal," she said from the door, wondering what kind of employment arrangement she had got into with the household staff.

She went back to the study and sat down with WDS-Nepal's proposal, flipping through it, unable to concentrate. Her thoughts kept skittering over the emails.

I thought we'd be Av and Gav forever.

The connection we had that night.

Here's the address.

Why did the household staff sit on the floor to eat, and not at the dining table? Ava began to feel that renting this house — this mansion — was a mistake. She should break the contract and go back to the hotel. Or she should cut all her losses and quit IDAF and go back home...

Her phone pinged. What time was it in Miami — would Luke be up at this hour?

It was Kim Armstone's friend, Tomás Barba: *Ciao Ava! Meeting friends 4 a Newari-Russian dinner 2night. U free?*

A Newari-Russian dinner, whatever that was, with company, beat spending the evening alone in this house. *Hi there!* Ava messaged back: *I'd love to join you and your friends for dinner.*

Gr8! He sent directions. *Come anytime, m already here, at d bar.*

"**AND, OTHER THINGS?**" Gyanu asked just to keep Maleah online, to see her, if only in blurs and pixels, on the blue electric screen. He was in Butwal Bazaar, at an Internet café that had been set up at the back of an old grain store. Maleah was in a cyber café at City Centre. Gyanu had been to that cyber café often, waiting by as she Skyped with Crisanto. Now she was there Skyping with him. On the screen she looked impossibly beautiful, impossibly remote. Gyanu said, "Tell me — other things, meri maya."

"What other things?" Maleah folded the sheet of paper on which she had printed Crisanto's last email. She had read it out to Gyanu, as she did all her son's emails. This one had ended with a request for new building set. At age six, Crisanto loved to build castles with plastic blocks.

"Tell me how everyone is?" Gyanu said. "How is Jairus?"

Maleah told him that Jairus had come to the gift shop. "He talked and talked: for two hours he talked, mahal! Only about you." Quietly, she added, "He is keeping your room." Gyanu heard the unasked question in her voice. Then she told him about her roommates: "Jojo is going soon. The agent has found her a job in Germany, in Hamburg. Susanna's contract will end in four months," she said. "Same like me."

He knew that she wanted him to ask if she, too, was going to go to the agent, but he was afraid that she would say yes, so instead he said, "You will have to look for another roommate after Jojo."

But then Maleah came right out and asked him, "When you are coming back?"

"Soon, meri maya, soon." Gyanu closed his eyes. "I will come soon to you."

The days kept slipping by, one after another, yet the transfer of the land deed remained undone. Gyanu had discovered that there were generations of paperwork to update first: Ba and Thulo-ba had never transferred it from their father's name to theirs. After wasting a week at the land revenue office in the bazaar, Gyanu had had to appeal to Thulo-ba for help. "Ey, you haven't got it done yet, Babu?" his uncle had said, acting surprised; and then he had dispatched Jeevan Bhatta to help him. "He knows his way around government offices, Babu, let him handle it." Jeevan Bhatta did, indeed, know how to move the files. All he required from Gyanu was money. "Bribing officials is the only way to get work done," he had explained with a sheepish grin. Gyanu had already given Jeevan Bhatta twenty-five thousand rupees. For all he knew, the widower was pocketing it himself. What Gyanu did know for certain was that at this pace, the transfer wouldn't come through by the end of his month off.

As though reading his thoughts, Maleah asked, "You phoned Shantanu Kumar?"

Gyanu said nothing.

On the screen, Maleah turned away.

Gyanu couldn't bear to see her turn away from him. He should go to her at once, he thought. Sapana could follow up on the land transfer by herself: she and Chandra could do it together. No. Thulo-ba would easily stymie them: the old man would delay, he would lie, he would cheat. Gyanu wished Ba were still around, he wished he were back in the desert, he wished he had never come here. In the booth, he fidgeted, thinking: perhaps there was no ideal circumstance in which to talk about the future. He asked, "What do you want to do, meri maya?"

"I want to live with my anak."

Maleah been waiting for a chance to tell him this, he realized. He nodded. "You will talk to the agent?"

"Yes, mahal."

The thought was out there between them now, uttered and acknowledged: Maleah was going to leave the desert, with or without him. A sadness grew in Gyanu and began to spread. He tried to contain it. "If you want to go, then go, meri maya," he said. "Germany, anywhere. Where you go, I will come."

Maleah's face crumpled.

"I will come where you go," Gyanu said.

Maleah wiped away her tears, and reached into her shirt collar to pull out the gold coin. She was wearing it as a locket on a silver chain. It felt as though an age had passed since Gyanu had gone to Suleiman-bhai's shop in Deira. He watched Maleah put the coin to her lips. Four grams. A wedding ring. A dream.

After they hung up, Gyanu walked past sacks of lentils, pulses, and beans to the front of the store to pay for the computer time and a new thousand-rupee recharge card. He asked the shopkeeper, "Where can I find women's clothes — which are the best new shops, Sahu-ji?"

"For your wife, mother, daughter?"

"Sister."

"Children's clothes are there." The shopkeeper pointed across the way. "But if you're looking for ladies' fashions, there's a new shop one street over. All the pretty girls go there nowadays."

Outside, Gyanu scratched the PIN number on the recharge card and topped up his mobile phone. He had to call Shantanu Kumar today. He would do so later.

The grain shop was in the old part of the bazaar, which was as sleepy as it always used to be. A busy modern city had risen up around it. Every time Gyanu came back, he noticed new buildings, new streets, entire new neighbourhoods. The bazaar now sprawled across both banks of the Tinau River, where there used to be open fields.

Following the shopkeeper's directions, he turned into the next street. As boys, he and his friends used to come to this part of the bazaar to seek out the urban entertainments. There used to be a DVD shop here that screened Bollywood movies. It had long since closed. Gyanu and his friends had learned to drink at a cabin restaurant next to it. They had once talked to a prostitute in that restaurant, tantalized but too terrified to follow her into a back room.

The clothes shop, New Nepal Fashions, was on the ground floor of a shopping complex that was still under construction. Rods and pipes were sticking out of the sides of the building. The front window was lined with six headless mannequins in vermilion wedding saris. Inside, the clothes were stacked tidily behind glass shelves to protect them from dust. A young salesman took out each kurta individually and held it up, modelling it against his slim frame. Gyanu selected a simple one with blue stripes that would suit Sapana.

Leaving the shop, he came upon a row of empty plots: fifteen in total, each demarcated by a low concrete-block wall. He wondered how much the plots were going for these days. The price of land was rising so fast that even after years in the desert he couldn't afford to buy in Kathmandu. But maybe here in the bazaar... Perhaps he and Maleah and Crisanto would end up here one day, he thought. Maleah sometimes asked him about the prospects in Nepal. It was his own misgivings that kept him abroad.

Gyanu stepped over the concrete-block wall and went into one of the plots, where it was quiet. Then he placed a mobile call to Shantanu Kumar.

"Hello."

Gyanu could almost see Shantanu Kumar. He would be in his office: he practically lived there. He would be tapping on the desk with his ring-covered fingers, looking out at the glass towers across the road. In Hindi, Gyanu said, "Sir, it's Gyanu."

"Hanh, Beta, I've been expecting your call. When do you come in? Speak."

Gyanu confessed, "I'm still in Nepal, Sir."

Shantanu Kumar coughed. Gyanu could hear tapping on the desk. Then Shantanu Kumar laughed, gruffly but not unkindly. "You're a simple hill boy, huh? You have no duties, no responsibilities? You'll have enough to live on, there, in your village?"

"I need a few more weeks, Sir."

"But I told you, Beta, when you left: thirty days."

"I — Sir. I have to, my sister —" Gyanu struggled to find the right words in Hindi. "I have to make my sister secure," he said, thinking, again: maybe he didn't have to, maybe Sapana and Chandra could take care of themselves.

"And how do you intend to make your sister secure?"

"There's some official work, Sir, concerning my father's land."

Shantanu Kumar drew a sharp breath. "For a worthless piece of land in the hills you give up everything, Beta? What an innocent you are." He laughed. "You travel to faraway lands, you work day and night, you prove yourself, you advance — and then? You throw away everything for a fallow plot of land in the hills." Then he grew stern. "Where I come from in Bihar, Beta? There's nothing. My parents spent their whole lives working their landlord's farm. My mother died from poverty: we didn't have enough money to buy her medicine. Now look at me. Learn from me, Beta. Learn to be smart."

"I'm learning, Sir."

"You're learning too late."

"Just two more weeks, Sir," Gyanu begged. "If you have to replace me I can take another position — assistant chef, even kitchen assistant. I'll clean dishes, Sir, I'll wash the floors —"

"Thirty days." Shantanu Kumar's tone was final. "You know it's not easy what I do, managing a top restaurant like this. Think about it from my side: nothing can ever slow down, nothing can ever stop, everything must always keep moving apace, tak-tak-tak." Shantanu Kumar sighed. "You know I like you, Beta, you remind me of myself when I was your age, but I have my own constraints." Before hanging up, he offered some advice: "Free yourself from your entanglements there. The village is the past, it only holds you back. The future is in the cities, cities like Dubai. For people like us, opportunities don't come by easily, Beta. You have to take them when you can."

"Jairus?"

"Gyanu!"

"What will I do?"

"What happened, hey? Why are you calling? Where are you? Are you still in Nepal?"

Gyanu's throat hurt. He couldn't speak. If he opened his mouth, he would cry.

Shantanu Kumar was right. The village was the past. If he didn't leave, it would trap him.

Jairus could feel his distress over the phone. "Gyanu, don't worry, hey," he said. "Tell me what the problem is. Whatever it is, you know I'll do what I can from my side. I'll talk to Maleah, I'll talk to Shantanu Kumar, I'll talk to all the Nepali brothers and sisters here. Hey, Gyanu," he said, "you know who I ran into yesterday? Suleiman-bhai Sah'b. He was asking — did he make the ring, when's the wedding, what kind of feast will there be?" Jairus said, "Gyanu, you have so many friends, hey. Remember that. If you're in difficulty, everyone will help. So, whatever happened, don't worry, Gyanu. Hello, friend? Are you all right? Are you hearing me? Hello?"

AVA WOKE UP parched, her head throbbing and her body stiff. She had had too much to drink. Tomás was trouble, he really was. Every time they met, he led her on a tear — and why did she so willingly follow? Last night, they had started out at a low-budget den near his apartment. Then they had caught a cab to a Tibetan neighbourhood, Bauddha, to meet Tomás's friends: "Drukpas, nomads, yak herders — I met them last year on the Tibetan plateau." The nomads had turned out to be jean-clad hipsters who spoke not a word of English. At a diner overlooking a candle-lit Buddhist stupa, they had noodles and a fermented millet beer — tuba? Tumba? Something like that. Then Tomás took them to a nightclub, "The Rox, it's where Kathmandu's rich kids come to let off steam," where they had done tequila shots and danced to the relentless beat of Journey — "Don't stop believing, hold on to that fee-ee-ee-ling."

Ava couldn't quite remember the cab ride back, but recalled, hazily, that Tomás had accompanied her home. Yes. He had uncorked a bottle of wine, railing about international aid's complicity in perpetuating inequality in Nepal: this seemed to be his favourite subject when drunk. "This isn't a poor country, what it needs is a redistribution of wealth. Aid is preventing Nepal from having a proper revolution." Ava had suggested, several times, that they call it a night, but Tomás had gone on and on — "Only humanitarian work is justified in this country" — till she had excused herself to go to bed, leaving him ... where?

Warily, she glanced across the bed, and there he was, buried under a tangle of sheets, pillows, and clothes.

Jesus.

Ava slipped out of bed and went downstairs. The house was all hers today. Upon her insistence, Luna had stopped coming in on the weekends, though the landlady had come over to argue with her about it: "Sunday no holiday Nepal!" Ava had refused to give in to redoubtable Mrs. Thapa. Jaleswar came in only thrice a week. Harihar lived on the grounds, in a house by the gate — a servants' quarters — but he kept to himself. Ava saw him only when he opened the gate for her.

She went to the kitchen and made coffee, enough for Tomás too, when he woke up. Her thoughts lingered over Tomás. He quite intrigued her. He was half-Montreal, half-Venice, effortlessly cosmopolitan. He had left home early, and had worked in Sri Lanka, Indonesia, Afghanistan, and Haiti before coming to Nepal; and he was full of stories. He wasn't bad to look at either, with a lazy eye that gave him a dreamy look — though it was too bad about the gold tooth. He had had an incisor capped during a trip to Tibet, and it glinted, sickly and yellow, when he smiled.

Ava took the coffee and two mugs out to the garden. Mrs. Thapa's balcony was vacant this morning. The landlady was no longer as hawkishly watchful as she had been at the start, but every now and then she still came out for a stare.

Only after pouring herself a cup of coffee did Ava notice the view. It had rained during a recent cold spell, and the air had cleared, leaving the city scrubbed and clean. Its concrete maze looked delicate, even fragile, cradled by a ring of green hills. Above the hills were the dark, jagged mountains that Ava had seen at the resort at the stakeholders' meeting. And above those mountains shimmered some squat snow peaks.

The Himalayas. Ava couldn't believe how close they were. They were like a dream, a hallucination.

What a country this was, she thought to herself. What a strange, difficult, complicated country. By now, Ava had caught up on background reading: the indicators in relation to women were bad, even distressing. Women lagged behind men in health, education, income, mobility, opportunity, political representation. Many of the national laws violated international law. The statute of limitations on rape was three months, and the new constitution, if it were ever drafted, was likely to deny women equal citizenship rights. Nepali culture was defiantly patriarchal. It didn't make things any simpler that Nepal's citizenry was divided into more than a hundred identity groups. Women's indicators varied widely by economic class, but also by their caste, indigenous, and regional identities.

"Good morning, my dear." Tomás came out, rumpled and dishevelled and yet somehow elegant. He sat down beside her and poured himself a coffee. "Ah, look. Ganesh Himal. It looks close, doesn't it, but it's up near the Tibet border."

"Oh, tell me you've climbed it," Ava said.

"I had to give up climbing after I broke my leg in the Wakhan corridor."

She gave him a look.

He shrugged. "Some friends were going, I tagged along, but then I had to be rescued. It was embarrassing."

How could Ava not like him? "Hey, Tomás?" she said.

"Yes, my dear?"

"About last night."

"You should have kicked me out." He raised his hands, proclaiming his innocence. "I hope I didn't, um, you know."

"No."

"Our spouses will be relieved to hear that."

He was married?

He noticed her confusion and explained, "Violeta and I are waiting for an annulment. In any case, I've taken a vow of celibacy — things were getting out of hand."

"Oh." Ava couldn't help but feel disappointed.

"Hey, did you mean it when you said you'd be up for a trek in the spring?"

"Have we discussed this before?"

"Last night, remember, at the Rox? It'll have to be an easy trek, because of my knee. Maybe Langtang," Tomás said. He stretched, yawning widely, and his shirt rode up to expose a shapely belly. "So, what's for breakfast?"

"There's leftover dal-bhat in the fridge."

"Let's go to the organic market," he said, standing up. "I'll introduce you to Richard and Luisa. He's Australian, she's Argentinian, they have a goat farm, they make cheese with a method from the Ardennes."

A day that began with Tomás would surely end on another tear. "Another time?" Ava said.

"Of course." He leaned in to kiss her on the cheek. "See you later, my dear."

Ava watched him amble away, feeling a little sorry for herself. Tomás and she hadn't talked about her adoption, but the fact that he knew about it made her feel close to him, though in truth she hardly knew him. An annulment: was he an observing Catholic?

Harihar darted out of the servants' quarters to open the gate for Tomás, who stopped to talk to the guard. Tomás had taken language lessons, and spoke what he called "bazaar Nepali." He wasn't tall, but he towered over the guard. He patted Harihar on the shoulder and left.

After closing the gate behind him, Harihar turned to Ava with an expression that was — what was it? He looked slack-jawed and horrified.

Ava stared back at him, startled. Was the guard judging her for having a man over — in her own house?

Out of the corner of her eye, she caught a flash of red. Mrs. Thapa had come out to her balcony. An odd, uncomfortable emotion — shame — crept through Ava. It quickly converted into anger. Was she really expected to conform to Nepal's conservative social mores? Why would she? She wasn't part of this society. And she deserved privacy: she was paying enough for this house. The rent had seemed reasonable when she had signed the contract, but Tomás had blanched when he had found out how high it was: "I'm going to have to intervene," he had said. He had since loaned Ava *Lords of Poverty, White Man's Burden, The Bottom Billion, Dead Aid,* and two books by William Easterly — sharp critiques of aid, which Tomás derided as "the aid industry." Tomás himself lived in a small apartment in an unassuming part of town, though he earned just as much as Ava. It wasn't as though he couldn't afford a house like this. It was just a difference of lifestyle: what he saved on rent he splurged on satisfying his wanderlust.

The freshness of the morning air was fading. Ganesh Himal was disappearing into the usual grey fug. Mrs. Thapa was still staring out from her balcony. Ava decided to go in.

She had to comb through WDS-Nepal's proposal this weekend, ahead of a meeting with its largest partner, National Network Nepal. The proposal was so big, and so ambitious, that it intimidated her. She had asked Claire Ross-Jones for permission to conduct an assessment before approving the grant. Claire had asked her to write a one-pager arguing her case. Ava needed to send the one-pager to Claire first thing on Monday.

But when she sat down to work, she realized she was still upset — about the guard, about the landlady, about this absurd mansion.

She was already halfway down the hill by the time Harihar scrambled out of the servants' quarters to close the gate behind her. Picking her way past a pile of garbage by the neighbour's house, Ava walked to the main road, where a cab sidled up to her, the driver calling out, "Taxi, taxi, taxi!"

The driver looked ten years old.

"No," Ava said.

"Taxi, Sister!" The driver grew baleful. "Sister, Sister, and taxi."

Ava sighed. "Okay, okay." She got in. "Can you take me to … Bal Mandir?" She hesitated over the name. Then, as she had seen Tomás do, she tried to bargain: "How much?"

"And four hundred rupees, Sister!"

Unlike Tomás, she couldn't haggle over what amounted, in the end, to four dollars. "Okay," she said.

"Okay!" The driver cried out as they started off. "And you which country from, Sister!"

"Canada."

"And Sister, Canada is too far!"

He launched a spirited, if garbled, conversation. She answered his questions politely — "Yes, it's far." "Yes, it's nice." "I like Nepal too, it's also nice." — till the conversation stalled for lack of a common vocabulary.

Then the driver turned on the radio and sang along to a Nepali pop song as he careened through the pocked, bumpy streets, swerving to avoid pedestrians and motorbikes. A sharp stench arose as they crossed a bridge. Ava looked out in alarm at the befouled Bagmati River, which trickled below like an open sore, rank and infected. How could people put up with this?

Past a roundabout they shot across a stretch of government buildings: the National Archives, the Supreme Court, Parliament House. The centre of town had wide streets and large, glass-front storefronts. Ava saw a crowd forming around a man, a performer of some kind. At an intersection, a woman traffic police waved them on, her face hidden behind a dust mask. Two middle-aged women at a bus stop were poring over a newspaper. A motorcycle whizzed by, loaded down with a family of four. Ava thought back to how repugnant she had found all of this on that Christmas visit with Mom and Dad and Luke.

When they reached a less busy part of town, the driver announced, "Bal Mandir!"

Ava tensed up as he drove through an open metal gate. She was thirsty from last night's excesses. She should have brought a bottle of water.

The driver halted in front of a rambling old palace and asked, "And waiting here, Sister?"

"No," Ava said, then changed her mind. "Actually, yes. Could you wait?"

"Petrol too big price today, and nine hundred rupees!"

"Okay. Just wait for me here, I won't be long."

She got out, bracing for the possibility of pain. She saw that the orphanage wasn't quite the crumbling wreck she had remembered it as. It was palatial, if run down, and it was ornate, decorated with columns, arches, and balustrades. There were two entrances, each flanked by Greek-style fluted columns with Corinthian capitals. The paint on the façade was chipping, as it was on the doors and windows, but there was a faded grandeur to the building.

There was no one in the front lawn. Ava thought of the children who had been there that Christmas: how they had stared at her. That old wound prickled inside.

"Existential Earth?" a woman said from behind her.

Ava spun around, startled. A young woman was holding out a brochure.

"Oh, I thought — isn't this Bal Mandir?" Ava asked.

The woman pointed at one of the entrances. "That is orphanage side. This" — she pointed at the other entrance — "is Academy of Art side." She gave Ava the brochure. "Please you are welcome to see, exhibition is on theme: Existential Earth."

"Oh. Thank you," Ava said.

With a smile, the woman headed to the door to the Academy of Art.

Ava turned back to the orphanage.

The building was quiet, and felt preternaturally still. There was no movement in any of the windows. *This is where we first met you, honey.* Where were the children?

Not wanting to stand around, but not yet ready to leave, Ava went through the door where the woman had gone, to the Academy of Art. Through the entrance was a large, empty foyer with a stone floor. She remembered the stone floor from that Christmas, and recalled how cold the rooms had been. Dust motes swirled in a beam of sunlight from a side window. There was a sign pointing upstairs. The wooden staircase creaked as Ava climbed up.

The art show was on the second floor. It opened dramatically, with a life-size effigy suspended in thick black rope.

A large television screen beside the effigy projected the image of a woman, also suspended, swaying back and forth in the air. Sometimes the woman would raise her hands as if trying to fly, and at other times she would flail, unable to find her footing. Ava took a photo of the installation on her cell phone and emailed it to Luke: *Look, little brother, there's conceptual art in Nepal!*

The rest of the show consisted of what Luke would probably dismiss as retinal art: landscapes, figurative paintings, abstractions. Ava noted the prevalence of Hindu imagery in the paintings. There were several gods from the pantheon, which she didn't recognize, certainly not in these interpretive renditions. There were too many paintings to take in properly. They began to blur together after a while.

Seeing a balcony on the far side of the hall, she stepped out onto it for a break. The balcony looked over an inner courtyard of the building, with an enclosed yard directly below. The yard must have been part of the orphanage. A boy was there, he looked about seven or eight. He had on a school uniform, but no shoes. Ava watched as he raised his arms and launched himself into a cartwheel, letting out a triumphant whoop as he landed on his feet. He raised his arms again and was about to do another cartwheel when someone called out, and he ran in.

Mother passed in childbirth. Father is unknown. Name was given for official purposes. Abha.

She was glad she had decided to come here.

When she turned back towards the show, the woman who had given her the brochure was standing directly behind her. "Oh! I didn't notice you," Ava said. "Sorry."

"Please, you are welcome to see my art," the woman said.

She looked young, in her early twenties or perhaps even late teens. She seemed very sweet. "That is by me," she said, pointing at a pedestal with a small carving.

"Oh, you're one of the artists?" Ava said.

The woman smiled. "I am youth artist of Nepal."

Ava went up to her carving. It was about ten inches high, and made of clay. It was of a woman, maybe, though it wasn't clear. The style was — naïve? It had a kind of raw energy.

"It is, it is ..." The artist struggled with her English. "It is mother."

"Your mother?" Ava asked. Or did she mean a universal mother figure?

"My mother is living in Kirtipur," the artist said. "It is not portrait of her, but my imagination."

"Oh." Ava wasn't sure just what she meant. "It's an interesting piece," she said.

The artist smiled shyly.

Checking the brochure for a title — there was none — Ava caught the price, and on a whim, decided: "You know what? I'd like to buy it." She decided that it would be a memento of her visit — her return — to the orphanage.

The artist's eyes widened in delight. "Oh, I appreciate very much your support!" she cried. "It is a big support to youth artist, thank you for buying, oh!"

The artist got into a tizzy over the payment, writing up a receipt, counting Ava's money, making change. She asked for Ava's business card, and cradled it in her palms as though it were a precious gift. "I will deliver sculpture myself," she said. "I will deliver to your house after exhibition." With a glee that both gratified and embarrassed Ava, she placed a red dot beside the piece. "Oh, I am very happy today!"

Only when she was out in the foyer did Ava realize that she had left the brochure behind. She hadn't asked, and the artist hadn't told her, her name.

Was it a Nepali thing not to introduce yourself by name?

Outside, Ava took a final look at the orphanage. She was done here: she would never come back.

When she got into the cab, the driver said, "Too long waiting, Sister! And one thousand rupees, okay!"

Ten dollars.

"Okay," Ava said.

She desperately needed a drink of water. As they started off, she checked her email. Luke hadn't replied: it was the middle of the night in Miami. She didn't really want to go back home. She needed a distraction — any distraction — so she called Tomás.

"Hey, how was the organic market?"

"I picked up some two soft cheeses, a semi-soft with truffles, and a hard blue. What are you doing for lunch?"

"A cheese platter wouldn't go amiss."

"Come over. I found a cab sauv from Margaret River in my corner shop. I'll open it so it can breathe."

"LAU, GYANU-BABU, let me know if I can be of any further service to you," Jeevan Bhatta said as they crossed the bridge over the mad river. "Send word anytime through your thulo-ba. Anything the chairman orders, I'll do."

"We couldn't have done this without you," Gyanu said.

Sapana, trailing behind by a few steps, also thanked the widower. "We'll always remember your help."

The widower gave her his usual loopy grin. "My loyalty to your family goes back for generations," he said.

They parted on the shore. Gyanu and Sapana watched him go towards Thulo-ba's house. No doubt he was going there to report on his success. By the end, Gyanu had given him seventy-five thousand rupees to see to the stamping, sealing, signing, and fingerprinting of a thousand documents. The land transfer was finally done.

After he disappeared around a bend, Sapana suggested they go and look at the plot. Gyanu led the way, skirting around the feudal estates to reach the ridge. The corn was already standing tall: it would have to be harvested soon.

Sapana was in a wistful mood. "Dai," she said, looking out at the plot of land, "I agreed to sign the deed only because you insisted, but it's not my land, it's ours. It's yours as much as mine."

"You'll have to take charge of it. For now let the old agreement with Thulo-ba stand, but in the future —"

"I won't do anything without consulting you first."

Gyanu was just relieved to have got this done. Sapana would be all right: for the first time, he truly felt so. To ease his last niggling doubts, he asked, "Bahini, do you think you'd want to live elsewhere — in the bazaar, say?"

"Why would I want to do that?" She looked at him quizzically.

"Or — do you want to live in the bazaar? Is that what you're saying?"

"No, I was just wondering. I saw some plots for sale, that's why."

"Don't buy land for my sake, but if you want —"

"No, it was just a stray thought," Gyanu said.

Sapana kept looking at him, trying to read him. Then she gave up, and grew wistful again. "They're really gone, hai, Dai? Ma and Ba. I never thought there would be no one above us one day," she said. "I mean, there's no one older than us now: there's no one between us and our own end."

"It's the way of the world, Bahini."

"I hate it, Dai. I know we all have to go one day, but I really hate it, I hate it so much." She forced herself to smile. "Shall we go? Chandra's cooking, she'll burn everything if I'm not there to teach her."

"I'll come in a little while," Gyanu said.

"I'd better go before Chandra burns it all!"

After his sister left, Gyanu sat down on the ground, leaning against the stump of the old willow tree. He had received a message from Maleah when he was at the land revenue office. He took out his mobile phone and reread it:

Im going 2 visit agent 2day mahal.

He had shot back a quick response: *ok meri maya.* He looked at both messages now, feeling at a loss as to how to proceed from here. He had overshot his thirty days' leave by several weeks. Shantanu Kumar had given his job to someone else. He needed to find another job, and had telephoned the manpower agency in Kathmandu through which he had first gone to the desert. It had closed after workers were stranded in the war in

Libya. The manager had opened a new agency, though. With some difficulty, Gyanu had tracked it down. "Right now, I have a line on Saudi and Kuwait," the agent had said to him over the phone, "and there's money to be made in Iraq, but you'd have to go through India." The agent had no links into the UAE.

Now that he was free to leave, Gyanu had no way back to the desert. And by the time he returned there, Maleah might have left ... He couldn't complete this thought.

From where he was sitting, he could see the low blue hills. The jungles there were thickening as springtime approached. Below the ridge, the mad river was seething, the meltwater from upstream having doubled the river's size. It was called the mad river because it often flooded without warning when the snows far upstream, in the mountains, began to melt. Two boys were standing in the shallows, casting nets. From the bridge, a man called out to them: "Have you caught anything good, boys, or is it all sidre fish?"

One of the boys replied, "We caught asala all morning!"

The man went to examine their catch and selected a long, lean trout for himself. After paying the boys, he came up the hill. Gyanu recognized his old friend and called out, "Kisne!"

Kisne looked up. "Oho, Gyanu, I heard you came for your ba, I didn't realize you were still here!" Kisne ambled over to him and sat down by him, laying the trout on a clean patch of grass. "I felt sad when I heard about your ba, but I guess the old man's at peace now," he said. "Are you going to stay on, Gyanu?"

"Only for a while."

Kisne had been a peculiar, though not unlikeable, boy, and he had grown into a peculiar, not unlikeable man. "I was sure you'd be gone by the time I got back," he said, picking a blade of grass and chewing on it. "There was a wedding across the border, our aunt's son got married, I had nothing else to do so I went." He let out a sudden, braying laugh. "It was crowded and dirty — and the heat! It reminded me of the time I used to work in Bombay. I guarded a shop there. Did I ever tell you I went to Bombay?" He shook his head. "Everyone called us Bahadur, Bahadur: that's how it is in India, isn't it, Gyanu? The shop sold refrigerators and stoves, all kinds of electronics. There was a separate machine to heat bread, a separate machine to cut vegetables, a separate machine to mix spices. I worked there for more than four years," he said, then laughed again. "What haven't we done, hai, Gyanu? In our lives? What haven't we done in our lives?"

Gyanu smiled. He asked after their friend Ram: "I heard he was in Kathmandu."

"He's still there, working at an office, an insurance company. Did you hear what happened to Bisnu?"

Their other friend had fled the bazaar after a pyramid scheme he operated collapsed, bankrupting hundreds of investors. "He ran away to Kathmandu — he lives in a seven-storey house, re, made all of glass. That's what people say," Kisne said. "Bisnu's not like you and me, Gyanu, he always knew how to make money." He went on: "Me, I've worked as a guard in Bombay, as a waiter in Allahabad, as a cleaner in Goa. Ey, Gyanu, did I ever tell you about the time I went to Japan?"

"Tell me."

"These boys I knew in Goa, they used to go there to pick apples for a few months, and then came back to work on the cruise ships — I decided to go with them to Japan. I'd heard so much about Tokyo, Tokyo, but my luck? We ended up in a village on an island all the way up in the north!" He brayed again in laughter. "Nobody spoke our language except for us:

all the apple pickers were from home. The pay was good, but it was freezing! I worked for one season and never went back. What about you, Gyanu? How have you fared in the desert? I heard you were working in a five-star hotel?"

"I've been lucky."

"Is it true that your uncle is building a hydro plant upstream?"

"Is he?"

"That's what I heard. It's going to earn ten lakh rupees a day, re, that's what everyone's saying. You're fortunate, Gyanu, you have him, he'll help you with anything you need. People like me, we have no one. Ey!" he suddenly cried. "Can you connect me with a manpower? What else is there to do but leave this land? Give me a telephone number, Gyanu, I'll try it, I'll try anything once, though these manpowers — which are honest, which are cheats? One never knows." Kisne narrowed his eyes. "You know Jiten from the bazaar? He went through a manpower, it took him to Doha, but there was no job, he had to come back, and he lost all his money. I have a cousin in Malaysia, maybe it would be better to go there, what do you think?"

"I've only been to the desert."

"And you've never been cheated?"

"Lots of people suffer, you're right to be careful."

They heard a ripple of laughter nearby, and turned to see two of Sapana's friends, Ritu and Namrata, crossing the bridge. The girls were absorbed in their own conversation and didn't notice them.

Kisne watched them walk by, then asked, "You're not going to get married, Gyanu? What about your sister — how old is she now?"

Gyanu changed the subject. "Come by the house sometime, and I'll give you the number of a manpower agency."

Kisne was still looking at the girls. "Womenfolk," he said, "they have their own difficulties, and we menfolk, we have our own, don't we?" He tossed aside the chewed-up blade of grass and got up. "I'll come and visit you, hai. Who knows? Maybe you and I will end up together in the desert, haha!"

He picked up the trout and left.

Gyanu remained on the ridge, rereading Maleah's message and his reply.

I m going 2 visit Jojo agent 2day mahal.

Ok meri maya.

He thought about what Kisne had said: *What else is there to do in this land.* Kisne was right. As was Shantanu Kumar: *The village is the past.* Gyanu would call Maleah tomorrow, they would make a plan, a life plan. If they couldn't be together in the desert, they would find a way to be together elsewhere.

He looked again at the blue hills, and, out of nowhere, vividly recalled a day from boyhood:

He and Kisne and Ram and Bisnu had skipped school and gone to the hills to pick ainselu berries. They were scrambling through the brush. Ram was talking about a tiger that had killed a goat in the village. Gyanu was correcting him, "A leopard, not a tiger," but Ram was insisting, "No, my cousin saw it, he said it was a tiger," when Kisne shouted: "I think it's been here, there's a dead goat here!"

Everyone scrambled over to Kisne and saw the remains of a carcass, pale and half-rotted in the underbrush.

"That's not a goat," Bisnu said.

"What is it?" Ram poked at it with a twig.

"It's a dog."

"No, it's a baby!"

They crowded in to see.

"It's a dog."

"It's a baby! Someone threw away a baby!" Kisne screamed.

A terror gripped them; they panicked all at once and began to run away, screaming.

"Leave it! Don't touch it!"

"Its ghost is going to curse us!"

"Let's go, let's go, let's go!"

"IT WON'T TAKE long," Sapana said, leading the others through the bazaar. "Rudra-sir will help us. You'll see."

"Good, because I have so many chores at home," Rama-bhauju said.

"Me too," Laptanni Budhi said, though this was clearly untrue. Waited on by a retinue of daughters-in-law, she never had to do any work herself. "I also have chores," she said.

Sapana felt sorry for her. The women's committee was taxing old Laptanni Budhi. She had been so relieved when Sapana had taken care of the accounts that she had passed the report straight on to Jeevan Bhatta. Now she was back to complaining about him.

"My nephew, since boyhood all he's done is to bother his elders. He told me this morning that the CBO is going to hold a big meeting, re. One of us will have to make a big speech." Laptanni Budhi pinched Rama-bhauju's arm. "As the secretary, you'll have to do it."

"What? You're the chairperson, you make the speech," Rama-bhauju said.

"My nephew forced me to be the chairperson — I swear I'm going to resign!"

"Why doesn't Sapana-bahini make the speech?" Rama-bhauju said.

"Me?" Sapana was intrigued. "But I'm only the treasurer, Bhauju."

"Do it, do it," Laptanni Budhi said. "All you have to do is praise the committee. There'll be foreigners at the meeting, re, and if you impress them, they'll give the CBO money for another study tour next year."

"As the secretary, I second the proposal that Sapana-bahini make the speech," Rama-bhauju said.

"Then it's decided," Laptanni Budhi declared.

Sapana laughed at the two older women. They were shameless about making her do all their work. A speech. She had never made a speech before, but having met all twenty-two members, she knew more about the women's committee than any of the other members did. The committee had done surprisingly well, though Rama-bhauju hadn't yet repaid her loan, and at least two other members would probably default: they had frittered away their money on household expenses. But Naina-di had earned twenty thousand rupees selling goats. Jethi-didi had planted an entire orange orchard. Even the poorest members had recovered their investment: Chandra's muwa had just repaid her loan, and from here on, all the earnings from the sales of her pickles would be hers to keep.

When they arrived at the bank, Sapana led them in through the front door, past the security guard. It was the start of the month, and the line was long. Sapana asked the others to wait by the side and went to Rudra-sir's cubicle.

Rudra-sir was busy with a client. He was wearing a green shirt today: he always wore green shirts on Wednesdays. Whenever Sapana came to the bank, he came out of his cubicle to help her. When Ba had fallen ill, Rudra-sir had taught her how to manage the family's account. He always expedited Gyanu-dai's transfers from the desert, and he liked to talk to Sapana about money management, stressing the importance of saving. Sapana could tell from Rudra-sir's attentiveness towards her that he liked her: even a blind man could see that, it was that obvious. After he finished helping her, he always said, "Let's have tea," and sometimes she said yes.

When he was done with his client, he left his cubicle and came to Sapana. "What can I do for you, Sapana-bahini?"

Rudra-sir wasn't handsome, but his eyes were a curious golden-brown that shifted hues in the light.

Sapana said, "We want to open an account, Sir. I'm the treasurer of a committee. I've brought the chairperson and secretary."

"Is the committee registered? Have you brought the registration papers?"

"Yes, and our citizenship cards."

"Then I'll just have you fill in some forms." Rudra-sir escorted the three of them to a side office, and methodically helped them write down all the information. "Complete the top part of this page. And I'll need you to sign on that line. How many signatories do you want on the account? Will you need cheques? Can you come back to pick up the chequebook, Sapana-bahini?"

"I can."

It took a while: and Laptanni Budhi and Rama-bhauju grumbled throughout. But when they were done, they were proud of what they had done.

"Our little committee has a bank account!"

Rudra-sir escorted them to the front door. "If you need anything else, come to me," he said to all of them, though he was looking at Sapana. "Are you sure there's nothing else I can do for you today?"

Sapana said, "That's all for today, Rudra-sir."

"If there's anything."

"I'll come to you."

Laptanni Budhi was deeply impressed by the ease of the transaction. After leaving the bank, she said, "If we had known it was so simple, we'd have done this years ago, hai, Rama?"

"Haaa!" Rama-bhauju laughed. "It was easy only because —

did you see how that boy was looking at Sapana-bahini? He wants to marry her!"

Sapana smiled knowingly. "A plain boy like that is lucky to talk to any girl!"

"He seems like a good boy, Bahini."

"He's the father of two grown sons!"

"Tchee, then why was he flirting with you like that? What a terrible boy!"

Before returning to the village, Rama-bhauju had to go to a medical shop; but first, Laptanni Budhi wanted to buy some rice. They turned into a grain store, and were about to go in when Sapana heard someone calling her name. Rudra-sir had come out of the bank, waving a sheet of paper. Sapana sent Laptanni Budhi and Rama-bhauju in and waited outside for him.

When Rudra-sir reached the grain store, he stopped to catch his breath. A delicate flush spread on his cheeks. "I thought we'd completed all the formalities, but —" He looked softly at Sapana with his golden-brown eyes. "I needn't bother the others, but if you have a moment, Bahini... do you have a moment? There's a little bit of information I still need."

Sapana saw the way he was looking at her, and she saw the power she held over him, and she liked it. She said, "I suppose I could catch a bus later," she said. "Let me go and tell the others?"

Inside, Laptanni Budhi was haggling furiously with the shopkeeper:

"Why would I pay so much, Sahu-ji, when I can go to another store and pay half that amount?"

"Go, then, go to another store if you can find a better price!"

"I'll pay you half the amount."

Unable to catch Laptanni Budhi's attention, Sapana told Rama-bhauju that the two of them would have to return to the village by themselves. She said, "I also want you to call a new meeting, Bhauju. I think the committee should open cooperatives, like the ones we saw on the study tour."

"Yes, yes, cooperatives — why not?" Rama-bhauju said, distracted by all the haggling. "And don't forget about the speech!" she cried out, before turning back to join forces with Laptanni Budhi: "Sahu-ji, we'd rather die of hunger than pay that much for your stale, broken rice!"

Rudra-sir, standing outside, had overheard Rama-bhauju. When Sapana rejoined him, he asked, "What speech is that, Bahini?"

Sapana told him about her thulo-ba's CBO, and about the meeting they were going to hold. "There are going to be foreigners there, re."

"A brilliant girl like you, I'm sure you'll give a great speech," he said.

Sapana could tell that he was just appealing to her vanity. "Do you really think so?" she said coyly.

"I have no doubt," he said. Then he opened his mouth to say something else, and Sapana already knew what it would be. He said, "Do you have some time to spare for me today, Bahini? If so, let's have tea first, we can fill out the forms afterwards ... but only if you have time."

"I have time."

"Then let's have tea."

WOMEN WERE FOOLS, they were imbecile-moron-dolts, naïve and gullible, willing to give up their most intimate selves to the first man who said, "I love you." They were simpletons, dunce-chumps, halfwits, saps: nothing but idiot-fools.

Durga had gone and got herself pregnant by the vegetable vendor. "Hajoor, I should take poison and die," she had wailed on the night of the dinner party. "No one will have me now. Muwa will kick me out when she finds out: aaaai, aaaai! Then, what will I do? Where will I go?" The girl had got so worked up that she could hardly breathe. "I should die, Hajoor," she had said, keening like a wounded beast. "I should take poison and die!"

Indira shuddered to remember it. She was in the waiting room of a private clinic, waiting for the girl to come out. It had fallen on her, naturally, to help the idiot-fool. "Tch, tch, tch! What are you saying?" she had said that night, her mind galloping in all directions all at once like a herd of wild elephants: how was she going to solve this, what if Muwa found out, what was she going to do with Durga? "No one's going to kick you out, you're part of the family," Indira had said to the girl. "Don't cry, girl. There's no use crying now. The time for crying has passed."

"Aaaai!"

Fool.

The girl had gone into the doctor's office more than two hours ago. There was no one else in the waiting room, thank the gods. For extra precaution, Indira had chosen a clinic in a poor part of the city, where no one was likely to recognize her. She hadn't told a single person about this, not even Uday Sharma, because if he found out, he would blab about it to Muwa, and Muwa would definitely kick out the girl.

The door to the doctor's office swung open after a while, and the girl shuffled out, dull-eyed. They must have given her sedatives. Indira rushed to her side.

The doctor came out behind her. "It was quite far along, I had to go in twice," she said brusquely, snapping off the rubber gloves. "You're her guardian? Who are you to her?" She appraised Indira with a withering glance. "You must be her master."

"I'm like a mother to her."

"Then you should educate her about birth control!"

After paying a thousand rupees for the procedure, Indira led Durga out of the clinic. The girl was unsteady on her feet. Indira had to hold her by the elbow so she wouldn't trip.

"This way, girl. How are you feeling? Don't worry. The medicine will wear off, you'll be back to normal soon."

The intersection by the clinic was choked with traffic. They crossed it slowly, and turned into a quiet side street, which was all shadows and discretion. There, behind a gate, was a concrete-block building with the sign: Heaven Hotel.

The hotel's front desk was unmanned, but Indira had already paid in advance for a three-night stay. "Here we are." She led the girl to the room at the end of the hall. The room was sunless, but it had a TV with a satellite connection. Indira helped the girl into bed and took out an extra blanket from the cupboard. "There." She tucked her in. "Don't do anything for a few days, Durga. Just lie here and watch TV," she said. She sat by the bed and grew solemn. "Now, listen: no one knows about this at home. I told everyone you've gone to the village to meet your family, understand?"

"My family," the girl mumbled, "has forgotten me, Hajoor."

"Just tell everyone you went to meet them — if they ask."

"My family has forgotten I was ever born."

"Tch." Indira held the girl's cool, clammy hands. "Look, Durga, I'm your mother-father, your guardian, your friend. Do you know what I've done for you here? I found you a doctor, I got you a hotel room, I took the whole morning off to be with you," Indira said, though this wasn't, in fact, true. She would have to leave before long for a meeting at Vishwa Bista's cousin-sister-in-law's NGO, National Network Nepal. "You know what else I've done?" she added. "I've lied to my family, Durga. Never before in my life have I lied to my family." Neither was this true. "I know things have been difficult for you, girl, but now you have to forget everything and move on."

Durga lay there like a broken doll.

"I'll get you some food," Indira said. "You just lie in bed and watch a movie." She went over to the TV and pressed the button, but it wouldn't turn on. She checked the lights: there was a power cut. Oof. "Why don't you just – sleep," she said. "Take a nap, Durga. You need to recover your strength."

She left.

Outside the hotel, on the main street, a taxi honked, a bicycle whizzed by, people jostled through the crossroad. It was dusty, the dry season was here, and they would have to start trucking in water to the house. On the far end of the block was a fast food place called Tandoor & Kebab. That would do.

A little boy was minding the counter while an older man cooked in the open kitchen. The menu was painted in enamel on the restaurant wall. Indira placed her order with the boy: "One whole tandoori chicken, one dal tadka, and four aloo parathas. And saag paneer, give me saag paneer, and do you have yogurt? One order yogurt. All for home packing."

The boy took her payment, then said, "It'll take twenty minutes, Auntie."

"Twenty minutes!"

"So? You want to cancel the order?" he asked, suddenly querulous. "Cancel the order, then, go ahead."

"No, no. I'll wait."

Indira went to a table splattered with oil stains and waited. The scent of fried cumin arose as the man put the tadka in the dal. Indira checked her watch. She was going to be late for the meeting at National Network Nepal. She didn't even want to attend the meeting. Why did the Canadian want to meet Vishwa Bista's cousin-sister-in-law? Perhaps she had noticed irregularities in the WDS-Nepal proposal... To Indira, the entire proposal seemed to be written in red and highlighted in yellow, signaling its own corruption. Vishwa Bista had to get it approved, and swiftly.

Indira fished out her mobile phone and texted Vishwa Bista: *Family emergency pls excuse me from meeting 2day Vishwa-ji, So sorry Indira.*

He texted back immediately: *Very very sorry 2 hear.*

Very very sorry to have ever heard your name, Indira thought bitterly.

"Auntie!" The boy called out from the counter. "You want sweets with your order?"

"What kind of sweets do you have?"

"Rasgullas."

"Pack four."

"Only four, Auntie?"

"All right, six."

"Take a dozen, Auntie. What's a dozen rasgullas for a nice, rich auntie like you?"

"La, pack a dozen," Indira said. She resigned herself to spending the morning with Durga. It was the least she could do for the girl.

Poor Durga. She was ruined now, Indira thought. Just as Indira herself might have been, for had she not, in her day, also been an idiot-fool? Yes, she had. She had given herself to Uday Sharma a fortnight before the wedding because he had said he loved her so much, he needed to show her how much. They had gone to a dirty hotel in the tourist district, and in a dirty room in that dirty hotel she had endured Uday Sharma's clumsy groping, mortified at the thought that other couples in the dirty hotel were doing the same dirty thing in their own dirty rooms. Indira should have refused, she should have kept herself safe till marriage. For even though everything had worked out in the end, anything might have happened, Uday Sharma might have left her; and she was only a woman. She could have been ruined, like Durga.

"Ready, Auntie!" The boy held out a plastic bag and a bill.

"But I already paid for the food!" Indira glared at him.

"Haaa, Auntie, you asked for rasgullas, did you forget?" the boy sneered. "Or did you think they were free?"

Snotty little bastard.

Indira paid him and went back to Heaven Hotel.

Thinking: maybe Durga needn't be ruined by this — little mishap. It wasn't fair on women, really. Nepali society wasn't fair. Maybe the girl could be whole again. Was it possible? Of course. Maybe not. It would be hard, but she should try to help Durga be whole again.

When she got to the girl's room, the lights — and the TV — were on. The girl was engrossed in a Hindi tele-serial. Good.

Indira sat down on her bed. "I hope you're hungry, girl, I hope you're really, really hungry, because I think you're really going to like what I've brought you."

"**YOUR'RE RIGHT TO** take precautions, Ava, but don't forget: when the assessment's done, you'll need to double the budget for the Five Year Outlook."

"Oh, I won't forget," Ava said. How could she, when Claire ended all her conversations with this reminder? She said, "Thanks, Claire," and picked up her attaché case and left Claire's office with just enough time to make it to her meeting at National Network Nepal.

On the way out of the fort, Ava stopped by the washroom to freshen up. She was feeling better now that Claire had approved the assessment of WDS-Nepal. The assessment would give her an additional six weeks to pick through WDS-Nepal's proposal. She could also use the extra time to double the Five Year Outlook. The Women's Empowerment Program needed to develop an annual budget of more than four million pounds. The prospect of drawing up such a budget was daunting. Ava washed up, and after drying her hand, poked the rubber breast in the washroom: each time, the underside felt stickier, and the lump lumpier.

Herman Banke was just outside the washroom door when Ava came out.

Without any preliminaries, he said, "Can you have women's empowerment without inclusion, Ava?" His face was red, his mien charged. He had lost his appeal to have the Social Inclusion Program reinstated, and was working on the short-term project on resilience while spending his days lobbying to turn it into a long-term program on inclusion. "Is women's empowerment not part of the inclusion agenda? What do you think?"

"I'm, um, just stepping out for a meeting," Ava said.

"Can women really be empowered only through employment generation, or" — Herman snorted — "peacebuilding? What is Jared going to do, build peace with the PEON, the Permanent

Establishment of Nepal? Don't you know, Ava?" Herman stepped in so close that Ava could feel his breath on her face: "This country is run by high-caste men, fifteen percent of the population, who have always, historically, monopolized power in Nepal by excluding all other identity groups. And don't even talk to me about women!"

"Look, I've read your social exclusion index, Herman. I understand, but —"

"There can be no buts!" Herman shouted. Then he took in a deep breath and stepped back. "I'm sorry, Ava. I have a tendency to get carried away. My wife is taking me to a meditation retreat next week, maybe it will help." He bared his teeth in a pained smile. "It's just that if you were a Nepali woman, Ava, everything would be determined by your gender and caste. If your family were rich, you would have some mobility, but otherwise — what you eat, what you wear, what you say, what you do: everything would be determined by your birth."

Ava thought back to what the official had said, that Christmas. *Caste is unknown.* "I know inclusion is important, Herman," she said. "It's just that I have a meeting to go to right now."

He said, "Are you going to Jared's dinner party tonight?"

"I, well —"

"He invited everyone from the office except me," Herman said, sounding hurt, like a child ostracized at school.

"Let's meet when you're back from the mediation retreat?" Ava said.

"Ten days of complete silence." He grimaced. "I don't know if I'll survive it."

Vishwa had gone ahead to National Network Nepal to debrief its director, Preety Rana, on Daphne Muirwood's implementation strategy on aid effectiveness, which all of IDAF's national partners were required to comply with. Ava was to meet him there.

The SUV that she had requisitioned was waiting at the front door. The driver took her a block along the main road and turned into an alley, steering through a narrow lane into a neighbourhood of high brick walls and tall metal gates. It turned out that National Network Nepal's office was within walking distance. They stopped at a tall gate, and the driver honked. The gate opened to reveal a second, taller gate inside. The security guard who had opened the first gate scurried to open the second one.

Past the second gate lay a half-built high-rise towering over a construction site littered with cement sacks, oil drums, wood planks, iron rods, and bricks. The high-rise's front door was as yet unfinished. The cavernous lobby inside smelled of wet cement. By now Ava had been to several NGO offices for meetings, and they could feel rudimentary — but the provisional, thrown-together air to National Network Nepal's office was of a whole other order. There was a reception desk in the lobby, but no chairs. National Network Nepal was, according to WDS-Nepal's proposal, one of the country's leading NGOs for capacity enhancement. Its director had a good reputation and was very well connected. "You should know," Vishwa had told Ava this morning, "that Preety Rana is married to the former finance minister. He's still very powerful in his party."

A man appeared out of nowhere, his face cloaked by a grey woollen muffler, and led Ava to an office complex at the back of the building.

There, in an inner sanctum, in a warm, sun-drenched office complex, was Preety Rana. She was sitting at her desk, across from Vishwa. They both stood when they saw Ava. Preety Rana was in her forties, and dressed in a sari. She had a polished manner and an impeccable British accent: "I'm sorry about the state of the office, they raised the rent on our old office, so we're camped here like refugees." She showed Ava a chair beside Vishwa. "Will you have coffee or tea, Ms. Berriden? I'd recommend our masala tea with ginger — our helper makes an excellent brew."

"That sounds wonderful."

Preety Rana placed the order with the man in the muffler, then turned back to Ava. "Mr. Bista tells me you're from Canada. I've been there," she said. "To Montreal. It was beautiful, but very cold!"

"You were there to study federalism, didn't you?" Vishwa said.

"That's right."

Vishwa said, "You know, Ava, Preety Rana was a member of the first constituent assembly. The one that was dissolved."

"Without drafting a constitution." Preety Rana laughed.

Vishwa said, "By the way, Indira Sharma called, and she won't be able to make it to the meeting. I'll debrief her afterwards."

When the tea arrived, Preety Rana started the meeting: "I've consulted on women's issues for over two decades, Ms. Berriden." She named the organizations she had worked for — "ADB, DFID, World Bank, UNDP" — and rattled off the titles of reports that she had authored — "Increasing Empowerment through Capacity Enhancement. Mapping the Mainstreaming of Gender Creating a Matrix for Inclusive Development. New Measurement Paradigms for Sustainability. You can keep this copy." She slid a hefty report across her desk. "I wrote this for the Canadian Cooperation Office, before CIDA collapsed. It's a pity that the Canadian government has cut back its involvement in the world, isn't it? Canada has no presence left in Nepal, they even downsized their consulate. That report is out of date now, but I thought you might be interested, as a Canadian."

"Thank you."

"You're welcome," Preety Rana said. "Now, as you know, Ms. Berriden, National Network Nepal is less than a year old, but as its director, I assure you, we're deeply dedicated to customizing the results log frame. We aim to partner with stakeholders at all levels, all over the country. For WDS-Nepal, we're proposing to conduct capacity enhancement workshops nationwide. In fact, I just came back from a workshop in Cape Town. We trained thirteen NGOs from all over Africa, including from sub-Saharan Africa, on microfinancing."

"On that subject," Ava said. She took WDS-Nepal's proposal out of her attaché case and flipped to an index of community-based organizations that National Network Nepal was proposing to partner with at the village level. "Can you tell me which of these CBOs does the best work on microfinancing?"

"All of our local partners are excellent," Preety Rana said. "That's why we partner with them, Ms. Berriden."

"Well, Vishwa and I are going to the field soon, and we'd like to visit some of them," Ava said.

"I'm sure Mr. Bista can find you a good CBO to visit."

"Maybe you could join us on the trip?" Ava asked her.

Preety Rana smiled. "Unfortunately, I'll be on assignment in Bangkok for the next two months."

"Oh. Well, I hope we can count on you to cooperate with an assessment we'll be conducting of WDS-Nepal and its partners."

"A what?" Vishwa said, sharply. "An assessment? Is there a problem with the proposal, Ava?"

"No, I just — it's such a large grant, I wanted to —"

"You should have discussed it with me first!"

Why was he so upset? Had Ava breached protocol? Was she supposed to have passed the assessment by Vishwa before taking it to Claire?

"I'm sorry," Ava said, flustered. "It's just a routine — I didn't mean to — I'm really sorry, Vishwa. Let's talk about it after the meeting."

"Yes, we must!"

Preety Rana was observing the exchange coolly. "Of course I'll cooperate with the assessment," she said. "Do you know, Ms. Berriden, that I've worked in all seventy-five districts of Nepal?" She slid across another report. "Here's the proposal we submitted to WDS-Nepal."

Ava had already read through the proposal. She leafed through it now as the other woman began to speak about deliverables, quantifiables, indexes, measurements, and matrixes. Preety Rana was extremely articulate. Yet something about her rankled. Was it that she was too professional, too polished? That wasn't fair.

"My personal mission," Preety Rana was saying, "has always been to empower the poor with tools to uplift their socio-economic status. Over my career, I've seen the fortunes of an entire family transformed by the empowerment of a single woman. As a Nepali woman, I dream of ordinary women — mothers, wives, daughters — being agents of change. In my own family," she said, growing passionate, "I'm the first generation to study beyond high school. My mother was a housewife, and I'm a PhD from the University of Leeds. I really believe, Ms. Berriden, that women are the ones who create change, lasting change, the kind of change that transforms society."

By the time they left, Vishwa was no longer upset about the assessment. "I know a consultant," he said. "John Barnett, he's the best — we'll have to get him to do the assessment."

"Would you look into it, Vishwa? That would be really helpful," Ava said.

"Sure, sure."

They were both going to Jared's party after that, so after stopping by the office to drop off some documents, they shared a ride over. Jared lived close to Ava, on a leafy side road at the bottom of the hill. A guard opened the gate and let them into a sprawling estate, where a crowd of expatriates — and one or two Nepalis — stood around a lawn.

There was a self-serve bar at one end of the lawn. Vishwa got them two gin and tonics, then fell into conversation with another Nepali man at the bar.

Ava went back out to the lawn and circled around, looking for Jared or anyone else from IDAF. The expatriates in Nepal came in several varieties, she observed. A few, like she, wore ordinary western clothes. Most accessorized their outfits with splashes of local colour embroidered silks, flowing tunics, dramatic Tibetan jewelry, embroidered pashminas. Yet others were dressed in flowing silks and woollen robes finer, and more delicate, than she had seen Nepalis wear.

There was a woman commanding the attention of a small crowd. Ava stopped to listen to her. The woman was swathed in maroon robes and her hair was shorn: were it not for a glass of red wine in her hands, she would pass as a Buddhist nun.

Or perhaps she was one. She was talking about sacred hidden valleys and secret Tantric teachings.

Then, spotting Daphne Muirwood by the bar, Ava went over to her. Daphne was scowling at her cell phone.

"I need some advice from you," Ava said, knowing better than to waste the other woman's time on small talk. "I've started to draw up WEP's Five Year Outlook, and want to achieve higher performance without simply throwing money at everything. Could I come into your office to talk, sometime, about your implementation strategy?"

Daphne nodded curtly. "I'm in the process of expanding the modular component of the implementation strategy," she said, when her cell phone pinged. She scowled and checked the message, then looked back up. "I'm aligning more closely to the principles of Accra and Busan, in particular —" Her cell phone pinged again. "One moment. Can you give me a minute, Ava?" She typed a brief message. "I'm sorry, where were we?"

"The modular component."

"Yes. I'm aligning —"

Her phone pinged.

Daphne's jawline tightened. "I'm sorry. I should turn the phone off, but it's urgent — it's a personal matter."

"We can talk about this in the office."

"I'm in the middle of negotiations, you see." Daphne bit her lips, frowning. "My future ex and I are working out custody for our son." She peered at Ava, as though noticing her for the first time. "Are you married, Ava?"

"Separated. No children."

Daphne said, "You're lucky — about the no children part, I mean. Was separating hard for you?" she asked. Then, without waiting for an answer, she mused, "Sometimes it feels like something will be unbearable, but when you go ahead and do it, it's not. For me, it was a relief to separate, but the divorce is thornier. My son is seven. He'll remember this time in his life, he'll remember his mother being abroad, his father being home with him." She scowled again. "I should have stayed in London till it was sorted out. I shouldn't have left headquarters till we settled."

"It must be difficult for you."

"It's what it is." Daphne shrugged. "Now, where were we?"

"Daphne," Ava said, "If you want to talk, I'm a very good listener. Why don't you come over for dinner sometime? I've got a nice garden, we can sit out and look at the view."

Daphne stiffened. "I'll have to look up my schedule and get back to you about that," she said.

"Oh. Of course."

Daphne's phone pinged again. "I'm afraid you'll have to excuse me, Ava. I really should go and deal with this."

Ava milled about, feeling out of place, even though the expatriates were, in a way, her tribe in Nepal. At the centre of the lawn, a man with a ponytail had pulled out a guitar, and was crooning Bob Dylan songs. Ava listened to his off-key rendition of "Tangled Up in Blue." When he started an off-key rendition of "Lay, Lady, Lay," she decided to leave.

"Excuse me, I'm sorry." An elderly woman in a red brocade gown passed by, trailed by the soft scent of marijuana.

Ava found Jared by the gate.

"You are already leaving, have you eaten?" he asked her.

"Yes," she lied. "Thanks for inviting me, that was lovely."

Jared said, "What Herman has said to you about my program, it is not true, Ava."

Ava's heart sank.

"Poverty is this country's biggest problem, not social inclusion," Jared said. "I am not a Marxist, Ava, do not think I am endorsing Marxism, but it is universally acknowledged that class struggle is the primary means to human progress."

"But I understand that some identity groups have historically —"

"That is dangerous talk, Ava, you must not listen to Herman, he is wrong."

"Why don't we talk about it at the office?"

Jared said, "It is not true that I wrote 'poor and marginalized' in my report because the government of Nepal told us to do so. Yes, the government did ask us to do so, but I agreed because I believe that 'poor and marginalized' is a more neutral category than "excluded.'"

I don't care, Ava wanted to say, but of course didn't.

"What Herman says about me is simply not true, Ava," Jared said.

Ava listened to him for a while longer and left, realizing that she would never be friends with her colleagues at IDAF.

DURGA WAS GOING to kill her, she really was. The girl was refusing to eat, saying, "I don't like it, it's not good," though how could anyone not like tandoori chicken? So Indira had bought her lamb kebabs today. Lamb kebabs for a servant girl! Never mind. The girl was doing a lot better physically, though she was showing little sign of recovering emotionally. When the power was on, the girl would watch Hindi tele-serials, but during the hours-long stretches of load shedding, she would lie in bed staring vacantly at the ceiling, despite Indira's exhortations, "Go for a stroll, get some fresh air, it'll do you good." Durga didn't even wash or get dressed, which was frustrating, because what more could Indira do for her? It was already two nights, three days. Indira couldn't keep skipping the office. She would take the girl home tomorrow, and that would be that.

Indira marched into Heaven Hotel, passing the unmanned lobby to reach the girl's room. The door was locked from inside. She rapped on it. "Open, ey, Durga." She had a one-on-one with Rick Peede this morning, and she was to tell him that she had applied to replace him as the director of WDS-Nepal. She was going to ask him to support her application. The arguments she was going to make kept running in a loop through her mind: WDS-Nepal had never, in its history, had a Nepali director — or a woman director. This was the twenty-first century. It was time.

Indira rapped again on the door. "I don't have all day, girl. Open the door!"

There was no reply.

Oof. Indira wondered if she should leave the food at the door but then someone might steal it, and Durga would go hungry all day. There would surely be an extra key in the lobby — if only someone were there. "Open the door, Durga!" She banged on the door. "Open, I said!" Nothing. She jiggled the doorknob.

She kicked the door once, twice. Then a terrible thought came to her, and she hurled herself against the door in a mounting panic.

The door flew open and Indira tumbled in and saw Durga unconscious in bed with a bottle of — what? — lying empty beside her. The whole world wobbled. The lamb kebabs went flying out of Indira's hands. She ran to the bed and felt for the girl's pulse, but her own heart was hammering so loudly, she couldn't feel anything. Indira screamed.

Then a burst of energy swept through her. She ran out of the room, past the unmanned lobby, to the street. At the crosswalk, she yelled at three loafing men. "You! You! You!"

"What happened, what happened?" A crowd quickly gathered around her.

"There's been an accident, come and help!"

The men swept back to the hotel with her, and carried Durga out. "Let's go, let's go," Indira cried. "Someone fetch a taxi!"

A taxi arrived. The men placed Durga in the back seat, and Indira squeezed in beside her.

The driver turned on the blinkers and raced to the hospital, which was on the other side of the crosswalk. Even though the driver was a wrinkled old man, he helped Indira carry the girl into the emergency room, where an orderly laid her out on a gurney.

"Here." Indira thrust a hundred rupee note at the driver.

He refused it. "Use it for the girl's treatment, Bahini."

The orderly wheeled Durga to a room.

Indira followed behind, shouting, "Doctor-nurse, doctor-nurse! Where's the doctor-nurse?"

"Wait here," the orderly said, and slipped out.

A nurse came in shortly and took the girl's vital statistics. Durga was unresponsive — was she even alive? Indira hovered over her, babbling, "She took something, Nurse. There was a bottle in her hand when I found her. Was it poison? Where would she have got it? Will she live? Will you pump her stomach, will she need medicine, shall I fetch her water, or saline for an IV drip? What should I do?"

"If you would just wait outside."

"Tell me what to do, she's like a daughter to me, I'll do anything, anything, Nurse."

"Wait outside."

Reluctantly, Indira went out to the waiting room. Her mouth was parched, as if she had swallowed sand. She bought a bottle of mineral water and gulped down half of it, but there was still sand in her mouth.

Her meeting! Oof, this world, her life. She fished out her mobile phone and called Rick Peede's secretary, her voice emerging in an ugly rasp: "Neha, there's been — I can't come to the meeting this morning. I need to reschedule it."

"How about tomorrow, Indira-ma'am?"

"Tomorrow we have a meeting at IDAF. How's this afternoon?" Indira said, wondering desperately whether she would be able to leave the hospital at all.

What if Durga were to die?

"Rick-sir is out most of the afternoon, Ma'am, and then he has a meeting with Chandi-sir."

Why was Chandi Shrestha meeting Rick Peede? Was he applying for the director's job too? "Schedule me before Chandi-ji," Indira rasped.

"I can't, Ma'am, but I can fit you in tomorrow morning before the IDAF meeting."

"No, I have to meet him before Chandi-ji!"

"Sorry, Ma'am, tomorrow morning is the only opening I have."

"Lau, then."

Why was everything so hard? Indira hung up and took another gulp of water.

Durga had better not die.

The waiting room smelled of disease and disinfectant. In one corner, a family was swarming around a pale, wilting man. A boy was sitting with his emaciated mother on another side of the room. A woman was weeping quietly beside Indira.

It was more than an hour before the doctor came out to talk to her. He was young and tall and upright, with an arrogant manner. "So how did she get a hold of rat poison?" he demanded.

"Is she all right, Doctor Sah'b, how's she doing, will she live?" Indira asked.

"If it wasn't a suicide attempt, it'll turn into a criminal case, you know."

"Of course it was a —!" The implication! "I'm the one who —!" Indira cried, "I found her and — are you saying I tried to kill her?"

"The things we see in here you wouldn't imagine," the doctor said drily.

"Is she, Doctor Sah'b, the girl —" Was Durga even alive? Indira couldn't even ask the question out loud.

The doctor said, "You'll have to answer some questions before leaving."

He put her in the hands of a nurse, who was kinder.

"The girl will be fine, don't fret," the nurse said. "She just needs a good night's rest." Then she sat Indira down and asked her some extremely unpleasant questions: who was Indira, where did she live, what was her home life like, what did her husband do, what were Durga's circumstances, had the girl ever been abused, beaten, raped?

"I'm the deputy co-director of WDS-Nepal, I work in the field of women's empowerment!" Indira protested, handing the nurse a business card. "The girl, well, she had a mishap, Nurse, she's sad, her engagement ended, and — I've been helping her. I'm all she's got in this world. I'm like her mother-father, in fact."

"We'll discharge her tomorrow unless it turns into a criminal case, in which case ..." The nurse said, "Come back first thing tomorrow morning."

Indira said, "I can't come in the morning. I have a very important meeting in the morning!"

"Then — how old is the patient?" the nurse said. "We can discharge her into her own custody."

"No, no, don't do that! I'll come. I'll come."

A nightmare. This was a waking nightmare, it was. Indira staggered out of the hospital and got into a waiting taxi.

It turned out to be the same one as before.

"How's the girl?" the elderly driver asked. "Is she all right, Bahini?"

"She'll be all right, Dai."

"May God keep her safe," he said.

Indira was grateful for his gentility. "Dai," she said, "I have to go Patan side."

"Patan side?" He shook his head. "There's trouble in that area, Bahini. A demonstration. They're not letting traffic through."

"But it's an emergency; it's a big, big emergency!" Indira said, and tears sprang to her eyes: tears of tension, exhaustion, distress. "I have to get to the office, or — I'll die!"

The driver turned around, aghast. "Don't cry," he said. "I hate it when women cry, Bahini. Women are always crying in this land. I don't ever want to make any woman cry."

"I have so much to do at the office!" Indira sobbed. "My boss will be angry! I'll lose my job! Then how will I feed-clothe-house my family?"

"My mother, in the village, she spent her whole life crying," the driver said sadly. "It made me feel so helpless." He sighed, turning back, and started the engine. "What's a few rocks hurled at a battered taxi, right, Bahini? The human heart, that's what matters. Lau, I'll get you to your destination through the back alleys. Just, I beg you, Bahini: don't cry."

THERE WAS A power cut, and the lights were off. Tomás had lit up a single candle. His apartment had no heating, and Ava was freezing. She pulled up the bedcovers and leaned in till Tomás's collarbone jutted, bony and satisfying, against her face.

"And you believe him?" he asked.

"I don't think he would lie about it."

Gavin had written again. *It wasn't a date or anything,* he had said, after mentioning that he had run into Leez Anne Williker. *We passed each other outside the bank on King Street, we didn't even stop to say hi. But it made me wonder — should I wait for you anymore, Av? Have you met someone? Is that what's going on? Do you have any intention of returning to Toronto, to our marriage?*

Ava had fired back a one-line reply: *It's only fair to tell you that I'm seeing other people.*

This wasn't exactly true. Her brief romance, or one-night stand, or whatever it had been with Anthony, had petered out due to distance. And what she had with Tomás wasn't a relationship, though it did bear many of the marks of one. They were spending most of their weekends together, as well as some weekday nights, though out of respect for Tomás's vow of celibacy Ava never acted on her sexual impulses with him. She did feel them. Maybe he didn't, though. It was hard to tell, with him.

"From everything you've told me, Gavin sounds very boring," Tomás said.

"He'd be happier with Leez Anne Williker — she's an equity sales director."

"You shouldn't drag out the divorce." Tomás had a bottle of red wine in his hand. He took a swig from it. "I dragged out my annulment, it was a mistake."

"Why did you want an annulment, anyway?" Ava asked.

"I have a problem with intimacy. Hey, did I tell you? I'm applying for a job in Myanmar."

"Oh." What? "You're leaving Nepal?" What was an intimacy problem?

"Nepal is passé," Tomás said, and took another swig of wine. "Things are changing really fast in Myanmar — you should come too. I mean, fuck IDAF, right: and anyways, you hate this job."

"Have I mentioned the size of my annual budget?" Ava said.

"Fuck the aid industry, all it does is enrich the global elite," Tomás said.

For a while they lay silent, he drinking, and she musing over everything she had read in the past months at IDAF, and everything she had written. All the meetings she had sat in, all that had been said to her, all that she had said. The presentations she had listened to, the presentations she had given. WDS-Nepal's proposal. That dinner at Indira Sharma's house. Vishwa, explaining things to her. All the meetings at IDAF. So many words.

"I'm looking forward to my trip," she said. "I've waited too long to get to the field."

"You should really switch to humanitarian work, Ava, it's the only ethical intervention in poorly governed countries like this."

"The only one?" she said.

"There'll be lots of openings in Yangon. I'll help you find a job there. We can move there together," he said, as though they were a couple.

Ava liked him so much. His wandering eye and dreamy expression always charmed her, as did his rants about the aid industry, as doctrinaire as they could be. Tomás made her feel like she was living in a world of ideas that mattered. And he was her touchstone in Nepal, neither a lover nor just a friend, but something else, something intimate if uncategorized. It did occur to Ava, when she was in bed with Tomás, that he was a married man — though they weren't having sex, so it didn't matter. Or perhaps it did. What was Tomás's intimacy problem?

She rubbed her face against his clavicle. He smelled of warm, sweet skin. She could really use the kind of magical night she'd had with Anthony. Or even — she missed the certainties she'd had with Gavin. But at least she could talk about anything with Tomás.

"Hey, Tomás?" she said. "What caste do you think I am? I mean — what caste was I when I was born?"

"Fuck knows: you'd have to ask a Nepali. They carry around all that useless information in their heads."

"I kind of like not knowing my roots," Ava said. She had told Tomás about her visit to the orphanage. She talked about it again. "I saw a boy there. He was — I don't know — eight or nine years old. He was the only person I saw there. Otherwise it was — there was nothing there for me."

"What were you hoping to find, my dear?"

"I don't know. It was following a kind of instinct in coming to Nepal. Maybe the instinct was wrong."

"So come with me to Myanmar," Tomás said. "IDAF is a collusion between the international and national elite." His voice rumbled pleasantly through his chest. "It's criminal," he said, "though they're all complicit."

"All of them?"

"This country needs to take responsibility for itself. You know the risks it faces. This entire region is overdue for — well, it's already a socio-political disaster. But imagine what's going to happen when the Big One strikes. All this," he gestured, and the wine sloshed in the bottle, "will vanish. None of these houses, these streets, this shitty infrastructure, will remain. The only international airport will close. The government will be paralysed — I mean, even more paralysed than it already is. There'll be no water, food, shelter, medicine. People will have to fend for themselves — and the powerful, the strong, will prey on the weak and vulnerable. That's what aid should help the country prepare for, Ava: preventing the worst-case scenario when — not if — disaster strikes."

Ava balked at the vision.

"All of this," he repeated, "will vanish."

"Shut up," she said.

"This country's doomed, Ava."

"Tell me about Myanmar," Ava said. "Tell me why I should switch to humanitarian work and move with you to Myanmar."

"Nepal is completely doomed."

INDIRA GRABBED HER purse from the security guard and rushed down IDAF's driveway. The receptionist — what was her name, she used to know it — recognized her from her visits to Catherine Christy and trilled, "Namaste, Indira-ma'am! Rick-sir and the rest are already here — please go up."

"Thank you!" Indira hurried up the stairway. She was half an hour late. This whole Durga disaster was going to kill her.

Indeed, Rick Peede was in the conference hall, as were the Canadian and Vishwa Bista — and why was Chandi Shrestha at this meeting? Indira's rival smiled at her unctuously as she took a seat.

"There you are, Indira," said the Canadian, looking far too young to be IDAF's director of WEP. "I'm sorry, we had to start, but I'll fill you in afterwards."

"Sorry, I — little emergency at home," Indira said.

"Oh, is everything all right?"

"No — yes! Just — sorry." Indira tried to catch Vishwa Bista's eyes, but they were hidden behind his floppy hair.

Rick Peede returned to the discussion that Indira's arrival had interrupted. It was to do with capacity enhancement. Rick Peede had a way of droning, and even after all these years of working together, Indira found his accent hard to follow. In any case, she was too agitated to pay close attention.

She had got Durga discharged from the hospital this morning — without incident, thank the gods — and had installed her back in Heaven Hotel. "You have to be good, Durga," she had pleaded with the girl, who lay bloodless and bereft in bed. "What more can I do for you? What will make you better? Tell me, girl. Tell me what you want."

The girl had whispered, "I want a life."

What did that mean? "Well, spend a few more days resting

here, then we'll take you back home," Indira had said. "And don't try to kill yourself again, Durga. You know how hard it's been for me to manage all this? No one at home knows anything, I've kept everything secret. And at the office I've got so much pressure right now, I don't need —" She had had to catch herself. "Now I'll go and get you some lamb kebabs. I'm sure you'll like it. And even if you don't, eat it, Durga. I beg you, girl: you have to be good."

She had rushed to Tandoor & Kebab, then rushed back to the hotel and pleaded with the girl some more, and then rushed over here.

Rick Peede kept droning on about capacity enhancement. Indira stared at him vacantly: that big head, the red hair. These expatriates were so unencumbered, so free. They could do anything they wanted all the time. Indira had met Rick's wife Misha at office parties. Misha was even taller than her husband. They had three children: the youngest was only two years old. An image came to her of Rick and Misha Peede having sex: there would be legs everywhere.

"Wouldn't you concur, Indira-ji?" Rick Peede asked, turning to her.

"Yes." Indira sat up. "Yes, Rick-ji, I fully concur."

And even though no one had asked him, Chandi Shrestha piped up, "As the other deputy co-director of WDS-Nepal, I also concur."

"Ava, I can't emphasize this enough," Rick Peede said, turning back to the Canadian. "In our annual appraisal last year, WDS-Nepal identified five key areas for prioritization..." Again, he droned on.

What if Durga tried to kill herself again, Indira thought. What if the girl were taking rat poison right now?

She fussed with her purse, she shifted around in the chair, she wondered if she might excuse herself to go out and call Heaven Hotel. Then Rick Peede suddenly stopped talking, and everyone stood up. Indira also shot to her feet, all of her ambitions frothing up like overheated milk: what had happened, had IDAF approved her proposal, was she going to become the next director of WDS-Nepal?

Rick Peede and Chandi Shrestha left after a round of handshakes. Vishwa Bista slunk away, muttering about a meeting. The Canadian turned to her with a smile. "Shall we go to my office, Indira?"

"Yes, why not?" Indira said, confused.

Catherine Christy's old office used to be cozy, with family photos up on the wall. Now it was stripped of decor. Indira remembered Catherine Christy's words: *you must become the first Nepali woman director of WDS-Nepal.* Catherine Christy used to sit with Indira on the sofa, like a friend, but the Canadian invited her to sit on a hard-backed chair across her desk.

"Would you like tea or coffee, Indira?"

"I will have tea."

Catherine Christy used to make her a special goji berry tea: it stimulated the libido, she used to say with a wink. The Canadian brewed her a weak, watery cup of milk tea. Then she sat down at her desk and spoke:

"Before you arrived at the meeting, I was telling Rick and Chandi that IDAF is undergoing an internal exercise to enhance the implementation of the Paris Declaration on Aid Effectiveness. I've been discussing this with Claire — do you know Claire Ross-Jones?"

"Of course, many times I have met her."

"And we've got Daphne Muirwood in from headquarters.

She's innovating an internal implementation strategy for the country offices of the Asia Pacific Region." The Canadian opened WDS-Nepal's proposal and turned to the section on the budget. "As I said when I came over to your house for dinner, Indira, I'm new to this field. My background — I used to work on mergers and acquisitions in a large law firm in Toronto. And I've only ever worked with organizations in Canada, so I may be bringing in my own biases, but, well." She frowned. "WDS-Nepal has so many partners, and they're so very different. Some work at the village level, and others in the districts, and others seem to — I can't quite figure out what some of them do. National Network Nepal, for example." She pointed at Vishwa Bista's cousin-sister-in-law's NGO. "It's slated to receive almost a quarter of your budget, and — well, you couldn't make it to the meeting, but I met the director, Preety Rana. Now Rick has explained that WDS-Nepal places a special emphasis on capacity enhancement, but, you see, I'm on my own mission for Gender Responsive Budgeting at IDAF, and Claire is really hoping to highlight the Post-Priority Themes going forward, so there's a lot I'm grappling with here." She smiled apologetically. "You'll have to bear with me, Indira. I'm wondering why you've chosen to partner with National Network Nepal. I want to know why them, specifically."

Why National Network Nepal, why National Network Nepal? Indira's mind slid from thought to slippery thought, searching for one she could land on safely.

"Ava, there is a big difference among our partners," she began. "They are all different in their mandate and methodology. The work is all — different." Indira pointed at another partner on the budget. "For example," she said, "this NGO is not an implementing agency. It partners with NGOs who do implementation.

Whereas this one" — she pointed at yet another partner — "it does direct implementation. Understand? National Network Nepal supports other partners, small ones, NGOs and CBOs in the field, to enhance capacity. It does not do direct implementation itself. So, it is like that, Ava."

She studied the Canadian's face to see if this had convinced her.

The Canadian was frowning delicately. There was a drawn-out pause before she spoke. "I'll probably see all this for myself on my upcoming field trip, but I guess the question I keep asking, Indira, is, what value do NGOs like National Network Nepal add? They should add value, right?"

Value?

"Value they add." Now Indira was irked. How little these foreigners understood. "Ava," she said, "there are four thousand villages in Nepal. Big international NGOs like WDS-Nepal, we cannot help every CBO in every village, that is too micro in scale, and also, our mandate is not for that. Understand?"

"Yes, of course." The Canadian pointed, again, at National Network Nepal. "So what will National Network Nepal be doing, other than disbursing funds to partners in the districts and villages? Because if that's mainly what it's going to do, that's akin to, well, to subcontracting, isn't it?"

Why this fixation on National Network Nepal?

"That one," Indira said, "has a sector-wise approach, Ava."

"What's its sector?"

Was the Canadian a complete idiot? "Capacity enhancement for the empowerment of women, of course."

"Oh, right, I meant — that wasn't what I was asking, of course I knew that." Now the Canadian was flustered. "Sometimes I feel a bit dense, Indira, like I'm just not getting it. It's just that if we approve your proposal, it'll be our biggest collaboration outside of the Government of Nepal. I've read everything I could find — though maybe I just need to stop reading and get out there, to see the work myself."

"You still have not gone to the field even now?" Indira said.

"Vishwa and I are going next week. We'll visit several CBOs that National Network Nepal is proposing to support, CBOs in" — she mangled all the names of the villages — "near a town called Butwal." She pronounced the town's name butt-wall. "So I'm going to wait to make my decision on your proposal till after I return. In the meanwhile, Claire and Daphne have allocated a special budget to conduct a review."

A review? "A review of what?" Indira stammered.

"Our partnership with WDS-Nepal." The Canadian smiled to soften the blow. "I'm sorry, Indira, I know it's an imposition on you, but it'll be clarifying to me as I draw up the Five Year Outlook. Vishwa's already lined up a consultant, he says he's very good — he's an anthropologist, John Barnett."

John Barnett. John Barnett! John Barnett was still in Nepal? "I know John Barnett!" Indira said. She had worked with John Barnett at Help more than twenty years ago. Indira remembered him as a chocolatey-handsome man with bright blue eyes and eyelashes as long as a girl's. He had been an intern, or no, he was writing a thesis back then. He was fluent in Newari and Tamang and several other Tibeto-Burmese languages. His thesis was on the indigenous management systems of — the Tamangs? Or maybe the Newars. Indira said, "Tell John Barnett to meet me, Ava. I will give him whatever information he may need."

"That would be wonderful, thank you, Indira. I'll tell Vishwa to put you two in touch. Vishwa's in charge of the review."

Of course. Vishwa Bista would handle this, Indira thought. He had done things like this before. Feeling better now, she asked, "Is that all, Ava?"

"Thanks for your cooperation, Indira."

They stood. Catherine Christy used to embrace her, but the Canadian reached over for a handshake, cold and impersonal. Anyone could tell, just from looking at the Canadian, that she had no special sympathy for women.

Out in the hallway, Indira tried to regain her composure. She wiped her face, patted down her hair. Would Vishwa Bista really clean up this mess? He had to — he had created it. And she had to make sure he would.

She turned into his office to confront him.

She opened his office door to find him sitting on a couch with a woman in a sequined miniskirt.

"Indira-ji!" he cried, springing up as though she had caught him doing something dirty.

Indira sprang back from the door. "Sorry, sorry!"

"No, no!" Vishwa Bista said. "Please come in and meet Shakuntala Shree Shakya. You must have seen her on TV. She's sure to win the title this year. She is our future Miss Nepal."

The future Miss Nepal smiled at Indira.

"Yes, of course, I recognize the name," Indira lied. "And, who wouldn't recognize the face?"

"I'm mentoring Shakuntala Shree-ji to be an ambassador for women's development," Vishwa Bista said. To the young woman, he explained, "Indira-ji is highly knowledgeable on the subject. You must learn from her about women's development."

"I would like to learn about women's development," said the future Miss Nepal.

"Come by my office any time," Indira said, giving her a business card. Then, to Vishwa Bista, she said, "About the assessment —"

"Leave all that to me."

"Thank you, thank you!" Indira said, wondering why she was thanking him, when it was he who had dragged her into his filth. "Thank you so much, Vishwa-ji!" she said.

"You're welcome, Indira-ji."

Indira left, loathing him viscerally, and loathing herself too. Excrement, filth.

Downstairs, the receptionist trilled, "Namaste, Indira-ma'am!"

"Namaste," she said, wondering what the receptionist's name was.

Out in the driveway, Indira's thoughts returned to Durga. There was so much to do at the office, but how could she possibly work? She would take the day off to look after the girl.

SHULINBABA WAS JUST a rock, and a misshapen one at that — he wasn't even a fine carving like the Hanuman statue beside him. Yet everyone was elbowing each other aside to kneel down before him. The temple bells were pealing, the air was thick with incense. It was hard to see anything. Sapana found an opening in the inner sanctum, and knelt before the rock. She closed her eyes and prayed: *Shulinbaba, help me make a good speech at the CBO meeting. Let me speak clearly and remember everything I have to say.* The whole village was going to attend the meeting. After the speeches, there was going to be a feast for the foreigners. Then all of the CBO's beneficiaries, including the members of the women's committee, would show the foreigners how they had benefited from the CBO's work. The occasion would be truly momentous. Sapana prayed: *let my words have power, Shulinbaba. Let them impress the foreigners.*

"Ey, aren't you finished?" Ritu nudged her from behind. "You're not the only one who needs a husband, you know. Namrata's getting desperate back here."

"How could you speak like that in a temple?" Namrata hissed.

Someone had offered marigolds to Shulinbaba. Sapana took one and put it in her hair. Then she got up to let her friends take her place.

She had to shove through the crowd to leave the temple. Outside, the devotees' queue snaked all the way down the hill to the mad river. Women from surrounding villages came here on this day, the unmarried to ask for grooms, and the married to ask for their husbands' longevity.

Rama-bhauju, who was standing in line with her brood of four, said, "You're already done, Bahini?"

"It'll take you an hour just to get in!" Sapana said, wondering why Rama-bhauju would bother praying for the longevity of a husband who had taken a second wife.

When Ritu and Namrata came out, the three of them ran down the hill, Ritu talking, as always, about boys: "Listen, girls, if we don't marry soon, all the good boys will be taken, and we'll have to settle for the leftovers. You know that monkey who lives across from my house? The other day he told me I'm too proud, I'll learn my lesson when I end up as his bride. You know what I said?" She crooked a pinkie finger, mimicking a limp penis. "I said, 'Eeeeh!'"

"Tchee!" Namrata giggled.

"I got a marriage offer the other day," Ritu said. She told them about it. The boy's family was from the far-west, but he had an office job in Kathmandu. Her relatives were acting as go-betweens, arranging a meeting for them in the bazaar. "I'm worried," she said. "What if he's not handsome – or rich?"

"Then say no. You get to say no," Namrata said.

Chandra had refused to go to the temple, and was waiting for them at the bottom of the hill, by the river. She scoffed when she saw them. "You're done praying for a husband?" She linked arms with Sapana. "The old widower just passed by, he said he wants to talk to you about the meeting."

"Again? I spoke to him only this morning!"

"He just wants to look at you." Ritu snickered. "You know, he doesn't look so old if you look at him from behind."

"Tchee!"

They crossed the bridge, then parted ways, Ritu and Namrata heading towards their homes and Sapana and Chandra walking back up through the village.

Gyanu-dai wasn't home when they got there. They sat at the kitchen table and waited for him. They had grown so spoiled, having him cook for them every day, that they just sat around, doing nothing, when he wasn't there. Gyanu-dai was spending less and less time at home nowadays. Sapana had thought he would have more free time now that the land transfer was done, but he went into the bazaar every day — to make phone calls, he said. He seemed distracted, or unhappy, somehow. Sapana sometimes caught him sitting all by himself on the ridge by Ba's plot, lost in thought. When he was home he kept busy with tasks that he assigned himself to improve the home. Since coming back, he had stocked the larder with expensive spices, oils, unfamiliar herbs — till the whole house smelled like a garden. He had hired a woodworker from the bazaar to replace the chipped laminate on the table and repair all the chairs. The pots and pans now sat in an orderly row on a new shelf. This week he had finished sandpapering the doors and windows. He was going to paint the house himself.

"Mmm." Chandra was leafing through a book of poems. "I like this, listen to it." She cleared her throat and recited:

> What grows in these still villages
> But death. To stay is to die.
> To leave is to die too. Mother!
> Save me. I'm fading.

Then she reread the poem, and frowned. "Actually, the poet seems a bit depressed, I've changed my mind, I don't like it."

"Read me a love poem."

"This poet doesn't know how to write love poems."

Dusk fell. A tranquility descended over the house. Sapana stirred, at last, turning on the kerosene lamp so that Chandra could keep reading. Then, because she was up, she started to cook dal-bhat-tarkaari for the evening meal.

Gyanu-dai arrived when she was halfway through. He was carrying a sheaf of papers under one arm. He put them on the table and came over to help her. "What are you making, Bahini?"

"The usual. What else do I know how to make, Dai?"

"It needs a bit more — here, let me do it." He put down the papers and began to cook.

Sapana happily returned to sit with Chandra at the table.

The papers Gyanu-dai had brought were from the Electricity Authority. He told them, as he cooked, that he wanted to electrify the house. "It'll be good not to use a kerosene lamp anymore. I meant to do it last time I came, but, well." He told them he would go to the bazaar tomorrow to hand in the application form and make the payment.

Listening to her brother, it struck Sapana that he was always looking for some task to occupy himself with. He seemed to need to always be doing something. She had an idea.

"Dai," she said, "at the CBO meeting, after the speeches, there'll be a feast. Maybe you could make the food — something that foreigners would like."

"You want me to work for Thulo-ba?"

"If we impress the foreigners, they'll give the CBO money, re," Sapana said.

"And will that money come to you?" Gyanu-dai asked, his tone suddenly brusque.

It took Sapana aback.

Gyanu-dai said, "What, actually, has the CBO done for you, Bahini? You're doing all this work for the women's committee. Are they giving you a salary? No. Are they training you? No. They took you on one small study tour — and did they do it for free? Do you know how much Thulo-ba must have pocketed for that tour?"

He was being so negative that Sapana didn't even want to respond.

Chandra had looked up from her book. She said, "It's true, Sapana. Your thulo-ba wouldn't have conducted the study tour for free."

"Yes, but the women's committee is doing good work." Sapana refused to give in to their cynicism. "You know that, Chandra. Your own muwa is a member. And Dai, you'd be surprised. I've talked to all the members, and — we saw so many cooperatives on our study tour, we're thinking of opening one here."

"And is that enough?" Gyanu-dai left the stove and came over to them. "A cooperative. That's really enough, Bahini?" Now he sounded puzzled instead of angry.

"The main thing is to find a market," Sapana explained. "Everything they've done out east, we can do here."

Chandra looked from one sibling to the other, and moderated between them. "The women's committee is good, Gyanu-dai. It's not going to create a revolution, but having it is better than not having it, I guess."

Gyanu-dai took this in with a nod. "It's just that I worry," he said.

"You love us, that's why you worry about us, Dai." Sapana reached for his hand. "But we're not like other girls, Dai, we don't want to have the lives of our mothers, we want to be modern, truly modern." She said, "The world has advanced so much. We want to advance too." To make her point, she borrowed a few lines from her speech. "If we don't make things better here, who will? We're the youth, we're the future, we're the hope of the nation. If we work together, there's nothing we can't do."

Gyanu-dai still looked sceptical, or maybe conflicted. He always had difficulty saying what was on his mind. He finally confessed: "It's just that I won't be here much longer, Bahini."

Ey. This was what it was. He was leaving. Somehow, this hurt. Sapana let go of his hand.

"I have to go to Kathmandu to talk to some manpowers," Gyanu-dai said. "I lost my old job in the desert, I'm looking for a new one." He looked at Sapana. "Will you really be all right living here by yourselves?"

Sapana refused to answer.

Chandra spoke for her. "We'll look after each other, Dai. We'll be fine."

But Gyanu-dai wanted Sapana to say so too. He wanted her permission to leave, she realized. He kept looking at her, but she refused to say what he wanted to hear.

"Now that the land is in your name," he said to her, "your rights are secure, Bahini."

Her rights. Sapana didn't know why this upset her so much. "My rights?" she said, her voice coming out cool and steely. "What about your rights, Dai? What are you, a stranger to this house?" She didn't hold back: "You worry about me, but maybe I should worry about you, Dai. You wander the world as though you're homeless; you come back here only to perform last rites; you feel as though you don't belong, Dai. But aren't I your sister? Aren't you and I of the same blood?"

Gyanu-dai hung his head.

"Isn't this your home too?" Sapana cried.

At this, Gyanu-dai took out a photograph from his wallet and placed it on the table. It was of a woman with a soft face and a trusting expression. She was sitting on a bench beside a river, or maybe the sea. She was dressed in a simple tunic and jeans, and she was smiling. Gyanu-dai said, "I'm going to marry her, Bahini."

Sapana picked up the photograph.

Her brother explained that he had met the woman in the desert. She worked there. She was from a country called the Philippines. She was a widow. She had a young son. His name was Crisanto Balana and hers was Maleah.

Why had Gyanu-dai kept this from her, all these months? Why was he so private, so unknowable? Why was he a stranger to his own family? Looking at the photograph, Sapana was struck by an unfamiliar emotion — resentment, or maybe jealousy.

What about me, she wanted to say. You're leaving me. Of course, I have Chandra, but don't you love me, Dai? You're my only family.

Gyanu-dai said, "I don't know where we'll end up, but I'll follow Maleah anywhere. That's why I have to leave, Bahini. I have to leave because I want to marry her."

This wasn't true, Sapana thought. Gyanu-dai was leaving because he had always felt like an outsider in their family, and in their village. Otherwise why not marry this woman and bring her and her son here? Gyanu-dai's life from before Ma married Ba still haunted him. It had driven him out of the village at a young age, and it kept him away after his studies, even though all of them — Ma, Ba, she — had always made him feel wanted. When he had come for Ba's funeral, he had never intended to stay on. He had transferred the land to her name, and had made improvements to the home, so that he could leave with a free conscience, Sapana realized.

Gyanu-dai was still waiting for her to say something conciliatory. "I'll stay for your speech," he said. "I know it's important to you, I'll talk to Thulo-ba, I'll help with the feast."

Sapana couldn't say anything. The sadness that she had refused to feel after Ba's death swelled up inside her now. She wished she could reverse time, she wished she could have Ba and Ma back, she wished their family would return to being whole again. With difficulty, she reached for Gyanu-dai's hand. It was warm, he was here, but she already missed him.

This was the end of her childhood, she realized. She desperately wished she could have it back.

GYANU DIPPED THE brush in the paint, scraped off the excess, and drew its bristles evenly over the post. The deep sea-green brought back the endless days of childhood — Ba reading out loud, Ma listening on with baby Sapana slung on her back. Family happiness, precious and fleeting. The fulfilment Ma and Ba had found together, the fulfilment they had shared with him. He painted the doorpost, using broad strokes at the centre of the post, taking care at the corners.

When the post was done, he started on the jamb. He had already painted the rest of the house. Only this door, which opened onto Ma and Ba's room, remained. The house looked almost as proud as it once used to. It satisfied Gyanu, in some deep physical way, to restore it; and the diversion helped quell his anxieties. Sapana was still angry at him, she wasn't talking to him. And she was right to be angry. For he wasn't simply leaving; he was leaving her. He understood the betrayal, but had to get back to Maleah while he still could.

Maleah and her roommate Susanna had gone to the agent that their other roommate, Jojo, had used to find work in Germany. The only jobs on offer were for certified child minders. The agency offered certification. Susanna had decided to train, but Maleah was uncertain. She had renewed her contract at the gift shop for another year. "Come soon, mahal," she had said. "I do not want to lose you. Come back, and let us marry."

After painting the outside of the door, Gyanu entered Ma and Ba's room. He hadn't been in here since Ba's passing, and neither had Sapana or Chandra. Through some unspoken agreement they had avoided the room as a way of evading their grief.

The air was stale inside. The bed lay stripped bare in the corner. There was a film of dust and two framed photographs on a table. One was a black-and-white of Ma and Ba, taken at a studio in the bazaar on the year of their marriage. Ma was young in that photograph, and ethereally beautiful. Ba was serene, holding Gyanu's hand as he, in shorts, stood in front of them staring wide-eyed at the camera.

The other photograph, faded and sepia-toned, was of the entire family in the same studio several years later. Gyanu was seven years old by then. Sapana was a newborn, swaddled in cloth in Ma's arms. Gyanu remembered going to the bazaar to take this photograph. It had been a festive day, a family celebration, a private triumph for Ba and Ma. After leaving the photographer's studio, they had eaten samosas at a tea shop. Ba had bought Gyanu jalebis. Gyanu remembered how complete they had felt as a family on that day.

Above the table, on the wall, hung a small mirror. It too was covered with dust. Looking into it Gyanu saw his reflection, and behind him, Sapana. He turned around, and immediately realized that it wasn't Sapana: it was Ma.

She placed a hand on his face the way she used to, her hand soft, a wisp. Gyanu felt her presence with him. Through all the difficult choices she had made, he felt her tenderness for him.

I couldn't even give you your own identity.

She had said this to him on her deathbed. She had also said what she said to him now: *You had to give up your past so I could live.*

He whispered back, "You gave me my whole life, Ma."

After a while, when he could no longer feel Ma's presence, he turned away from the mirror. And as he turned, in the dark edges of his memory, he located a few lost shards of the past:

He saw a large, open yard with a date tree. He smelled dust, heat, tar. There was a house with a chicken coop.

He saw himself racing past the coop, through the yard, to the front door of the house. He heard the bellow of a man's voice, and also a woman's cry. He felt his own terror, and saw himself turning around and racing across the yard to hide in the chicken coop.

To change anything in this room felt, to Gyanu, like an erasure of Ma and Ba. He decided not to paint the rest of the door.

When he stepped out, there was a visitor in the kitchen.

It was Kisne, sitting at the table with a girl. From the resemblance, it was clear that she was his daughter. Gyanu put down the can of paint and brush and wiped his hands on his pants.

"I didn't hear you come in," he said.

Kisne grinned. "I came for the number of the manpower." To his daughter, he said, "Chhori, say namaste to Gyanu-kaka."

The girl was about three, and shy. She hung her head and didn't respond.

"Where are your manners?" her father said, prodding her. "Say namaste."

"Let it be." Gyanu went to the stove. "I'll get you the number, but first, let's have tea."

"Sure, let's try the tea of a five-star hotel." Kisne laughed. "Hai, Chhori?" He scooped up the girl in his arms. "Let's see what five-star hotel tea is like, hai, Chhori?"

The girl squealed.

"Hai? Hai?" He began to tickle the girl.

She squealed again. "Stop, Baba, stop! Don't tickle — stop!"

"Hai?"

They made a sweet picture, father and daughter. Kisne, tickling the girl, "Hai, hai, hai?" and the girl, squealing, "No tickling, Baba, stop, stop, stop!"

The whole house rang with the girl's laughter.

"Stop, Baba, no tickling! Stop, Baba! Baba, stop!"

IN HER STUDY, Ava clutched the newspaper, reading the story over and over. The words slipped and slid around, impossible to take in.

The director of the Bal Mandir orphanage, as well as another official, had been arrested the day before, and charged with multiple counts of rape.

She read:

The officials were accused of organizing "wedding parties" at the orphanage on Saturdays.

They gave alcohol to autistic girls, they showed them pornography.

They dressed them as brides, in red saris, and made them dance.

They sprayed them with water, forcing them to undress.

They took them to bars and groomed them as prostitutes.

She reread the story.

The arrested officials were proclaiming their innocence.

The words slipped and slid.

She reread the story in shock.

She reread the story again.

THEIR HOTEL WAS damp, with a hint of mildew in its dark, clammy corners. It was a relief to step out into the sunshine. Ava moved slowly, feeling shaky, as though something might give underfoot and she would tumble.

She had known, of course, that conditions were poor in the orphanage. And she knew that life was cheap in Nepal. Everything she had learned at IDAF underscored this truth, and she had felt it instinctively, in her bones, since that Christmas visit to Nepal. After joining IDAF, Ava had come to understand that Nepal's girls and women were especially vulnerable; and yet the news about the orphanage had struck her with a force that had gutted her, making it hard for her to breathe.

The hotel's front gate opened onto Butwal town, which was smaller than she had expected. Outside its central core, it had the sleepy air of a village. Or perhaps the hotel was in a quiet residential part. Ava walked down to the main road.

Driving into town last evening, she had seen that the residents were moderately well off, or at least not abjectly poor. Now, too, she noticed new, westernized clothes on a man passing by, and sturdy shoes on the feet of two girls who were playing marbles by the side of the road. A woman in a nightdress strolled by. She had a thin gold chain around her neck. Ava observed her own relief at these tokens of prosperity, and wondered what she was doing: looking for signs that not all Nepalis were suffering? Allaying her guilt for having survived this society, for having thrived in Canada...

Past a row of empty lots, she entered a busier part of town. There were small businesses here: shops, banks, boutiques. Six headless mannequins in bright red saris stood in the window of a shop called New Nepal Fashions. Those were bridal saris: the sequins glinted, stabbing the air with light. They brought to mind the wedding parties at the orphanage mentioned in the news report. A horn blared at a nearby bus station. A conductor was yelling to attract passengers to a departing bus.

On the other side of a row of parked vehicles was a river. Ava had seen it yesterday, driving in. She walked to the bridge over the river and stood at the centre, looking down. The slow moving river was wide and clear. The water looked clean. She wondered whether people swam in the rivers in Nepal. There was no swimming in Kathmandu's befouled Bagmati River. Yesterday, on the highway, they had driven alongside two rivers: one large and wild, its water crashing down massive boulders, and the other one narrow, with swift, deep rapids. There had been no one on the banks, perhaps because the water was too dangerous, or too cold. Here, below the bridge, Ava saw a man ambling along the pebbly bank. A woman was washing clothes at the water's edge. A flock of birds — starlings, perhaps — swooped down from the far shore and glided back up into the sky.

She was glad for a chance to be alone. Vishwa had talked non-stop throughout the drive yesterday. "Finally, the real Nepal," he had said as they drove out of Kathmandu Valley, launching into tales about every single town, every single village, they passed: "Now this area, Ava, is very inspiring. They've had a successful open defecation–free movement. It's set a real example for the rest of Nepal."

"There's a big Hindu temple nearby here, Ava."

"This area is famous for organic farming. They've banned all pesticides here."

He was only being helpful, and Ava hated to be so uncharitable, but she was in pain over the news about orphanage. She would have given anything to take in the countryside in silence and to let all the emotions that were churning inside her settle down.

"That village, up on the hill? It's where my ancestors are from. Now, if we were to continue on this road? We'd get to Pokhara. You must go to Pokhara sometime, Ava. It's much nicer than Kathmandu."

Nepal's countryside was astonishing: the land was riven with cliffs and canyons and gorges, breathtaking, and utterly unworkable. Ava stared at lone huts high up in the hills: how would they ever get electricity or drinking water? Why would anyone choose to live in such isolation? The thought — it could have been me — recurred like a nightmare she couldn't shake off. Nodding politely at whatever Vishwa was saying, she thought: I could have been born in any of these huts.

I could have been one of those girls in the orphanage.

The high mountains had eventually given way to hills. The highway followed the course of the rivers, breaking through to the southern plains. They drove along a stretch of low blue hills overlooking flatlands.

"Now in this area, Ava, IDAF supported many peacebuilding initiatives during the Maoist conflict."

By the time they reached Butwal, Ava had been exhausted.

On the bridge, from behind her, now, came a sudden burst of laughter. She turned to see four young women walking by, holding hands. They were dressed in grey-and-pink tunics: school uniforms, or — how old were they? — perhaps college uniforms. They looked so confident in their youthfulness, their beauty, their intelligence. One woman called out, "Namaste!" to her, and then they walked on, following the course of their lives.

Ava remained on the course of her life. She remained very much on the course of her life, her life of — she cringed at the word, it was strident and unsubtle — privilege. It had been impossible, on yesterday's drive, not to see how shielded she had been all her life from the country of her birth. She had been shielded by family love, by Mom and Dad's financial stability, by everything that came with a childhood in Overwood: an education, health care, and things she had never even thought about not having, like running water and electricity. She had been shielded by her law degree, even by her marriage, and by the heft, the solidity, of her former job at the law firm. Being in Nepal threw her privilege into stark relief: her salary at IDAF afforded her a mansion, three household staff, trifles, and luxuries. How much ought a person have to buffet themselves against — others? The poor. Reality. Bleakly, Ava had thought: here she was, at last, in the real Nepal, completely fortified against it.

"Ava, Ava, there you are, Ava!"

A lasting fatigue washed over her as Vishwa strode up to the bridge.

He said, "I've been looking for you everywhere." He had dressed for the trip in outdoor gear: a tangerine North Face jacket, a wide-brimmed hat, new Merrell boots. Ava had dressed, as always, in a suit. She was carrying her attaché case. She felt very conspicuously foreign.

"How are you this morning, Ava?"

"I'm fine, Vishwa."

"Did you sleep well? Did you have breakfast? Should we get you something to eat?"

"I'm fine."

"It's nice out here, isn't it?" With a toss of his hair, Vishwa looked out at the river and made a sweeping gesture with his hands. "This is called the Tinau River. Did you get a chance to look around this morning? There's a strong industrial economy in Butwal, though of course there's still poverty among the marginalized. See there, across the river?" He pointed to a few mud huts on the shore. "Sometimes, I really feel so helpless, Ava. After decades of aid, well, there's been progress for sure, but there's so much left to do. You'll see what I mean when we get to the villages. Are you ready? The driver's waiting. It's an hour's drive to the first CBO."

THE SKY WAS silver-grey, and the birds were chirping outside the window. Sapana rolled over and shook Chandra. "Ey, get up!"

Chandra groaned.

"The sun's already out," Sapana lied.

"Let me be," Chandra groaned, drawing the quilt over her head. She had stayed up late reading a thick book on social science, and would have trouble waking up.

"Sleep all day, then," Sapana said, springing out of bed.

She went out to wash, and afterwards, came and changed into the kurta that Gyanu-dai had bought for her. Sapana had been saving it for a special occasion. She checked herself in the mirror and approved: the blue stripes really suited her.

Chandra was snoring underneath the quilt. Some revolutionary she'd make! Sapana went and shook her. "Ey, don't I look pretty?"

Chandra groaned. "I said, let me be."

"I look really good in this new kurta, Chandra."

"Stop being so vain." Reluctantly, Chandra opened her eyes. "You always look good," she said. She yawned, stretched, and sat up. "Lau, I know it's your big day, I'll go and make you something to eat." She straggled out of bed, her hair tangled and her nightdress crumpled.

Sapana went back to the mirror, combing her hair back in a tidy braid, lining her eyes with gaajal and placing a black tika between her brows. She had to look completely mature and responsible today. She had been feeling mature and responsible: she would have to take on all family duties once Gyanu-dai left. She could: she and Chandra had been doing so anyway. Gyanu-dai could leave. They would be fine by themselves.

Out in the kitchen, Chandra had made tea, and also Sapana's favourite: spiced potatoes and roti. "Eat." She put a plate on the table, then sat down beside Sapana. "Gyanu-dai's already gone to prepare the feast," Chandra said. "You know what he said? The CBO bought a gas cylinder at an inflated price, re. Your thulo-ba's taking a cut off the gas, the loose tea and milk, sugar, even bottled water." She sat back and became philosophical. "That's how it is with the feudal classes. They capture all the resources, ey, Sapana. That's what this book on social science says. We need a revolution to overthrow your thulo-ba." She laughed. "Though look at the Maoist revolution: even that didn't dislodge him, hai? You know the poet I was reading? The depressed one? Sometimes I think he's right to be depressed."

Sapana wasn't paying attention. "Make sure your muwa's ready to meet the foreigners, Chandra."

"You're really going to show them her stupid pickles?"

"I should go and make sure everyone's ready." Sapana got up.

"But you hardly ate anything!"

Sapana was already out the door. "Come soon, hai, Chandra, come and find me wherever I am!"

The season of morning mists had given way to incandescent springtime. The bottlebrush trees were red with flower, the sun was blazing, and the breeze was sweet. On days like this, even life's biggest challenges seemed like light refracted through crystal: and the whole world glittered.

Sapana went to Naina-di's house first, because it was the closest. Naina-di was in the kitchen, cooking. Her sari was stained, and her face was smeared with dirt.

"Di, your face!" Sapana cried.

Naina-di laughed, wiping dirt off with the end of her sari. "I spent all morning cleaning the stall. The goats look better than me."

It was true: in the stall behind her house, her goats were lustrous and lively. Naina-di squatted down to pet a frisky kid. "They're a mix of khari and jamunapari, but I hear that boers breed faster," she said. "A group of us should get boers, Bahini. That cooperative you've been talking about? Let's make it a goat farm."

Sapana said, "I'll talk about cooperatives in my speech, Di. Now make yourself as clean as your goats, or the foreigners will think you're a jungly animal."

As she left Naina-di's house, she saw Chandra ahead of her. Chandra hadn't changed out of her nightdress or even combed her hair: what a slob! Little Tara was scampering behind, trying to keep up with her older sister. The pair turned past the bottle-brush trees and went into their muwa-buwa's house.

Jethi-didi lived in one of the concrete houses by the fields. She was on the front porch chatting with Rama-bhauju, who lived next door. "Bahini, you have to convince Rama," Jethi-didi said when she saw Sapana. "I've been telling her to forget about her Jersey cow and plant an orange orchard instead."

Rama-bhauju laughed. "All I want is to go on another study tour. Remember the fun we had, Jethi?"

"How we sang on the bus ride back!"

"I can still taste the yogurt we had on the last day, it was so good."

Sapana interrupted them to ask if they were ready to meet the foreigners.

Rama-bhauju laughed. "Haaa, stop worrying, Bahini. I'll show them my Jersey, Jethi will show them her orange trees. Everyone else knows what to do too. You needn't worry about us."

"Really?"

"You go, go and practise your speech."

Sapana had memorized her speech, but she was eager to see the preparations. "Lau, hai, I'm counting on you!" she cried as she ran off.

The lower part of the village looked entirely festive today. Thulo-ba's house looked like a fairground. A multicoloured tent had gone up in the front yard. There was a wooden stage in the front half of the tent. Thulo-ba's political workers were strutting about, barking out orders to one another. Some were setting up a podium on the stage, others were carrying over a sofa from Thulo-ba's house. One worker was wiring up a microphone. Jeevan Bhatta was supervising them all.

"Sapana-nani," he called out. "Go up to the stage, let's see if everything's in the right spot."

She did as he said, standing behind the podium. Jeevan Bhatta walked from side to side, staring at her, ostensibly to assess the placement of the podium. The poor old widower, Sapana thought. It was mean the way Ritu joked about him, but she was right: he did ogle her a lot.

"The podium's all right where it is," he said at last, "but move the sofa forward, ey, boys. And make sure there are enough plastic chairs on the side for all the board members."

Sapana remained behind the podium, imagining herself making her speech. Everyone in the tent would be able to see her, even from the back, because of the height of the stage. And everyone would hear her because of the microphone. She mustn't be nervous. *Shulinbaba,* she prayed, *give my words great force.*

From the podium, she spied a makeshift kitchen at the back of the tent, and went there. Gyanu-dai was stacking plates on a table where he would serve the feast. He was subdued. She felt a pang of guilt, making him work for Thulo-ba's CBO. She knew how much he despised their uncle. And she had also been cold to him. Wanting to make up, she helped lay out cups and saucers. "The women are ready," she said, "but I don't know about the men, Dai."

"The men are always ready to make money," he said.

Trying to leaven his mood, she said, "Did the CBO really make a profit off the gas cylinder?"

"Would Thulo-ba let go of the chance?" he hissed back.

She wished her brother weren't always so cynical about everything. "Well, Thulo-ba let go of Ba's property," she said.

"I lost my job waiting for him to do that."

Sapana gave up, and they set up the table in silence.

At the end, Gyanu-dai said, "Did you see Chandra? She was here, looking for you. Has she told you?" He frowned. "They received a letter from Surya."

Sapana didn't understand what he meant. "What?" Had she misheard him? She said, "Surya-di's — she's alive?"

Gyanu-dai pointed towards the front of the tent. "Chandra went that way. She's very upset."

Surya-di was alive! This was good: it was great! Why then was Chandra upset?

Sapana raced off to find Chandra. The villagers had begun to gather. The crowd was thickening in the tent. "Ey, Sapana-nani, are you ready to make your speech?" someone called out to her. Sapana saw Chandra on the other side of the tent — her hair was still tangled, she was still in her nightdress. Just then, someone yelled, "They're here! The foreigners are here!" and the entire crowd surged.

Sapana was shoved out of the tent. She saw that across the mad river, a jeep was racing up from the highway, kicking up a cloud of dust. "Make way, make way!" A commotion ensued as

Thulo-ba, dressed in a crisp, ironed labeda sural, muscled his way through the crowd. The CBO's board members followed close behind, carrying marigold garlands. The board consisted of Jeevan Bhatta and other party workers, as well as Thulo-ba's youngest daughter-in-law. Sapana looked around for Chandra, but couldn't see her from here.

She turned back, craning her neck to watch as the jeep halted by the bridge. Three people got out of the vehicle. The driver stayed behind and the other two crossed the bridge, where Thulo-ba and the board members were now standing in a row to greet them. The crowd strained to watch as they offered garlands to the foreigners.

Thulo-ba then led them back up to the tent. There was a new charge in the air. To Sapana, everything suddenly felt like a show, a play, that she too had a part in. As he passed by, Jeevan Bhatta grabbed her arm and led her onto the stage, sitting her down on a plastic chair. Only after the foreigners were seated did Sapana realize that one of them was a woman. The woman was wearing pants, that's why Sapana had thought she was a man. And her hair was short like a man's. She was small and dark, with black eyes: you could tell she was foreign only because of her bearing, which was confident and smart, and not at all Nepali. Sapana had expected white Americans with yellow hair and blue eyes, but even the foreign man wasn't like that. Then she heard him speaking to Thulo-ba — "How long will this take? We have two other villages to visit" — and she realized that he was actually Nepali.

Was the woman Nepali too? Now Sapana was confused.

Thulo-ba sat with the guests on the sofa as Jeevan Bhatta rushed around, seating everyone else. "Here, this is your seat." He placed Thulo-ba's daughter-in-law beside Sapana.

The crowd in the tent quieted down when Jeevan Bhatta went to the podium. Leaning over the microphone, he cleared his throat.

An enormous crackle burst out of the speakers. Everyone gasped.

"Forgive me!" Jeevan Bhatta turned away and cleared his throat before beginning his speech: "Respectable international as well as national visitors, honourable CBO Chairman-jyu, distinguished board members, and esteemed assembled residents of the village, it is my great honour, as the secretary of our great CBO, to welcome you to this august gathering."

THE MAN'S VOICE thundered through the mic, insistent and declarative. Ava had no idea what he was saying. She didn't even know who he was, because no one had bothered to introduce him. The only introduction she had received was to the traditionally costumed chairman of the CBO, whose air of authority intimidated her for some reason. He was like a relic of some ancient way of life that was inaccessible to her. He didn't speak English. Did anyone here do so? Vishwa, seated beside her on the sofa, was nodding in agreement with the speaker, who was saying — what? Asking for funding. Begging, Ava thought. And who was she to say yes or no?

The stuffing in the sofa was flabby. Ava was sitting low to the ground, and her knees stuck up inelegantly. Everyone else was seated in plastic chairs, presumably signalling that they were of lower status. The formality of the event — the formality of all Nepali events — was mind numbing. The garlands prickled her neck. The crowd was gawking at her, as though they had never seen a foreigner before: though how could that be? A coil spring chafed against her thigh. She squirmed.

The man thundered on and on. How many more speeches would she have to sit through? Ava saw that there were only two other women on the stage: a teenage girl and a middle-aged woman. Otherwise it was all men — of which caste? She would have to run the CBO's board members' names past Herman Banke when she got back.

She looked from person to person, trying to read them. From the chairman's costume, and his demeanour, he seemed quite well off. The rest of the crowd looked distinctly less so, perhaps because they were farmers, or peasants. The women's faces were chapped. The men looked worn down. At the edge of the tent was a group of children with flyblown hair. Why weren't they in school? Was there a school in the village? The tent blocked the view of everything but an electric pink house. Ava wondered whether that was the CBO's office.

When the speaker finally finished, the crowd clapped, and the chairman took his turn at the podium.

The chairman spoke commandingly, in a voice that boomed over the tent. The crowd sat at attention. Ava kept squirming. Why, she wondered, was she expected to sit here, uncomprehending, as everyone talked in Nepali? Why was this considered reasonable? How was she to figure out whether IDAF should fund WDS-Nepal, so that it could fund National Network Nepal, so that it could in turn fund this CBO, if she couldn't even understand what the speakers were saying?

She leaned in to Vishwa and asked, "What's he saying, Vishwa?"

"He's talking about the CBO's work in the village."

"And who was the first man, Vishwa?"

"The secretary of the CBO."

"Did he say anything interesting?"

He waved vaguely. "He said the CBO had done a lot of work and can do even more if they get more funding."

That was all the secretary had said? Ava persisted: "And what's the chairman saying now?"

"He's saying that the productivity of people's fields have doubled with a new variety of seeds that the CBO has promoted."

After a while, the chairman's voice rose into a crescendo.

Ava leaned back towards Vishwa. "What's he saying now?"

A hint of irritation flickered over Vishwa's face. "He's saying that the CBO cured a man who was going blind, Ava."

"You're kidding, right?" Ava balked.

Vishwa shrugged. "It was at a health camp that the CBO organized. There was a man who was going blind, he was cured."

"Is that true?"

"Why would he say it if it weren't true?"

The chairman spoke on, shaking a fist. He wagged a finger, thumped the podium, punched the air. It struck Ava that this was a performance. It was in keeping with the theatrical nature of so many of her dealings in Nepal. Nepalis seemed to adhere primarily to form: content was secondary. What the chairman was communicating, she saw, wasn't as important as the need to communicate it properly, in this case by making a fiery speech.

A longwinded, fiery speech.

Ava sat, growing increasingly uncomfortable as the speech continued on. Even Vishwa began to glance at his watch. The coil spring in the sofa chafed against Ava. The chairman thundered on — till, with a flourish, he stopped.

There was another burst of applause.

Then the teenage girl came up to the podium.

She, Ava wanted to hear from. Ava shifted to the front of the sofa so that she wasn't sinking down so low. Maybe the girl wasn't a teenager; maybe she was an undernourished woman. Ava couldn't tell. The young woman reached the podium and turned to Ava with an earnest, determined expression.

Ava asked Vishwa, "I'm really sorry, would you mind translating? Not just the gist. I want to know exactly what she's saying."

"You want me to be your interpreter?"

Was that an imposition? "Would you? I'm sorry," Ava said.

"Sure, sure. I can interpret. If it'll help you understand. Of course."

SAPANA FELT LIGHT, as though her body weighed nothing, and she were afloat on the stage. The foreign woman had a sympathetic face. Sapana really wanted to impress her. The microphone was high. She lifted her head to speak. And then she saw Chandra at the back of the tent with little Tara..

Chandra's arms were crossed, her face was dark, her eyes were red. She was crying.

Sapana forgot what she was supposed to say.

In confusion, she turned to the foreign woman. The woman was looking straight at her, as was Thulo-ba. Jeevan Bhatta nodded, indicating that she should begin. The whole crowd was waiting for her.

Sapana said, "Namaste to my elders." She felt weak, her knees trembled. From a corner of her eyes, she saw the Nepali man whispering to the foreign woman. She realized that he was translating her speech into English.

At this, her nervousness dissipated, and the words she had memorized came back to her.

Sapana told the foreign woman about everything: the funds the women's committee had collected, the loans it had given, the profit its members had earned, and the few losses they had incurred. She told the foreign woman about the dreams the women had seen on the study tour, and their vision to develop Nepal. "We want to form a cooperative," Sapana said, and the microphone echoed through the tent, giving her words a certain poetry. "We're young, we have the energy and the determination to develop our country," she said. "Everyone says there's no hope for our country. Everyone wants to give up, everyone wants to go abroad to work in a foreign land. But if we, the youth, don't build our own house, who will? We are the future of this nation," she said. For emphasis, she repeated the line:

"We are the future of this nation. Believe in us. If you help us, we can work together and develop Nepal, and make it rich, like America."

At the end, she ran out of breath.

Everyone clapped. The foreign woman was smiling, as was the man who had translated her words. Sapana was pleased at how she had spoken; but now she really had to go and find Chandra. Instead of sitting back down, she left the stage.

"You spoke well," someone in the audience said to her. Someone else patted her on the back.

Sapana slipped out of the tent and went to the other side, to where Chandra and little Tara were waiting for her.

"Gyanu-dai told me," Sapana said.

She led them to an open patch of grass so that they could talk.

Chandra was carrying Surya-di's letter. She gave it to Sapana, and began to cry — in relief, and in grief for all those years of thinking her sister dead.

"Don't cry, Di," little Tara said; and then she, too, began to cry.

Sapana read the letter carefully.

Surya-di lived in a town called Ghaziabad, near India's capital, Delhi. This was where the middleman had taken her right at the start. She worked as a maidservant in the house of a wealthy master. Over the years, she had worked for other masters too. Her present masters paid her modestly, but didn't work her too hard.

Sapana read every line of the letter several times.

One of the other girls who had gone with her had been unlucky, Surya-di had written. She had also found work as a maidservant, but she had got pregnant by a fellow Nepali, a doorman at the same house. The doorman already had a wife back in the village. Their masters kicked them out when they found out. The middleman took the girl to another town to work, and she had fallen out of touch after that.

Surya-di was still in contact with the third girl, who worked as a maidservant in another part of Ghaziabad. On Saturdays they would meet at a park and reminisce.

"All these years, Surya-di was sending us letters," Chandra said tearfully. "The middleman threw them away, thinking that she would want to come back if she kept in touch with us." This time, Surya-di had met a Nepali who was coming directly to Butwal. He had left the letter with a shopkeeper, who had sent it to Chandra's muwa-buwa in the hands of a mutual acquaintance.

Chandra took the letter back before Sapana was even halfway through. She folded it and tucked it away in her nightdress, and said, "She wants me to come, Sapana. She says she can find work for me."

"As a maidservant?" Sapana said.

Chandra looked down. A loose strand of hair fell over her face. She tucked it behind her ear. When she looked up it was clear that she had already made up her mind. "Surya-di's given us her master's telephone number," Chandra said. "Little Tara and I are going to go to the bazaar to call her."

"I'll also go with you," Sapana said.

"To India?"

"No, to —" Was Chandra really going to go to India? "I'll go with you to the bazaar," Sapana said. "I meant I'll go with you to the bazaar to call Surya-di."

Chandra nodded.

Little Tara, who was still crying, said, "When I grow up I'll also go to India!"

"Be quiet," her sister hissed.

This only made little Tara cry harder.

"Tch." Chandra gathered her sister into her arms. "I didn't mean it. Don't cry, little one. Forgive me, I shouldn't have said that, that was wrong of me."

They were still consoling little Tara when Jeevan Bhatta came rushing out of the tent. "Ey, this is no time to sit around gossiping," he said to Sapana. "The speeches are almost done. Come at once!"

Sapana took Chandra by the hand. "Come with me."

"I haven't even changed. I'm still in my nightdress."

"Don't leave me, Chandra."

Chandra looked at her. "Come with me, Sapana, let's go to India together."

THE YOUNG WOMAN had spoken in tones so rousing that Ava's speech was bound to be flat by comparison. Not that anyone understood what she was saying. Feeling futile, Ava spoke about IDAF's mission in Nepal, the Millennium Development Goals, and the Post-Priority Themes. She might as well have been lecturing the village on rocket science. She had meant to highlight IDAF's partnership with WDS-Nepal and National Network Nepal, but she skipped over those parts, and indeed over most of her speech, rushing to the conclusion. "This is my first field trip since coming to Nepal. I'm very pleased to get a chance, today, to see the work that IDAF hopes to support through its national partners. Thank you very much."

People were kind. They clapped for her, as they had for the previous speakers.

Then the chairman stood, and everyone else on the stage scrummed up to the sofa. A hand guided Ava as the chairman and the rest of the board members herded her off the stage. The crowd parted to let them through. Ava had assumed that they were going to see the CBO's work, but they led her to a table laid out with an elaborate display of kebabs and rotis and crisps and patties and puddings and what appeared to be a baklava: a thin roll with nuts. Smiling nervously, the middle-aged woman on the board offered Ava a plate.

Vishwa produced hand sanitizer from his pocket. "Want some?"

"We're eating?" Ava said.

"The chairman has organized a feast in our honour. We'll have to eat quickly and leave, we're running behind schedule."

What? "I'd rather skip the meal and see some work," Ava said.

"That would be very rude, Ava." Vishwa glanced at the chairman, who was waiting for Ava to serve herself, and said, "We can interact with some beneficiaries as we eat."

"No," Ava said. "I'd like to see some work."

"Ava —"

"I mean it, Vishwa. I didn't come here to eat."

Vishwa checked his watch. "But we have two more CBOs to get to today."

Jesus. Feeling helpless now, Ava pleaded, "At the very least, let's see what the women's committee has done."

"Let me ask." Vishwa turned to the chairman, and they got into a protracted conversation full of questioning, hemming and hawing, declaring. What was there to discuss at such length? Was it a Nepali thing to talk so much? In response to what they were saying, a man at the buffet table began to put the food away, covering some dishes and moving others to a room at the back of the bright pink house. The man's expression jarred Ava. His eyes were turned down, and his lips were pursed, as though he could barely conceal his contempt.

At the end of the discussion, the chairman issued an order, and the secretary stepped up with the young woman who had made the speech. The young woman was holding hands with two other girls, one tall, with a shock of uncombed hair, the other one younger, around nine or ten years old. The two girls looked different — racially, or in terms of caste, or identity — from the first young woman. All of them looked distressed: had they been crying?

After another lengthy discussion, the chairman and the secretary announced that the young woman would show them the work of the women's committee. Only at this point was the young woman introduced to Ava. She was the treasurer of the women's committee. With a refreshing lack of diffidence, she reached out to shake hands with Ava. Her hands were small and hard and rough: a worker's hands. Her name was Sapana — Car Key?

"Car Key?" Ava asked Vishwa.

"K-a-r-k-i."

Ava felt calmer, and more in control, once they left the tent. Past the bright pink house, the crowds fell away, and the village came into view. It was idyllic, with all the romance that a village could evoke. The path in veered away from the river, along a stretch of terraced fields. There were hills on the horizon. The air smelled sweet. There were electric poles along the side of the path, though not all the houses were connected to the line. Ava remembered, from all her background reading, that less than five percent of rural Nepal was electrified.

Sapana led the group to a concrete house that looked neither rich nor poor, but decidedly middle-class by Nepali standards. Their arrival threw the residents into a flurry of bowing and scraping as they laid out straw mats in the courtyard. Following some intricate hierarchy, the chairman sat on one mat and Ava, Vishwa, and the secretary on another. Sapana and the other girls sat with the woman of the house on a third, more tattered, mat.

The woman of the house was dressed in a cotton sari and wore a gold ring in her nose. Ava couldn't even begin to guess how old she was. Upon Sapana's prompting, she began to talk, mainly addressing the chairman.

Ava asked Vishwa if he would mind translating.

"Sure," he said coolly, making it obvious that he minded, but would oblige her. After listening to the woman, he started: "When I came to this village as a bride of sixteen, I knew this area was famous for its oranges. That's what I had heard ever since I was a little girl in my village. Of course, not everything you hear is accurate, but everyone always said —"

The secretary cut in, and the woman stopped talking. Then Sapana said something, and the chairman replied to her. A sharp exchange followed. Ava asked Vishwa what was going on.

"The secretary told her to hurry up and get to the point."

"Tell her to take her time. We're here to listen to her."

When Vishwa conveyed this, the woman swallowed hard, and, glancing from the chairman to Ava and back, continued.

Vishwa translated for her: "As a new bride, I missed my mother and father, I missed my brothers and sisters. My husband and his family were strangers: I cried every day for six months. But how long can a woman cry? It's our lot, when we marry, to move to an unknown house. We have no choice but to adjust.

"There were orange trees in my neighbour's house. When I had my firstborn, I cut a sapling and planted it in the yard. The oranges were juicy, with a fine skin and very few seeds, not like the oranges that you get in the bazaar. Everyone in my family loved them. So when the women's committee began to give out loans, I thought: why not plant an orchard? The land behind our house is lying fallow. My husband said, 'Do it, I'll talk to the Sahu-ji in the bazaar to help sell them.' So I planted sixty saplings."

The woman took them behind the house and showed them the very first orange tree that she had planted. Beyond it lay a field with smaller trees, spaced evenly in rows. She showed them the oranges, which were still green on the branches. The woman had dug an irrigation canal to keep the roots properly watered. The first year the trees had borne fruit, she had earned more than twenty thousand rupees.

Ava asked Vishwa, "Did she really get married at sixteen?"

Vishwa translated the question.

The woman covered her mouth with her hands and laughed.

Vishwa translated her answer: "I was fifteen going on sixteen. I had my first son at seventeen, and four children after that."

At twenty-eight, she was younger than Ava.

From there they went next door, to another concrete house, though this one was smaller, older, grubbier. Ava would have liked to go inside, to see what the living conditions were like, but it didn't seem to be the village way to invite guests into the house. Here, too, they sat on straw mats out in the courtyard.

The woman of this house spoke as though making a speech, though her voice quavered throughout.

Vishwa translated for her: "I come to this village from Bhairahava town, from a well-to-do family. My family sold milk to the dairy, so I grew up knowing it's profitable work. I never thought of doing it here, though, till the CBO set up the women's committee. The loan I got wasn't big enough, so I added my own money and bought a Jersey cow. It just birthed. I've been selling milk to friends and neighbours. It's been helpful. I'm raising four children all by myself."

As she spoke, a girl came out of the house and served everyone glasses of milk. Ava took a sip. The milk was warm, and it tasted — not unpleasant, but too creamy and rich.

Afterwards, they went to the cowshed, beside the house. Tethered to a post, her cow was chewing impassively on cud. Its calf cowered behind, looking out at them with wide, startled eyes. With the birth, milk production had increased, and the woman would repay her loan at last. She was, she confessed, more than six months late.

"But I don't want you to think badly of the committee." Vishwa translated for her. "I'm the only member who hasn't repaid the loan on time. I told the chairperson to fine me, but she said, no. But I insisted: I'm the secretary of the committee, you have to fine me, otherwise everyone else will also be tardy. So the chairperson said, 'All right, I'll fine you'; but she hasn't set the fine yet."

Sapana told them that the committee would set the fine at the next meeting.

Then the chairman announced that the board members were waiting for them, they had to go back for the feast.

"But we've only just started," Ava said, turning to Vishwa.

He said, "It'll all be like this, Ava. You get the general idea."

It took Ava a moment to realize that she really didn't like Vishwa. "No," she said. "I'd like to continue, Vishwa."

He sighed. "If you'd wanted to spend this much time at each site, you should have scheduled a week for the trip, not three days, Ava."

After a discussion with the chairman, they decided that the chairman would go back to the tent and the rest would continue with the tour.

"But we can fit in just one more house," Vishwa said.

"Okay," Ava said, wondering why he got to decide, when she was, in effect, his boss.

As they set off, Sapana and the secretary got into a discussion, which soon escalated into a full-blown argument. Vishwa explained that the entire women's committee was hoping to meet them. "They don't know what to show us: there's goat rearing, there's chicken farming, there's vegetable farming, there are lots of other things. Is there anything in particular you want to see, Ava?"

She didn't even have to think about it. "I'd like to see what the poorest member of the committee has done with her loan," she said.

Further up the village, the houses grew raggedy. Concrete gave way to mud, tin roofs gave way to thatch. A hut lay rotting by the side of the road. The atmosphere here was moribund. They turned by a copse of tall, willowy trees with bristly red flowers. Beside it was a hut, or a hovel: its walls were flimsy, of bamboo and mud, and the thatch on the roof was bald.

Sapana's girlfriends went in and brought out an emaciated woman. It was obvious from the resemblance between them that she was their mother. A blind man also emerged from the hovel, and squatted at the door as the mother and daughters laid out mats.

In their yard, Ava felt blatantly, unforgiveably, wealthy. She wished, especially here, that she could go into the house. These were the poorest people she had ever met in her life. How did they live?

After they sat, the woman laid out a row of jars, big and small. She began to speak, and her face scored with wrinkles. Her voice was low. All the girls leaned in to hear her.

"My family, we're unfortunate, we've suffered." Vishwa translated again. "My husband lost his sight as a young man, and I, unlucky woman, couldn't give birth to a son. Nowadays, they say it's the same thing, daughters and sons are the same, and I love my daughters dearly, but it's not the same thing. My elder daughter went to India to work. These others" — she pointed at her two daughters — "they'll go too, one day, otherwise what will they eat, how will they live?"

The effort of talking seemed to drain her. She wiped her face with the back of her hand before continuing.

"When the women's committee formed, I didn't even know what it was for, or why we should pay a monthly due. A hundred rupees is a lot of money for a wretch like me. But then I thought: how long can I support my family working in the fields of rich landlords?

"I waited to take a loan. I watched what the others did with theirs. Some made good investments, others didn't. I kept looking for my best option. I don't have enough land for a goat stall or cowshed: I don't even have enough land for a chicken coop. What I do have are some rich relatives in the bazaar. They have a shop: they sell everything in that shop. Now everyone in the village knows I make tasty pickles. Everyone says my pickles are delicious. So I asked my relatives if they would sell them in their store. They said, all right, but it's not enough to make tasty pickles, you have to put them in jars so they don't get mouldy, you have to stick bright labels on them so that people will want to buy them. I said, give me a few jars, but they said, no, you have to buy your own jars. I bought a hundred glass jars with my loan. Then I went to my relatives and said, here, here are the jars. Now teach me the rest."

She laughed feebly and continued.

"Rich folks — why would they help the poor? But I pestered them, and they finally had to give in. I began making pickles last winter, with dried cauliflower and fermented greens. When it became warmer, I used cucumber and fruit. Then I made other pickles, with lemon, fenugreek, mustard seeds, chilli, and green mango. Some sold, and others didn't, but I earned enough to repay my loan. My relatives told me to make only three or four of the bestselling pickles. That's what I'm doing now."

With that, she held out a jar of her bestselling pickle as a gift for Ava. Ava took it, feeling guilty: surely she should be the one giving, not the one receiving.

At this point, Sapana turned towards her. "Madam," she said, and to Ava's surprise, she broke into English: "What is country from where you are?"

"Canada," Ava said. "I'm from Canada." The other two girls were listening closely: they seemed to understand a little English. "Do you know where Canada is?" Ava asked them.

They shook her heads no.

"Ava, we should go now," Vishwa said.

Ava ignored him. "Do you know where America is?" she asked the girls.

They nodded.

"Canada's north of America," she said. "It's a big country, it goes all the way up to the Arctic. I'm from — have you ever heard of the city of Toronto?"

Sapana said, "No, Madam."

"It's on Lake Ontario. Do you know about the Great Lakes?" She didn't.

Vishwa said, "We really have to go now, Ava."

But then Sapana reached for her with her hard, rough hands, and began to talk in Nepali. Begrudgingly, Vishwa translated for her:

"The women's committee wants to do so much more than we're doing, Madam. The CBO has helped us, and we're grateful, but we can do these things — making pickles, rearing cows, starting an orange orchard — by ourselves, using the money from our monthly dues. What we want is some help doing much bigger things. As I said in my speech, we want to open a cooperative. Teach us how, Madam. I'm saying this on behalf of the entire women's committee. Believe in us. We'll prove ourselves to you. If we work together, there's nothing we can't do."

With that, Vishwa stood. "Okay, we absolutely have to go now."

Ava couldn't hold him off any longer.

After they said their goodbyes, Sapana and her friends lingered behind as they left. Ava was sorry to lose their company.

Back at the tent, the chairman and the CBO's board members were waiting for them by the buffet table, where the woman board member immediately set about serving them food. Ava didn't want to be subjected, right now, to this particular form of Nepali hospitality, as well meant as it was. She excused herself and slipped away to an outhouse behind the bright pink house.

The reek of urine assaulted her before she could even close the door. She held her breath, scanning the under lit room in alarm. To one side was a squatting commode, or not even that: a hole. A tap was dripping beside it. The floor was slippery. Ava couldn't get herself to squat over the hole. She stayed there till her breath ran out.

Outside, she felt at a loss for what to do. She didn't want to go back to the chairman, she didn't want to eat, she didn't want to hear about all the good work the CBO had done. Behind the outhouse was a ledge facing out, towards the river and hills. She went there.

It was a relief to have a moment's silence. From the ledge, she could see a few houses: they were large, like this one. Their residents were prosperous, or if not exactly prosperous, upper middle-class by Nepali standards. Ava thought of the woman in the last house: the hovel. How emaciated she was. She thought of her blind husband and her daughters, bound for India. How much could the woman possibly make selling pickles? Nepal's poverty level was defined as an income of less than a dollar a day.

Then she heard a movement beside her, and realized that there was someone else on the ledge. A man had been watching her, waiting for her to notice him. It was the man who had put away the buffet earlier.

"Oh, I — I was just ..." Ava felt as though she had been caught playing hooky. She pointed behind her, at the bright pink house. "Is this the office of the CBO?"

"It is house of chairman." The man's English was simple but clear. "You like to go in, Sister?"

"No, I was just taking a break." Ava tried to explain: "We went to see some of the CBO's work, it gave me a lot to think about."

He nodded. "You like the CBO?" he asked, pointedly.

She had to think about her reply. "I'm impressed by the women's committee," she said. "The treasurer — Sapana? — took us to three homes."

The man nodded. "Sapana is my sister. She is very idle. Always she is wanting to do big things."

He must have meant ideal; or idealistic. "Is she all right?" Ava asked. "She looked upset at the beginning. She and her friends looked like they'd been crying."

The man's face hardened. He seemed to want to say something, but held back. "Just it is life," he said. "For girls, for women, life is not easy in Nepal."

He was obviously being circumspect, and this made Ava want to draw him out. "Well, to answer your original question," she said, "yes, I do like the CBO." She was intrigued to see him grimace. "Why? Isn't it doing good work?" she asked.

He looked away, towards the hills. For a while he didn't speak, but when he did, it was with unexpected vehemence. "Will the women become rich with one-two cows, Sister?" he said. "Will that make big change in their life? What help the CBO gives, really? Where all the money goes?" He scoffed. "You are coming today, so everything is nice, Sister. It is just for show."

Ava recoiled. "Are you saying that everything I saw today was a lie?"

The man studied her, as though assessing whether or not to be honest with her.

"Tell me," Ava said. "How will I know if you don't tell me the truth?"

But she could almost see him deciding to hold back. After a pause, he said, "No, everything is not just for show. Sorry for saying," he said. "Don't mind."

Was that how he truly felt? Or was he tempering his outburst out of consideration for his sister?

"Well," Ava said, "I was certainly impressed by your sister. Please tell her that."

The man nodded.

Ava went back to the tent, feeling ill.

AFTER THE VISITORS left, the crowd dispersed, and the farce ended. Thulo-ba's lackeys pulled down the tent, disassembled the stage, and swarmed, like carrion, over the leftovers of the feast.

Gyanu walked to the highway and waved down a bus to the bazaar, finding a seat beside an elderly man and his middle-aged son. The letter from Surya had shaken him. Surya was two years younger than he. Gyanu remembered her as a feisty girl, like Chandra, but even more independent. He knew, from the letters that Nepali brothers and sisters sent back from the desert, that their letters could conceal the truth. He tried not to think about what Surya may have endured in Ghaziabad. How she must have cried over the years. There was something about Nepal, he thought, feeling desperate: this land made its women cry. Ma had cried in her day. Chandra was crying now. And if Chandra were to go to India and he to the desert, Sapana, too, would cry.

The thought tore at him inside.

Come soon, mahal, Maleah had said over Skype. *I do not want to lose you,* she had said. *Come back, and let us marry.*

Halfway to the bazaar, Gyanu's mobile phone caught a signal, and he got off the bus. Standing by the side of the highway, he placed a call: "Jairus, all I need are some permit papers — I'll do any kind of work to get back there."

A truck roared by in a haze of diesel.

Jairus said, "Gyanu, are you all right? You sound too worried, hey."

"Jairus, if I don't come back soon —" Gyanu voice caught. "Help me, Jairus. I'll do anything to come back."

"Gyanu? I'll see what I can find. God will look out for you."

After they hung up, Gyanu walked to the bazaar. A private

car sped by, blaring its horn. A truck roared past him, and another. He stopped at the bridge over the Tinau River. Maleah would be at the gift shop right now. She would be free in an hour. Gyanu sent her a message: *Skype, meri maya?*

After a while, she replied: *I am free tomorrow morning only mahal.*

He remained on the bridge, looking out at the water, clinging to Jairus's words. *God will look out for you.* He decided to leave for Kathmandu in a few days to meet the manpower agent. Sapana would have to move into Thulo-ba's house: there would be no alternative if Chandra were to go to India. From there, Sapana would have to find her own way forward. Gyanu had to believe that she could do it. He did believe it. Ma had done it: she had left one family and started another. She had been strong enough to do so. Gyanu thought about Ba's love for Ma, and Ba's acceptance of a stranger's son as his own. There was good in this society. Sapana would have to find it, or create it. She was strong, like Ma, or she would have to become so now. He wasn't his sister's guardian: he couldn't be.

He closed his eyes and saw Maleah as he had first seen her, in church: the white lace, her bowed head. He heard her whispered prayer. *Our Father who art in heaven.* She had saved him with the miracle, the mercy, of love.

He saw his earlier life: the large, open yard, the date tree. The house, the chicken coop. The dust, heat, tar. The bellowing of a man and the crying of a woman.

That was all he'd had before Maleah: an origin he could never get back to. A memory of loss.

"Our Father," he murmured, standing on the bridge. "Our Father."

"**MADAM DEPUTY CO-DIRECTOR** of WDS-Nepal, Indira Sharma-ji."

It was him, it was really him, it was John Barnett, after all these years. His body had thickened and his hair had thinned, but his eyes were still bright blue, and his eyelashes were as long as a girl's.

"John-ji!" Indira was aflutter at her desk.

He took her hands and held them to his heart, as a boyfriend would. "I always knew you would go places, Indira-ji."

Flattered, pleased, embarrassed, Indira withdrew her hand. "What would you like to have, John-ji — coffee or tea?"

"Pukka Nepali tea with milk and sugar, the way we used to have it at Help — remember?"

Indira remembered, yes, she remembered it now. "Of course." She put in the order, and they sat looking at each other fondly.

John Barnett shook his head. "Can I make a confession? I always wanted to say something to you, Indira-ji. I hope you won't take offense."

"Please say whatever."

"I was head over heels in love with you at Help."

Indira blushed. "So long ago." She hardly knew where to look. That was a few years before she got married. A fancy passed through her mind, a thought of what might have been ...

"But I was also terrified of you!" John Barnett laughed. "I was afraid to even talk to you. Every day I'd tell myself: say something to her, but I couldn't. You were such a proper, pukka Nepali girl!"

"You know how things were," Indira murmured. "Everything was strict, not like now."

"True: I didn't have a single Nepali female friend before I met my beautiful wife, Vidya. Ah, Indira-ji. Tell me," he said, "what have you been up to?"

Then he launched into the story of his life.

At the end of his internship at Help, John Barnett had stayed on in the country, researching his PhD thesis on the indigenous natural resource management systems of the Newars of Bhaktapur. He had met his wife, a Newar from Bhaktapur, during this period. "Oh, how her family objected! A queeray, a white man — the dishonor I brought upon them!" He laughed the full, throaty laugh of a man whose troubles were far behind him. After winning her family over, they had had a traditional Newari wedding. Their eldest child was in her first year at Oxford. The other two were studying at the British school here.

A reedy boy — a new peon? — came in with two cups of tea. When he left, John Barnett resumed his life story, and Indira mused over the life choices we make.

John Barnett's wife didn't work. "Vidya's a simple woman, a woman with a good heart, but, well, she's not like you, Indira-ji. She has nothing outside of the family," he said. "For her, we are God." They lived in an old-fashioned brick house on his wife's ancestral property. "You must visit us, Indira-ji. Vidya will be so happy to meet you."

"And you must meet —" Indira said. With especial effort, she uttered her husband's name out loud. "Uday Sharma is under-secretary at the Ministry of Works and Physical Planning."

"A lucky man! And children? You must have children. Tell me about your children, Indira-ji. Tell me everything, everything."

It was not possible, of course, to tell John Barnett everything. After mentioning Aakriti and Aakaash briefly, Indira steered the conversation towards work. "You know what it's like, John-ji, for Nepali women, even women like me. How we have to struggle at work, how we have to struggle at home." Indira pushed forward a stack of reports that she had compiled for him.

"Do you remember Ramila Singh from Help?"

"Wasn't she the only other woman on staff?"

"She had to stop working after marriage. Her mother-in-law-father-in-law wouldn't allow it."

"Isn't that terrible? Oh, that makes me so mad, Indira-ji. Ramila was a rising star!"

"My mother-in-law is also a very strict lady." Indira handed him a business card. "But this is the reality for all Nepali women, even we highly modern, highly professional, highly successful Nepali women, isn't that so, John-ji? Ke garne: what to do? Now, about the assessment, if you need any further information, or if you'd like to interview me or other staff, please call."

"I'll definitely call," John Barnett said. "Oh, there's so much to catch up on, Indira-ji. We'll have you over to our home very soon," he said. Then he stayed on for another hour and reminisced about old times:

"Whatever happened to Raju Sharma? Remember him? He was always cracking jokes."

"He is in the UN now, in Addis Ababa."

"And — who was the one in Social Mobilization? The fat one."

"Jeewan Khadka. He won the green card lottery. He is in America now, in Queens."

"Wow." John Barnett blinked, or maybe he winked; his eyes suddenly twinkled. "Just now, Indira-ji, when you were speaking, you looked exactly like you used to. I can hardly believe it. You're as stunning as ever."

"John-ji." She blushed again.

"It's true!"

Leaving, John Barnett again held her hands to his heart.

Afterwards, Indira could hardly stop smiling like an idiot-fool. What was wrong with her? She chided herself. Was it so rare to be admired by a man, a chocolatey-handsome man? All John Barnett had had to do was look at her with those bright blue eyes, and ... tchee. She grinned.

Indira was feeling better now, better than she had in days, weeks, months. If she could manipulate — no, guide or inspire, yes, inspire — John Barnett into giving WDS-Nepal a good assessment, things would be all right at work. Yes. If she could inspire John Barnett, and if Vishwa Bista could guide the Canadian director of WEP at IDAF, then: definitely. Maybe. Maybe not, too, but hopefully: hopefully things would be all right.

At home, too, things were improving gradually. Durga had come back, and had promised not to try to kill herself again. Every morning, before setting out to the office, Indira spent a few minutes with the girl, talking to her, pepping up her spirit, boosting her morale: "Everything that happened, Durga? That was nothing."

"Nothing, Hajoor?"

"Nothing."

Every now and then, she also slipped a little bit of money to the girl so that she could buy new kurtas and make-up and trinkets. Durga was rallying day by day: she was almost back to normal. And this restored normalcy to Indira's life. Which was crucial, because Indira had told Rick Peede that she expected him to support her bid to succeed him. He had assured her that if IDAF were to accept her proposal, no one could stop her from becoming the next director of WDS-Nepal.

The new peon came in to clear away the tea cups. He was a clean cut, good looking boy, a bit reedy, though that would change with age. Indira studied him, then asked, "What's your name, Babu?"

He snapped to attention. "Hira, Sir. My name is Hira."

Sir. How sweet. Indira watched him place the empty cups on the tray. "Hira," she said; and the tray rattled, and the cups clinked. "When did you join WDS-Nepal, Babu?"

"Sir," he said, and coughed. "It will be two weeks tomorrow."

"Two weeks. And how has it been? Have you enjoyed working with us, Babu?"

The fear on the boy's face was quite endearing. "I'm enjoying working at WDS-Nepal very much, Sir." He added, "Sir, it fills me with great pride to be working for an organization that helps so many poor brothers and sisters in — in this great nation of ours. It is very big work, Sir, and though I'm just a peon, it fills me with great pride."

His answer genuinely moved Indira "You can't be very old," she said.

"I'm going on twenty, Sir."

"And is this your first job?"

"In an office, yes, Sir. Before this —" He lost his breath and had to pause. "Sir, I've worked since I was a boy. In the village I worked on the landlord's fields, and in the city — I've done everything."

"And how did you find this job, Babu?" she asked.

"My uncle — my uncle." The boy stammered. "I was — I was working at a shopping complex, Sir, and my uncle, he's a driver here, he drives the car of the big white sir, the sir with red hair? He told me the office was hiring a peon. He helped me apply."

So his uncle was Rick Peede's driver. "Narayan is your very own uncle?" Indira asked. "Do you have a lot of relatives in the city, Babu?"

By now the poor boy was so nervous that he was shifting from foot to foot, desperate to bolt. "My uncle and aunt are all I've got here, Sir."

"And in the village? Who's left in the village?" Indira asked.

The boy's face brightened. "Everyone's there, Sir. My mother and father, my sisters and brothers... we're seven children altogether. I'm the oldest. The youngest is two years old."

Yes, she could see it all now. The loving but poor family in the village. The dutiful eldest son in the city. "So you're living with your uncle and aunt?" Indira asked. He would be sharing a corner of their rented rooms, no doubt.

"Yes, Sir."

"Very well." Indira dismissed the boy and watched him scuttle out the door.

Then she smiled. Men. Men were so... And yet... Her thoughts wandered back to John Barnett. She saw him as he had been when he was young.

You're as stunning as ever. He had flirted with her today — hadn't he? A little bit, yes. He had even winked, or blinked. There was nothing wrong with flirting — a little bit — as long as it was innocent. And it had been innocent. John Barnett was happily married, Indira was happily married: there was nothing wrong here. Romance was a part of life. It was natural, and necessary, even. It was a basic human right, or at least it was nice to have.

You're as stunning as ever.

John-ji.

It's true!

There was nothing wrong.

You're as stunning as ever, you're so stunning, you're truly stunning.

Oh, John-ji, you're just saying that.

It's true, Indira-ji, I mean it, can I confess? I hope you don't mind. I truly love you.

THE TREES SHOOK violently in the blustery springtime winds as Sapana rang the temple bell once, twice, thrice — and again. And again. Again. The peals echoed against the hillsides. She kept ringing the bell again. Again. Again: till the peals rose up to the sky.

She tossed away her slippers and stormed in. There was no one in the inner sanctum today, no devotees, not even a bird or an insect or a worm. She knelt before the deity, fulminating: *Shulinbaba, make everything right, you'd better make everything right, or else!*

Or else what?

Shulinbaba was just a misshapen rock, and Chandra was leaving, and there was nothing she could do. All of the energy drained out of Sapana, as though it were water, not blood, that was flowing through her veins. Her stomach churned, her body ached, her heart hurt.

Yesterday, she had gone to the bazaar with Chandra, little Tara, and their muwa to call Surya-di. At the grain store, they had dialled Surya-di's telephone number, and suddenly her voice was on the line, after all these years.

"Hello?"

The entire family had wailed.

"Ey, Muwa, ey — ey!" On the line, Surya-di had wailed; and in the grain store her muwa and sisters had wailed.

"Eeeey!"

Their emotions flooded like the mad river at monsoon time, a froth of white rage decimating everything in its path, including the pact that Chandra and Sapana had made to live together.

"Muwa!"

"Eeeey! Chhori!"

"Muwa!"

"Eeeey! Eeeey!"

It was a long time before they were able to talk.

When they did so, Surya-di repeated what she had said in her letter: Chandra should come to her in Ghaziabad. She would find work for her there. "It'll only be housework, but you wouldn't be idle, you'll earn, you'll stand on your own two feet," Surya-di had said. "How long can you depend on Muwa-Buwa, Bahini? You're not a child anymore."

Chandra had hung her head, listening, not saying yes, but also not saying no. Sapana could tell what she was thinking. Her muwa-buwa needed her to earn. Of course she would go.

And it hurts, Shulinbaba, it really hurts. It felt to Sapana as though a part of her were being ripped out of her, leaving her amputated and bleeding.

Afterwards, returning to the village, no one had said anything: the family had exhausted all their emotions. Sapana was in tumult: Chandra would go, and would she be all right in India, would she be safe?

Shulinbaba, she prayed: *look after Chandra, don't let any harm come over her in that foreign land, keep her safe. Keep her safe, or else...*

Or else, nothing.

Everything was going to change for Chandra now, and everything was going to change for Sapana too. Gyanu-dai hadn't said it because he was too much of a coward to ever talk openly about what was on his mind, but Sapana wouldn't be able to live by herself at home. She would have to move in with Thulo-ba and Thuli-ma, and what did they care about her future? They would force her to marry, and maybe there would be no choice, maybe she would have to marry, because that's what every girl did, in the end. Everything she and Chandra used to talk about — they were dreams, they were childish delusions.

Sapana felt like curling up on the floor and crying forever. But then she felt a familiar trickle of warmth between her legs, and shot up, cursing. Everything was hellish, this whole world was hellish. She ran out of the temple into the blustery winds, cursing the universe.

"**WHAT IF ANYTHING** were to happen, Jairus?"

"Nothing will happen, hey, Gyanu. Women have an inner power. Never underestimate them: they're much stronger than us menfolk."

"I'm betraying my sister. She's angry. She's won't even talk to me properly."

On the phone Jairus sighed. "In life there's only so much you can do for others, Gyanu. And how can you help your sister if you're weak? You have to make yourself strong first."

Gyanu nodded: he understood, of course, but couldn't agree.

"Now listen, friend, this isn't a fancy five-star hotel, it's a small place behind the spice bazaar. The restaurant is called Zafran. Irani food: chelo, kebab, polo, khoresht. The owners want someone who'll stay for at least two years. This is your fastest route back here."

"I'll go to Kathmandu to get the permit," Gyanu said.

"The owners are good people. You can marry your love, na. And I miss your cooking, hey." Jairus laughed. "When you come back, you'll see how thin I've got, friend. You can look for jobs elsewhere once you're here. You know, Gyanu, I've been thinking: I want to leave too. You and Maleah, me and my wife, let's all go somewhere else," he said. "I have a cousin in Australia, he's a chartered accountant, he lives in a little brick house. We can go to Australia and live in little brick houses, na."

Gyanu found his patter soothing.

"Jairus?" he said. "I'm grateful."

"Why such formality, friend?"

"I'm just grateful."

Jairus laughed. "Remember one thing, Gyanu. The world needs people like you. You're a trained chef from a country that everyone loves. Me? I'm a driver from Pakistan, but you know what? The world needs me too. The world needs all good people, Gyanu. Remember that. Now go, go and Skype your love. She said she'd wait for you at the cyber café."

"LUKE?"

"Big Sis, is that you? The line's kind of bad. Hold on? There's this really loud punk rock band."

"Is this a bad time?" Ava shouted into her cell phone. "I can call later."

"No, no. Okay, that's better. What's up? How are things going out there in your imaginary homeland?"

"Luke, you're right, I made a mistake," Ava said.

"What was that?" her brother said. "Sorry, I'm at a club and there's this band, it's fantastic, but — let me step outside."

"Never mind, I'll be back in Kathmandu tonight, we can talk then," Ava said.

"No, hold on, I've got news for you too. Shit. Let me cross the road, it'll be quieter there."

Ava waited on the bridge, looking down at the pebbly shore. There was no one by the river this morning, only a dog. It sniffed a rock, stopped to pee, trotted on. The river felt desolate. Everything felt bleak. This field trip — her entire time at IDAF, her decision to come to Nepal — had been a colossal mistake.

Yesterday, after the first village, she and Vishwa had gone on to two more villages. At both, they had been subjected to speeches so formal and empty that Ava had stopped asking Vishwa for translations. There had been tea and snacks at both villages, but no time to see any work. And the worst part was that Vishwa kept reminding her that it was her fault. He was right, too. Ava hadn't realized, when she had planned the field trip, that the villages would be so far apart. They had looked right next to each other on the map. Neither had she realized that they would be spending two full days driving from and back to Kathmandu. She should have asked Vishwa for help.

She should have scheduled a whole week for the trip. She didn't know what she was doing — at IDAF, in Nepal, in life.

"Right." Luke came back on the line. "Is this any better?"

Ava blurted out, "Remember, in Miami, at the beach, you said I was coming here because these do-gooder Canadians rescued me, and I wanted to repay my debt?"

"Oh, God, I was just saying that, I didn't actually mean it, Big Sis." There was some rustling on the line. Luke whispered to someone, then said, "Are you okay out there? What's going on?"

Ava sighed. "I'll be back in Kathmandu tonight, let's talk then."

"Yeah, 'cause I have something to tell you," he said. Then he whooped. "We're pregnant! We're going to have a baby, Big Sis, a baby!"

What? "Oh, my God, Luke! You and —?" The heavily pierced performance artist?

"Revolution Mary! We literally just found out!" Her brother whooped again. "We're out celebrating!"

At a nightclub? "That's amazing," Ava said. "Oh my God."

"I know, I know! Auntie Ava! I'm going to be a dad, can you believe it?"

Ava couldn't, quite. She said, "I want to hear more. Let's definitely FaceTime: how's my tonight, your tomorrow morning?"

"Don't make it too early. Oh, hey, Anthony's here. Want to rekindle your romance with him? Hey, Anthony! Anthony! It's Ava, she's in Nepal, she wants to say hi."

"No, Luke, hey —"

Before she could protest, he put Anthony on.

"Hi, there."

"Anthony! Hey. Hi." Ava cast about for something to say. "How are you doing?"

"I'd be a lot better if you were in Miami," he said.

She said, "Me too, actually," and laughed.

"You heard the news?"

"About Luke and, um, Revolution Mary? Yeah. Great news, huh?"

"You think your brother's ready for fatherhood?"

"Jesus. I guess he'll have to learn on the job."

"Hey," Anthony said, "where are you right now? What are you looking at? What's directly in front of you?"

"I'm looking at a dog on a river bank."

"I'm looking at a man in a dog collar. Coincidence?"

They laughed.

"It's nice talking to you, Ava," he said.

"And to you, Anthony."

"Come and visit."

"You know, I may just."

After they hung up, Ava felt completely lost.

She wanted her old life back.

She and Vishwa were going to head back to Kathmandu in an hour. She already dreaded all the talking he would do on the drive: the constant explaining of Nepal. The Mansplaining. Or Nepalsplaining. The wearying combination of the two.

The stray dog was still trotting along the shore. There was a trail near the bus stop that seemed to go down to the river. Ava decided to follow it, to see where it would lead.

THE BUS TO the village wasn't in. A newspaper lay crumpled on a bench. Gyanu picked it up and scanned through the usual grim news of strikes and closures, blockades and impasses, grandstanding in Kathmandu among the political parties. There was no sign of the constitution ever being drafted. Half the paper was filled with pictures of starlets. In a corner he saw an article about artificial intelligence, but most of it had been ripped out. He tossed the paper aside in disgust. Then, looking around, he saw the woman from yesterday: the foreigner.

Her suit and briefcase made her stand out in this setting. She had stopped at the top of a goat path down to the river, staring in consternation at the litter around her feet. This was where the neighbourhood threw its garbage.

Gyanu went over to help her. "Sister."

"Oh." Her face lit up when she recognized him. Then, perhaps remembering their exchange, she stiffened. "Hello, there." For a while, she just stood there awkwardly. Then she said, "I wanted to go to the river, not to swim, but – would it be okay, I don't know, culturally, to dip my feet in the water, do you think?"

"It is no problem, Sister."

"Please just call me Ava," she said. "I'm sorry, I didn't catch your name yesterday."

Gyanu introduced himself, then explained that there was a better path down to the river. "I will show," he said.

She didn't say much as he led her down the main path. She was tense, though she seemed to relax a little when they reached the water's edge. She crouched down on her knees and dipped in a hand. "Oh, that's gorgeous." She sat down on the shore and rolled up her trousers. After taking off her shoes, she dipped her feet in the water. "That feels incredible."

She became more sociable after that. "How's your sister doing?" she said. "Sapana, isn't that her name?"

"She is fine, Sister — Ava."

"Yesterday, her friend ... I didn't catch her name. The one whose mother makes pickles?"

"It is Chandra."

"Chandra seemed very upset. Both she and her — I think that was her younger sister? I kept thinking about it later on. What were they upset about?"

Gyanu wasn't sure how to explain it in English. He said, "Chandra has one older sister. Many years before, she — she went to India. They think she is dead." Seeing the alarm on Ava's face, he quickly added, "She is alive. Just: they are worried."

"Oh. Her sister's all right, then?"

"She is all right."

Ava frowned. "This is a high-risk area for trafficking, isn't it? I saw that in National Network Nepal's report. I really can't get my head around it: more than ten thousand Nepali girls trafficked annually." Her tone grew introspective, as though she were talking to herself more than to Gyanu. "They were so poor, Chandra's family. Later on, after we left the village, I kept wondering how they could live like that. I mean, they had nothing, you know?"

Her question struck Gyanu as naïve.

"They do little bit everything," he said. "Little labour, little farming, little business. In the village, everybody does little bit everything."

She looked at him. "What do you do, Gyanu?"

"I — I do not live here. I am chef in Dubai. Just I am visiting my sister."

"Oh." She studied his face, examining him for signs of — what?

236

"Yesterday," she said, "you told me that the CBO's work was a lie."

He demurred.

"Did the women's committee really do all the work they showed me?" Ava asked.

Gyanu had to calibrate his response. "The women's committee is good," he said.

"But?" She kept looking at him. "What's the catch? What are you holding back, Gyanu? How will I understand if you don't tell me?"

He looked into her eyes, trying to assess whether she wanted to know the truth. He decided to risk it. He said, "The CBO: what money they are getting, what money they are spending, what cut they are taking?" He hesitated. "The chairman — if he cannot take the cut, he won't have the CBO, he won't have the women's committee, he won't do any works. Maybe ten percent of budget is going to programs. The rest?" he said. "To the chairman."

Ava looked pained, as if he had landed her a physical blow.

"It is okay," Gyanu said, surprised at the force of her reaction.

Ava began blinking back tears.

Gyanu said, "Also the rich have to make money, yes? If no, why they will do any works for the poor?" He repeated: "It is okay, Ava."

"No, it's not okay," she said. "It's not okay, Gyanu. Jesus! It's really not okay." She turned away and cursed under her breath: "Fuck, fuck, fuck!" When she turned back, her expression was tormented. "Can I tell you a secret, Gyanu? I came here —" She paused. "I was born in Nepal," she said. "I was adopted by a Canadian family when I was a few months old. What I'm doing here isn't just a job for me, Gyanu. I could have been born in your village — and you know what? I don't think I would have survived."

Why was she telling him this? Now Gyanu felt sorry for her. "You did see, yesterday, how people survive," he said.

"I didn't see anything! I was hoping I'd really understand everything on this field trip, but there's been so little time, all I've seen is the surface." She let out a cold, hard laugh. "Even when I went to the homes of the women's committee members with Sapana, everyone was so open, they were telling me all these things, but — it's silly — I kept wanting to go into their homes, to see how they live."

What did she want to see? Something related to work, or something more personal? "I can show," Gyanu said. "I invite you to my home."

Ava looked at him. "The car's leaving for Kathmandu soon." She bit her lips. "Maybe I could hire a car to go back?"

"You can take the bus. I will help you."

"Is it safe?"

"There is tourist bus, that is safer."

"I'll have to tell my colleague," she said. "There's a ton of work I have to get to this weekend. What time would the bus get me into Kathmandu, do you think? Will I get there by tonight?"

"You will reach tomorrow morning."

She mulled it over, then said, "Fuck it," and punched in a message on her mobile phone.

SAPANA COULDN'T BEAR to listen to Chandra's muwa-buwa urging her to go to India. She got up and ran out of their house.

"Sapana, ey!" Chandra rushed to her feet and followed her. "Stop, listen!"

"I don't want to hear anything you have to say!" Sapana yelled.

"Just stop for a moment, ey!"

"Leave me alone!" Sapana ran through the courtyard and turned past the bottlebrush trees.

Chandra was faster than she. She had almost caught up to her by the time Sapana reached home. The two of them burst into the kitchen to find Gyanu-dai sitting at the table with the foreign woman from the day before.

Sapana stopped, surprised. Chandra collided into her. They both stood at the door, panting and out of breath.

The foreign woman stood to greet them with a smile. She had a notebook open in front of her. Gyanu-dai explained that she was here to find out more about the women's committee.

"She wants to meet the rest of the committee members," he said.

"They won't be prepared," Sapana said, surprised, "but — of course, Dai."

"Come and sit."

Gyanu-dai made everyone a round of tea.

The four of them spent the morning in the kitchen. The foreign woman — Ava-madam — had been dissatisfied by how little time she had spent here the day before. She asked Sapana about the committee, about the prospects of a cooperative in the village, about the CBO, and even about Thulo-ba.

Sapana answered her questions faithfully, and in detail.

Gyanu-dai translated between them, switching effortlessly between Nepali and English.

Sapana knew her brother spoke English in the desert, but she had never actually heard him speaking English before. With her rudimentary school learning, she couldn't follow everything he was saying, but she did catch a few words and phrases. At one point, Ava-madam said something that made Gyanu-dai smile. Sapana couldn't understand what she had said. Then they spoke among themselves for a long time. Watching them, Sapana found Gyanu-dai different, all of a sudden. He was open with the foreign woman. He was at ease. He didn't have the usual hard expression on his face. It was as though he were a different man in the woman's company, and this made Sapana wonder how well she knew her brother. Or — she knew him in the role he played in her life, as her brother, but this stranger speaking English to a foreign woman: this was Gyanu-dai too.

After a while, he threw together a fragrant noodle soup for their morning meal. Then they took Ava-madam to meet the committee members, going right into their houses. Some of the members were home, others were out. Ava-madam was interested in everyone's stories. She took copious notes, filling page after page as the committee members talked to her. She spent the entire day asking questions, listening to the answers, and writing them down.

At the end, back at home over a cup of tea, Ava-madam turned her attention to Chandra. When was she going to India? she asked. What was her sister doing there?

Chandra glanced at Sapana before responding. "Tell her, Gyanu-dai: she met my muwa-buwa yesterday, she saw how poor we are. How can I not go? I'm not a child any more. Shouldn't I earn?"

Her words were clearly intended for Sapana.

Ava-madam asked Chandra: Was it risky to go? Was Surya-di safe? Had she been under any coercion while talking on the phone?

She and Gyanu-dai and Chandra parsed over the matter, and by the end of the day, came up with a plan.

Ava-madam knew some NGOs in Kathmandu that rescued women who had been trafficked to India. She would ask one of them to check in on Surya-di. If Surya-di were in any danger, or if she changed her mind about staying on in India, the NGO would bring her home. But if she wanted to stay on in India, and if Chandra wanted to join her there, Ava-madam would help Chandra get to Ghaziabad safely.

"If you want to go, you should go, Bahini," Gyanu-dai explained to Chandra. "Her intention isn't to stop you, just to make sure you and Surya-bahini are safe."

Chandra kept glancing at Sapana for approval, but Sapana refused to return her gaze.

Gyanu-dai decided that he would stay on in the village till Chandra's plans were finalized. "After that, I'll have to leave," he said.

These words, too, were intended for Sapana.

Towards the end, it was mostly Gyanu-dai and Ava-madam talking among themselves again. Sapana watched them — they were attentive, animated — and an unfamiliar emotion, resentment, bloomed inside her like a strange dark flower. She knew she should be grateful to Ava-madam. Ava-madam was going to help Chandra. She was also going to help the women's committee. And she would surely help Sapana too. But the foreign woman's presence in the house heralded a change that Sapana wasn't prepared for, and it angered her. The more Sapana watched Gyanu-dai talking to Ava-madam, the more clearly

241

she saw how narrow the horizon to her life had been. From a young age, Gyanu-dai had had an independence that Sapana never even thought to have. Now that she thought about it, she wanted that independence too. She wanted the same broad horizon that her brother had had.

At dusk, Gyanu-dai said he would take Ava-madam to the bazaar to catch a night bus to Kathmandu.

Saying farewell to Sapana and Chandra, Ava-madam became quite emotional. She embraced them, and thanked them for letting her into their home.

Gyanu-dai translated for her: "I learned so much today, it's been very important to me. I'll always be grateful to you for what you've given me today."

It was a bit surprising.

Sapana and Chandra stood at the door, watching Gyanu-dai and Ava-madam leave. The sky was growing dark, darkness was engulfing the corners of the village, and Gyanu-dai and Ava-madam disappeared into that darkness.

Chandra put an arm around Sapana.

Sapana slapped it off.

For a while Chandra was silent, rebuked. Then she said, "You know you'll be all right, Sapana."

"Be quiet!" Sapana cried.

"You should enroll in the Plus Two. You and I aren't in the same situation. I would have never been able to afford it, but you should study, you should —"

"Don't tell me what I should do!"

"Listen." Chandra put an arm around her again.

Again, Sapana slapped it off.

"This woman will help you, Sapana. She'll help you start a cooperative in the village. You know the change, the progress, the revolution we dream of? It'll happen," Chandra said. "You'll make it happen. You can do it, you can —"

"You don't love me, no one loves me, you're all getting on with your own lives and forgetting about me!" Sapana cried.

ALL THE WAY across the house she heard a shriek, a bellow, the clatter of a pan flung across the kitchen.

"What's happening?" Indira rushed out of the bedroom.

A cloud of myrrh was swirling out of Muwa's bedroom door, which was ajar. Upon peeking in, Indira saw that her room was empty. The sitting room was empty too. The old witch was nowhere to be seen.

Indira found Durga in the kitchen, crouched on the floor and sobbing into her hands, her body shaking like a bud in a storm. The girl's hair was tousled, lipstick was smeared over her face and the gaajal on her eyes was running. The back door was open. From the telltale scent of myrrh, Indira could tell that Muwa had slipped out of there into the yard. The old witch had pummelled the girl.

"I should die," Durga sobbed. "I should just die, Hajoor. I should take poison and die."

"Tch, tch, tch. What are you saying?" Indira crouched down beside the girl. "Don't ever say that, Durga, don't ever say something like that."

A squeal emerged from the girl's mouth: "You told Muwa!"

"I never! I would never! I gave you my word!"

"She came in." Durga gasped for breath. "I was putting on lipstick. She grabbed my hair and called me a — a — a —"

"Tch, tch, tch, tch, tch." The girl had been doing so well, the last thing she needed was a setback. "Forget Muwa," Indira said, wiping the lipstick and gaajal off the girl's face. "Muwa's insane. She's losing her mind. She's been crazy from the day I married into this family, actually." What was she going to do about the old witch? "Remember," Indira said, to comfort the girl, "what you said to me at the hotel? I've been thinking about it, Durga, and you're right. You need a life."

The girl looked up at her with sad, doubting eyes.

Indira said, "I know what you're thinking, Durga. You're thinking, I'm just a servant girl, brought to Kathmandu by a father who couldn't feed-clothe-house her; what kind of life can I possibly have? But have I ever let you down? No, I've never let you down. I give you my word, girl. I'll give you a life."

Durga sniffled. "Will you raise my salary, Hajoor?"

What?

"Hajoor," Durga said, "You have to pay me minimum wage. I heard in the bazaar. It's the law, re."

Oof. Fair enough. The girl was right. Indira should have done this years ago. She had been meaning to, in fact, and had simply forgotten.

"All right, la," Indira said. "But don't tell Muwa, or she'll kick you out."

The girl sat up a little. "I also want one day off each week, Hajoor."

What was going on? Indira looked at the girl, and the girl looked back expectantly, all her hopes laid bare on her face.

"Lau, you can take Tuesdays off. I'll tell Muwa you're fasting for Lord Ganesh," Indira said.

The girl smiled through her tears.

"Now, be happy." Indira helped her get to her feet. "Look, Durga, I know Muwa's difficult, but what can I do? I'm just the daughter-in-law of the family, I have no power here. Just avoid her for a few days and it'll pass. Now" — Indira issued the instructions for the day — "don't forget to open the windows after Muwa's puja is over, I don't want the house stinking of myrrh. And what's in season in the bazaar? Buy pumpkin greens. Don't forget to make fresh yogurt — yesterday's batch was sour. Do you have enough money for the shopping?"

"I have enough left over from yesterday."

"Good. Now I'm off to office." Indira patted the girl on the back. "And you, you're already in your office, Durga. We, professional women, our work is never done, isn't that so?"

Oof.

Avoiding Muwa, she went out from the front door. Uday Sharma, who always absented himself during family showdowns, was waiting by his ministry car with Aakaash and Aakriti.

"Is everything all right?" he asked.

Cowardly man. "There's no problem whatsoever!" Indira declared loudly, for the benefit of the children. "You-all get going, now. Aakaash, Aakriti, be good at school. We'll have pumpkin greens for dinner."

Aakaash groaned. "I hate those!"

"They're my favourite!" Aakriti beamed.

After herding her family into the ministry car, Indira's thoughts turned towards work. Rick Peede was picking her up on the way to a seminar on Post-Priority Themes for the MDGs. After the seminar, they would drive back together to WDS-Nepal to conduct a multi-sectoral briefing on sustainability. On both rides, Indira would be able to reassure him about John Barnett's assessment, which was due any day now. Indira was sure — or at least hopeful — that his assessment would be positive. Yes, it would most definitely be positive. That was what she would tell Rick Peede.

With a honk, a Pajero arrived at the front gate, but instead of Rick Peede, Chandi Shrestha was sitting in the vehicle.

He gave her an unctuous smile. "Rick-ji said he would walk, you know how he hates sitting in traffic," he said. "And me, I'm getting a lift to ActionAid. You can drop me off — it's right on the way."

Indira got in with a sigh.

"Drop me off first, ey, Narayan," Chandi Shrestha instructed the driver, before turning back to Indira. "So! Vishwa Bista from IDAF told me there was some problem with your proposal?"

Vishwa Bista was talking to him about her proposal? "No, there's no problem," Indira said. "It's a routine assessment, Chandi-ji. There is absolutely no problem."

"Vishwa-ji also told me that IDAF's new director of WEP has some very strange ideas." Chandi Shrestha chortled. "He called me from the field, he said she has no idea what she's doing."

"Vishwa Bista called you from the field?" Indira asked.

"He was calling about something else, this just — came up," Chandi Shrestha said, suddenly becoming circumspect.

"Of course, you're free to talk about my proposal with Vishwa-ji or anyone else," Indira said tartly. "Women's empowerment shouldn't concern only women; men should care about it too. Indeed, I wish more men shared my passion for women's empowerment, Chandi-ji!"

Chandi Shrestha smiled. "You're so right, Indira-ji, women's empowerment is for all of us, men and women. In fact, as the father of two daughters, I feel that women's empowerment is more important for us men than for you women. We're the ones who are holding you back."

That male glibness: Indira had heard it all her life. Men were always patronizing her, talking down to her, telling her that of course she was superior, but also letting her know — through connotation, inference, signs, and body language — that they were in charge. All these glib men were always letting her know: I have a penis. I have a penis, and you don't.

"Anyway," Chandi Shrestha went on, "Vishwa-ji was telling me that the assessment will come in soon. He said the meeting with IDAF is next Friday?"

"I know that," Indira snapped, and immediately began to fret. A few days after their first meeting, John Barnett had called her. For more than an hour he had talked about himself and about his charmed life, his beautiful wife, their brilliant children. "I meant it when I said I'd like to have you over, Indira-ji," he had said at the end. "I can't wait for our families to meet. I'll call."

But he hadn't called.

He hadn't called, and now that Chandi Shrestha had brought it up, it was impossible for Indira not to fear the worst. John Barnett was giving WDS-Nepal a poor assessment. He had found out about the bribe, or worse: Vishwa Bista had told him about it. Or even worse than that: Vishwa Bista had conspired — with Chandi Shrestha, yes, of course, with her rival — to expose Indira as a giver of bribes, and get her fired.

The entire conspiracy fell horribly into place.

In fact, Chandi Shrestha must have put Vishwa Bista up to all this, Indira realized. He must have offered Vishwa Bista a bribe even bigger than hers. They must have met — they were men, they could meet anywhere — and hatched a plot to sideline her. Why else would Vishwa Bista phone Chandi Shrestha from the field? It had been a plot all along, a male plot against her: for she was just a woman in the end.

She didn't have a penis and never would.

Indira sank into the back seat of the vehicle like a deflated balloon.

Chandi Shrestha would replace Rick Peede as the director of WDS-Nepal.

Outside the window, the traffic was thickening. The city was a vision of the kaliyug: the age of destruction. This government was widening the road in this neighbourhood. The houses on the sides had been ripped open, and their rooms gaped open like the soft, exposed innards of freshly slaughtered animals. The traffic was kicking up clouds of dust. There was a snarl up ahead. The vehicle was barely moving.

"What's the problem?" Chandi Shrestha demanded of the driver. "Why are we stuck?"

The driver said, "Sir, there's a demonstration up ahead, Sir."

"Then why did you take this route? Turn off and take the bridge, the bridge is faster, take that!"

"Sir, it's blocked in every direction, Sir. That's what they were saying on the radio. There's a demonstration, it's like this everywhere."

"Tch." Chandi Shrestha looked at his watch. "I guess I'm close enough, I can walk from here. Lau, Indira-ji, sorry to leave you in this jam: and best of luck getting to your meeting on time."

He hopped out.

Indira sat back, dispirited, as the vehicle lurched and halted, lurched and halted.

All was lost.

Her dream was over.

She was excrement, she was filth.

At the centre of the traffic jam was a crowd of protesters, waving banners and flags. "What do they want?" Indira asked dejectedly, more to herself than to the driver. "These people, always demonstrating — for what?"

The driver replied, "Madam, they want a constitution, Madam. They're protesting the delay."

"The constitution." Indira scoffed. "Always, the constitution."

"Madam, the political parties, all they do is blame each other for the delay. I shouldn't say it, it isn't my place, I'm just a driver, but everything that's gone wrong with our nation? Is because of our political parties, Madam."

Indira looked at the reflection of the driver's face in the rear-view mirror. He seemed like a sensible man.

"Narayan," she said, "we've never really talked, have we?"

"Madam, why would a driver like me talk to a boss like you, Madam?"

A thought occurred to her. "Well, I'm glad we're getting a chance today," Indira said. "I want to ask you about that nephew of yours, Hira." She sat up a little to get a better view of his face in the mirror. What, she wondered, was Narayan's caste? "Hira seems like a good boy," she said.

"He is a good boy, Madam."

"The other day, he told me about his family in the village, and I've been thinking," Indira said, feeling reenergized by the thought that was forming in her mind even as she spoke. "I'd like to help him establish himself in the city, if I can. It would be good to see a young man like him flourish, wouldn't it, Narayan?"

The driver glanced at her in the mirror.

"Our youth are the hope of the nation, after all," Indira went on. "That's why I want to know, Narayan, what are your nephew's plans, ambitions, dreams? He told me he's twenty years old, and I'm wondering: is he by any chance in need of a pretty young bride?"

AVA FELL ASLEEP despite the jouncing of the bus, her head constricted by a spiky metal bar. She awoke with a crick in the neck when the bus halted to a screech. It was dark outside, and the air was dewy. The woman one seat over was asleep, breathing loudly through her mouth, a trickle of drool dribbling from her lower lip. Ava checked her cell phone and saw that it was five in the morning. For a while she couldn't tell where they were, but then she recognized the check post at the edge of Kathmandu. When the bus started up, the woman beside her awoke and started chanting — prayers? — beneath her breath.

On the descent into the valley, Ava looked at the concrete maze, feeling completely alert in an under-slept, somewhat unhinged way. In her somnolent vision, the concrete maze looked sheltering and secure, rather than squalid. Kathmandu was where Nepal's countryside came to look for fortunes, she realized. The countryside came here to rally resources, to move out into the world. If the city was ugly, it was because people spent most of what they had on personal advancement. They couldn't spare much for aesthetics.

The roads were already congested at this hour, though less so than usual. There was also less dust, and the air was mostly clean. The houses were still, and with only a few lights on. Kathmandu at dawn felt like a city of huddled dreams and sleeping ambitions.

The eastern horizon was glimmering to blue when the bus drew into an expansive bus stop. Here, the city was wide awake. Horns blared, people swarmed, all transactions teemed with urgency.

"Taxi, Madam?" The familiar refrain started up when she disembarked from the bus.

"Taxi, taxi."

"Taxi, Sister, taxi, you want taxi?"

Ava got into the nearest cab and gave directions. The driver started the engine wordlessly. She sat back, her mind ablaze.

All these months in Kathmandu, this was what she had been missing: the connections she had forged after running across Gyanu. The time in his home, the time in the homes of the women's committee members: that was what she had craved for. It helped her — it healed her — to know she could do something for a girl like Chandra. It wasn't, of course, Ava's job as the director of IDAF's Women's Empowerment Program to help individual women. This was something at a micro scale, or even smaller than that: it was personal. But it was clear to Ava in hindsight that this was why she had come to Nepal.

The driver turned into her neighbourhood and drove up the hill, stopping at the gate. Ava added a hundred-rupee tip to the fare. He pocketed it and left. She pressed the buzzer to the gate.

There was no reply from inside.

She checked to see if she could open it, but it was locked from inside. She knocked on the metal, and then banged, but there still was no reply. Harihar was probably asleep.

Ava waited around a while, wondering whether she should call the landlady. But then Mrs. Thapa would scream at Harihar, and Ava didn't want that. She scoped the compound wall, and saw that it was attached to the neighbour's wall, which was low.

She climbed it without much difficulty. The neighbour's dog began to bark. It was an Alsatian, and it raced out of the house towards the wall. Ava clambered up out of reach onto the adjoining compound wall. The dog started baying as she made her way to the wall of her own house.

After lowering her attaché case, she jumped, landing with a thud on the other side.

The neighbour's dog kept baying. Harihar never woke up. Ava let herself into the house.

John Barnett's assessment of WDS-Nepal had arrived in her absence. It sat on the desk in the study. She would have to read it this weekend, ahead of the final meeting with WDS-Nepal.

There was another package on the desk. Ava tore off the wrapping and saw that it was the sculpture she had bought at the Academy of Art: not a portrait of the artist's mother, but her imagination about her, whatever that meant. The artist had taped her business card at the bottom of the clay figure. Ava read her name out loud.

After making coffee, she carried the sculpture from room to room, trying to figure out where it should go. It was too small for the study or the living room. The dining room was so large that the sculpture just disappeared into it. She didn't want it in the bedroom. The house was simply too big, the sculpture didn't look right anywhere. She finally gave up and placed it back in its wrapping.

The sun rose. At her laptop, she scanned through a few work emails: several memos and a reply-all conversation that had gone on for days.

Congratulation!

Hearty congratulations to all on the team! Another laudable IDAF success!

Hats off to all of us!

Anthony had written immediately after their phone conversation.

Hey, any chance you're going to be in Toronto this May? My film's premiering at Hot Docs.

There was also a new email from Gavin. It was curt. *I haven't heard from you in forever, Ava. Wondering if you got my last email. I wanted you to know that Leez Anne and I are seeing each other. You and I need to talk.*

He'd written Ava, not Av.

Av and Gav.

Leez Anne and Gavin.

Ava shut the laptop and went out to the garden with John Barnett's assessment.

Spring had unloosed itself on the garden. The acacia and crepe myrtle trees had only just started budding a few days ago, but they were already dense with colour, a riot of pinks and reds and greens, effusive and unrestrained, right up to the jasmine hedge, which was an eye-dazzling yellow. Ganesh Himal was visible beyond: the morning sun casting it as hard edges of light.

The Himalayas. Ava would be up there, soon, in Langtang, trekking with Tomás.

She thought about calling him, but didn't.

She spent the morning reading the assessment, rereading WDS-Nepal's proposal, looking up NGOs working on trafficking, and placing a series of calls on her cell phone, starting with one to Claire Ross-Jones:

"Hello, Claire? It's Ava. Sorry to call you on a Saturday, but I need to meet you and Daphne Muirwood urgently about the Paris Declaration. Monday after the briefing would be great, thanks."

"Hi Shova, it's Ava. Could we meet this week about microfinance and cooperatives?"

"Herman, it's Ava. Could we meet soon to discuss social inclusion?"

"Andrew, it's Ava. I need your advice on donor shopping."

"Jared? Can we talk about peacebuilding?"

Vishwa called her mid-morning. Ava let the phone ring, and when it stopped, she sent him a message saying that she would see him on Monday.

By noon, Ganesh Himal had disappeared in the usual fug of Kathmandu. Ava got up to get something to eat, and saw Harihar at the gate, staring at her as though he had seen a ghost. She waved to put him at ease. The landlady, too, was staring at her from the balcony. Ava waved at her too.

There was leftover dal-bhat in the fridge. She ate it cold.

Then she returned to the study, and without letting herself think twice, wrote: *Dear Gavin.*

Steady.

I guess we should file for divorce.

I'm sorry, she wanted to write. *I love you, I'll always love you,* she wanted to write. She didn't. She pressed the send button and sat, stunned.

She spent the rest of the day napping, falling in and out of sleep, caught up in a dream in which the villages she had been to, and Butwal, Kathmandu, Miami, Toronto, Overwood, and Georgian Bay all came together in an unsolved jigsaw puzzle.

In the evening she awoke clearheaded. She poured herself a glass of wine and FaceTimed her brother.

"Oh, Luke, I still can't believe you're having a kid!"

"Neither can I, Auntie Ava!"

Revolution Mary was with him. She was radiant on the screen. "Hey, babes, don't you think Luke's going to make a great father?"

"Tell me more," Ava said. "I want to hear more."

"Mom and Dad are freaked out!" Luke laughed. "They're not ready to be grandparents. We're discussing names," he said. "We haven't found a girl's name, but if it's a boy we're going to name him Baby Jesus."

THE RECEPTIONIST TRILLED, "Namaste, Indira-ma'am."

"Namaste," Indira called back, wishing she could remember the receptionist's name.

Not that it mattered. Focus, Indira Sharma. All was not lost, all couldn't be lost, Vishwa Bista and Chandi Shrestha mustn't defeat her. She had to fight back, and furthermore, she had to win.

But her confidence collapsed when she entered the conference hall, because there was Chandi Shrestha: I have a penis. Why was he always, always at her meetings? Rick Peede was beside him, sitting across from the Canadian and Vishwa Bista. All three of them looked somber.

Only the Canadian was collected. "There you are, Indira," she said, her usual girlishness replaced, today, by a cool air of authority. She suddenly seemed older, in her mid-thirties, maybe because she was wearing a pinstripe suit.

She waited for Indira to sit before speaking:

"I'm going to voice my concerns very clearly," she said. "I've seen significant leakage in IDAF's work, and it's built into the way our funding is structured. We fund our partner INGOs, they fund their partner NGOs in Kathmandu, and they in turn fund their partner NGOs and CBOs in the districts and villages." She looked from person to person to make sure they were paying attention. They were. "I understand," she went on, "that neither we nor you can implement projects at the micro level, but in light of an IDAF headquarters directive to innovate an internal implementation strategy for the Paris Declaration, I've decided to demand a higher level of transparency."

Indira's mind went blank.

The Canadian was clearly expecting a reply.

Rick Peede offered one: "As you know, Ava, WDS-Nepal itself initiated the Transparency Matrix over two decades ago," he said in his droning way. "It has since been adopted by over two hundred NGOs in Nepal. All our national partners are required to sign it as a precondition to funding. And we've always observed the highest level of compliance in reporting, though of course we'd be happy to address your concerns."

The Canadian said, "Our assessment revealed that some of your partners have a thin presence on the ground. Our consultant, John Barnett, confirmed my own misgivings when I met with" — she consulted her notes — "Preety Rana of National Network Nepal. Now, Vishwa has pointed out to me that Ms. Rana has an impressive CV, but her organization is new." She turned to Indira. "To be frank, I'm puzzled that you chose National Network Nepal as your largest partner, Indira."

Indira glanced at Vishwa Bista for help, and caught him exchanging glances with Chandi Shrestha.

Penises!

Indira had to find something, anything, to say. She said, "You see, Ava, in the past," and had to swallow. "There were some" — her voice caught — "irregularities with our old partners. Not big irregularities, just: failure to comply with the transparency matrix due to an inability to customize the results log frame." Her heart began to beat wildly, like a trapped animal's. "So, we thought..." She said, "Preety Rana is very good, Ava."

At this point, Chandi Shrestha had the gall to contradict her: "But the previous partners were much better, Indira-ji. To be honest, I am also surprised."

Penis!

The Canadian leafed through her notes. "Talking about irregularities," she said.

Indira had to stop her before she could go on. "I want to say one thing!" she cried out.

Her voice rang out louder than she had intended. Everyone looked at her in surprise. Even Vishwa Bista was looking at her now, glaring at her from behind his floppy hair. Indira glared back at him with venom.

"I want to say one thing!" she repeated. But in truth, there was nothing to say. She had offered Vishwa Bista a bribe, but Chandi Shrestha had outsmarted her. He had obviously offered a bigger bribe. He would replace Rick Peede. She was done.

A roar burst out of Indira's mouth and ricocheted off the walls. She couldn't stop herself. She roared once again.

Mortified, she rushed up and stumbled out of the hall. Outside, she gasped for breath. Oh, Mother Earth, open up and take me in, as you did the goddess Sita in *The Ramayan*! Such humiliation! Never in her life –

Indira reeled into the women's washroom, where a rubber breast was sticking out of the wall. Disgusting! She locked herself inside a stall and wept.

"What do you want to do when you grow up?" her elders used to ask when she was a girl.

"I want to develop Nepal and make it prosperous," she used to say.

In the stall, Indira wept hopelessly, helplessly, till she ran out of tears, and then she wept some more. Her mind looped over the same thought: she was corrupt. Look at what she had become. Just look at her.

Excrement. Filth.

It took a long time for Indira to stop weeping. It took ages before she felt able to leave the stall. She did so despondently and saw, to her horror, that the Canadian had come into the washroom. She was standing by the wall, poking at the rubber breast.

"Oh! There you are, Indira," she said when she saw Indira. "I was worried. Are you all right?"

"Yes, I ... sorry." What was there to say? "I am having a little problem," Indira said, trying to come up with a plausible explanation: "At home, there is a girl. The girl who served the dinner when you came? She has ... problems, Ava, I am worried about her. I am experiencing too much tension at home."

"We've rescheduled for next week, everyone's gone." The Canadian was back to being her usual girlish self. "Why don't I make you a cup of tea?"

She led Indira to her office, inviting her to sit on the sofa. "You take your tea with milk and sugar, right?" she said. "I don't want to pry, Indira, but if you ever want to talk — not that you have to — I'm quite a good listener."

"Oh, it is too much a bother, Ava."

"It would be no bother."

So then — why not? Over a cup of weak, watery milk tea, Indira told her about Durga's misadventures. "She is a young girl, Ava, a village girl, very innocent. I am her guardian — I am her mother-father, her only family in this world. You see, Ava, the problem in Nepal is — women are idiot-fools. We give men everything, and these men: what do they do? Life is too hard for Nepali women."

"It really is, isn't it?"

"You don't know!" Indira said. "You see me, a leading gender expert of Nepal. I am modern, I am independent, but how do I live at home? Do you know, Ava, how many rules I must follow as a daughter-in-law? Like when you came for dinner: can I drink a glass of wine in my own house? And at work — am I equal? How much I have to struggle every day, just to be respected by men colleagues. These men, in public they say:

you are equal to us; but in reality? Always, in small things, in big things, they dominate us!"

"I've come to realize this." The Canadian nodded. "On my field trip I saw — and in Kathmandu, too — the gender balance is incredibly skewed." She thought for a while, then said, "It's hard for me to accept, given the way I grew up. I'd find it impossible to be a Nepali woman."

"Oh, it is too impossible!" Indira cried.

"Can I be honest with you?" the Canadian said. "I don't think I'd be able to do what you do, Indira. On my field trip I met these women, these incredible, strong, resilient women, they were so inspiring. And, I mean, some of them were so poor." To Indira's surprise, the Canadian's eyes began to moisten as she talked. "I kept thinking — if I were them, I don't know how I would have survived," she said, blinking back tears. "I'm sorry. I don't mean to be emotional. I just wanted to say — I don't know how you, all of you, Nepali women, do it. I really admire you."

Something tender stirred inside Indira. This Canadian, this Ava Berriden, wasn't so hard-hearted after all. "Ava, you are also a woman, you are also strong," Indira said in a warm, big-sisterly tone, a tone of woman-to-woman camaraderie. "All of us women are survivors," she went on, and as an afterthought, added, "The important thing is, we must always support each other against men."

"Well, that's what I'm hoping you'll do with my pilot project. But we can discuss it another time." Ava smiled. "I'd hate to force you to think about work in the middle of a personal crisis."

"No, tell me," Indira said. "Tell me right now. I must know!"

So Ava filled her in on what she had told the others at the meeting:

IDAF was going to launch a pilot project to increase aid effectiveness, a project that Ava was designing jointly with a consultant from IDAF headquarters in London. "I'm really hoping to partner with you on this, Indira," she said. The pilot project contained a direct implementation component, which would allow Ava to get to the field regularly. All she needed from Indira were a few amendments to the WDS-Nepal proposal. "I've had to work hard to convince everyone at IDAF — and between you and me, I've had to fight Vishwa in particular," Ava said. "He's completely against the pilot project. From today's meeting, it seems clear that Chandi's not in favour of it either, though Rick's open to it. So I'm counting heavily on your support."

Indira listened on, flabbergasted. Not only did Ava want to approve WDS-Nepal's proposal, she wanted to increase the budget so that WDS-Nepal could hire two full-time consultants to work with her on it. One of the consultants would be John Barnett.

Ava said, "In his assessment, John Barnett suggested that we cut out the middleman — National Network Nepal — and work directly with CBOs at the village level. That's what I'm hoping to do in the direct implementation component, Indira. I want to go directly to the women and support them — not just to bypass men, but also that," she said, becoming thoughtful. "Also to bypass men. Because they're everywhere, aren't they? Everywhere you look in Nepal, there are men."

"Always, men are there!" Indira agreed.

Ava smiled. "I've been lucky with the timing," she said. "I came in just as IDAF was drawing up its Five Year Outlook. IDAF headquarters has already given me a go-ahead. Daphne and Claire — I can never remember; do you know Claire Ross-Jones?"

"Of course, of course I know Claire, of course."

"They're both very supportive of the pilot project."

Indira said, "Me too, I'm also very supportive, Ava, I will back you fully on this pilot project."

"Oh, thank goodness!" Ava looked so relieved, it was strange. It was as though she didn't know that it was in her power to dictate the terms to WDS-Nepal. She said, "I'm really looking forward to working together on this, Indira. Maybe you could — why don't you come over to my place for dinner one day? We'll sit out in the garden and talk about everything over a nice glass of wine."

The two of them, sipping wine in Catherine Christy's old house. "Yes, why not?" Indira said.

"Wonderful." Ava got up. "Thanks for your cooperation, Indira." She reached over, and in a completely unexpected gesture, hugged Indira.

"No, no, thank you, thank you, Ava," Indira said, hugging her back.

"I'll call Rick now, and let him know what we've agreed on."

"Thank you so much, Ava, you don't know how much," Indira said, hugging her again.

"No, thank you," Ava said. "Thank you, Indira."

"Thank you, Ava. Thank you, thank you, thank you."

Indira strode out of the office, completely vindicated.

Victory was hers!

As it should be, as it should rightfully be, in the end.

With Ava's help, she had triumphed over men.

As was only just, and fair, and right.

She strode down the hall feeling like a queen, musing to herself:

Women always helped other women, didn't they? They really did. All her life, she had helped women, women all over the country, and also women at home: women like Durga. Durga, who was now getting a life — for after some cajoling, and with a financial inducement of two lakh rupees, Hira had agreed to marry the girl. At first, Durga had hesitated: "I don't want to marry an office peon, Hajoor, I want to be one." Silly girl. Indira had had to talk sense into her: "Which office will hire a class three dropout like you? Hira's a good boy. He has two lakh rupees in the bank. I'll build a new servants' quarters for you, you can live there together and start a family, even. You'll work for us, he'll work for the office, don't you see? It'll be perfect."

"Perfect, Hajoor?"

"Perfect."

The girl had eventually come around.

And now — and now! It was Indira's time to rise with the help of this — Ava Berriden.

Who would have thought that this young, dark, twiggy Canadian would help her rise? And keep rising.

Downstairs, in the lobby, the receptionist trilled, "Namaste, Indira-ma'am!"

"Namaste," Indira said. Then on a whim, she stopped. "Remind me, dear. What's your name?"

"Indira, Ma'am."

"No, I mean what's your name?"

The receptionist smiled. "Ma'am, my name is also Indira, though my friends call me Indu."

"Ey, your name is also Indira!" Indira exclaimed. Yes, yes, how could she have forgotten? She remembered now. She said, "Like India's famous prime minister, right? We Indiras, we're powerful women, aren't we, Indira?"

"Yes, Ma'am."

"Lau ta, Indira, namaste to you," Indira said.

"And namaste to you, Indira-ma'am."

THEIR LAST DAYS together were full of defiance. Sapana moved her belongings into a room in Thulo-ba's house and prepared to close up the family home, but she refused to feel sad, and in any case there was no time to feel sad. Everything was happening so fast.

A few days after reaching Kathmandu, Ava-madam got an NGO to locate Surya-di. Ava-madam telephoned Gyanu-dai to confirm that Surya-di was safe in Ghaziabad, and that it was all right for Chandra to go to her. Gyanu-dai and Chandra were going to take a bus to Bhairahava town tomorrow to meet an NGO employee who had agreed to escort Chandra through the border post at Sunauli, all the way to Ghaziabad. From there, Gyanu-dai would go on to Kathmandu to obtain a permit for his new job in the desert, staying at Ava-madam's house till the permit came through.

Gyanu-dai clearly felt very guilty about leaving. He kept asking Sapana, "Will you be all right, Bahini?" and she always replied, "Of course, Dai," refusing to show any weakness.

He was abandoning her, but Sapana was no longer as angry about it, because she was going to be doing something, something very important right here. Ava-madam was starting a new project in the bazaar to teach the members of the women's committee — here in the village, and also in surrounding villages — how to form cooperatives. Ava-madam was going to come to the village herself to discuss it with the committee. She had said as much to Gyanu-dai over the phone. "I'll tell you more after I meet her in Kathmandu," Gyanu-dai had said to Sapana, though Sapana didn't believe he would give it much attention once he left: he was already turned away from his past, towards his future with the woman he was going to marry in the desert.

Gyanu-dai spent his last day in the village taking leave of friends and relatives.

This was also Sapana's last full day with Chandra. She and Chandra woke up, washed and ate their morning meal together, not wanting to spend a single moment apart. After the meal, Sapana helped Chandra pack. Chandra was uncharacteristically indecisive, fussing over every detail:

"Will I need a sweater? Isn't it hot in India? What do you think, Sapana?"

"Take one just in case."

"I'll leave the rest for little Tara, she's growing up so fast, it'll fit her next year. Look after her, hai?"

"Do you have to ask?"

"And my muwa-buwa."

"Don't even ask!"

"Maybe I should take two sweaters. What if it's cold there? I'll take two," Chandra said, her thoughts racing to the adventures ahead. "Gyanu-dai said it's an overnight journey. I wonder if we'll take a bus or a train. It would be fun to ride in a train, hai. I hope we take a train."

They took the rest of Chandra's clothes to her muwa-buwa's house. The families of the other girls who had gone to India with Surya-di came by, hungry for news about their daughters. They asked about what had happened to Surya-di and their own girls. The mother of the girl who was still in Ghaziabad gave Chandra a letter for her daughter. The parents of the girl who was no longer in contact sifted over every detail, examining it, searching for possibility and hope: "Send word if you hear anything, Chandra-nani. Send word immediately."

"I'll track down that middleman, I'll find out what happened," Chandra said.

"We just want to know that she's alive."

In the afternoon, Ritu and Namrata dropped by to say goodbye. Both of them were sombre today.

Even Ritu didn't joke around as usual. "India's a big country, careful you don't get lost," she said. Her own plans were also set. She had met the boy from the far west, and they had liked each other well enough. Their families were consulting an astrologer to fix the wedding date. "We'll live in Kathmandu," Ritu said. "I'll only have to see my in-laws once in a while. What about you, ey, Namrata? What are you going to do?"

"I don't know. Maybe — I don't know. Should I join the women's committee?"

"Won't the foreign woman's project help girls pass out of school, Sapana?"

"I don't know," Sapana said.

"I should have studied harder when I had a chance," Namrata said.

Chandra was mostly quiet, but at one point she quoted the depressed poet: "What grows in these still villages but death." She repeated the line, and then recited the rest of the poem:

> *What grows in these still villages*
> *But death. To stay is to die.*
> *To leave is to die too. Mother!*
> *Save me. I'm fading.*

"Tchee, what a horrible poem." Little Tara made a face.

"The poet won a national award!" Chandra said.

"So? It's still a horrible poem, never recite it again."

The sun was still above the horizon when Sapana and Chandra went back for their last night at home.

"You really shouldn't go abroad looking so jungly," Sapana said.

She laid a straw mat on the porch, and brought out a comb and a bottle of coconut oil. Sitting behind Chandra, she unclipped her friend's hair. It tumbled down in thick shocks onto her shoulders. Sapana combed through it carefully, easing out the tangles, and then parting it to apply oil to the scalp.

The sunlight bore down, warm and golden. A crow cawed. The rich scent of coconut filled the air. Chandra closed her eyes. Sapana kept parting her hair and applying oil till the entire scalp glistened. Then she massaged Chandra's head, kneading the forehead, the temples, the jawbone, the neck. Chandra sighed.

Afterwards, Chandra turned around and took the oil and comb from Sapana. It was her turn to oil Sapana's hair and make her sigh.

For the evening meal, Sapana cooked Gyanu-dai's favourite dishes, the same dal-bhat-tarkaari she had made after the thirteen days of austerities for Ba: rice, black dal, potatoes, and cauliflower.

When he came home, they sat at the table and ate.

"This is the best meal in the world, Bahini."

Gyanu-dai was just saying so to make her feel better. Sapana said, "It's not as good as the food you cook, Dai."

"It's better."

Liar.

He spoke a little bit about his new job. "It's a small restaurant, it won't pay as well, but I'll look for something better once I get there," he said, adding, "I'll send money transfers, like before, Bahini. Don't tell Thulo-ba or Thuli-ma about the money, keep it to yourself." Then, as though admitting to a crime, he said, "We'll marry soon, Maleah and me. I — I don't know how long I'll stay in the desert," he said. "We might move to another country. We want to live with her son, as a family, somewhere."

Somewhere that wasn't home, Sapana thought.

Chandra asked, "Will we ever get to meet Maleah-bhauju?"

"One day, I hope," Gyanu-dai said. "I hope we can all come here for a visit one day."

Sapana didn't believe her brother at all.

They all cleaned up together, putting away the pots and pans for the last time. After that, Gyanu-dai went to his room, and Chandra and Sapana went to theirs.

They changed into their nightdresses, turned off the kerosene lamp, and got into bed. And in the darkness they reached for each other. When would they share a bed again? Attached by love, by need, by desire, they held on to each other. In the morning they would have to let go. Tonight they could still hold on.

"Don't forget me, ey, girl," Chandra whispered.

"Don't be an idiot," Sapana said, trying not to cry.

"Tomorrow?" Chandra said. "Let's be strong, Sapana. Let's not cry, hai."

"Let's never cry, Chandra."

They lay awake for a long time in the darkness, holding each other, thinking their separate thoughts. Sapana didn't think she could fall asleep, but Chandra drifted off soon enough. Her grip loosened, and her legs twitched. Sapana listened to her steady, even breathing. Every moment felt precious, she wanted to gather each last memory and store it away for when Chandra wouldn't be here. She didn't want to sleep tonight.

A harsh morning light clattered in from the window. Chandra's arms were still around her when Sapana's eyes opened. She could tell from Chandra's breathing that she was awake, too, but she also lay still, not wanting the moment to end.

But then the neighbour's cock crowed, and Chandra stirred, and Sapana also had to stir, because there was no stopping time. Soon they were out by the tap.

And after a quick round of tea, it was time for Gyanu-dai and Chandra to go.

There were no family elders to take leave from: there was no ritual to follow. Though he was the one leaving and she the one staying, Gyanu-dai placed a daub of red, powdery tika on Sapana as a blessing, simply because he was older.

"May you go as far as your heart desires, Bahini," he said by way of offering his blessings.

"You too, Dai." Sapana put tika on him. "Whatever you want— may you get it."

Then Gyanu-dai put tika on Chandra, saying, "Be safe, Bahini. Telephone me as soon as you get to Surya."

"I will, Dai."

Sapana also put tika on Chandra: "Don't ever forget where you're from, girl."

"How can I ever forget?"

Then Gyanu-dai and Chandra carried their bags out. Sapana locked the front door with a Chinese padlock that she had bought in the bazaar. Its key was tied to a silver chain, which she slipped around her neck.

They were beside Chandra's muwa-buwa's house when they saw a stranger marching up the path. He had a heavy bag strapped to his chest. He stopped in front of the rotting brick house and called out: "Where's the house with the lines to be connected?" The man's forehead was beaded with sweat. "I'm from the Electricity Authority," he said. "There was an application from this village."

"Ey, Sir," Gyanu-dai said. "There's been a change of plans."

He had forgotten to cancel the application he had put in. He explained as much to the man. "We don't need to connect the lines anymore."

"But I came all the way!" The man unstrapped the bag and hurled it onto the ground. "I've brought all the wires, all the equipment!"

"It's my mistake, Sir. I completely forgot."

"Do you know how long it took?" the man cried. "I had to wait an hour for the bus, I had to walk all the way from the highway, I had to walk up this village path in the hot sun!"

"Forgive me, Sir."

"You wasted half a day's work!"

The man calmed down only after Gyanu-dai paid him off, apologizing. "You went through so much trouble, we're grateful," he said, tucking several hundred-rupee notes into the man's hands.

"You really should have cancelled!" The man picked up his bag.

"The mistake is entirely mine."

Chandra's muwa-buwa were waiting for them in the house, with little Tara. They had packed food for the journey, and they put it into Chandra's bag, along with a new kurta for her, and another one for Surya-di. Chandra's muwa also slipped her an envelope with some money. Then both parents put tika on Chandra, offering her their blessings:

"Prosper, daughter. Like your older sister, find your own path forward. May the gods keep you safe."

As Chandra knelt down and bowed at her parents' feet, little Tara began to cry.

"Don't cry, little one. Don't cry." Chandra got up and held her sister for a long time, and then released her to their muwa-buwa's arms.

Sapana escorted Gyanu-dai and Chandra to the bazaar. She would have gone all the way to the India border if she could have. She and Chandra held hands on the bus ride, and got off in the bazaar still holding hands.

The bus to Bhairahava was already there when they arrived. The driver was honking; the conductor was yelling to attract passengers; there was no time for them to linger over their farewells. Gyanu-dai and Chandra scrambled on as the bus engine started up.

Sapana watched anxiously from outside as they found seats at the back. When the bus lurched forward with a groan, Sapana's heart leaped. She looked wildly at Chandra, and Chandra looked at her.

The bus began rolling away.

Gyanu-dai called out, "I'll telephone from Kathmandu, Bahini!"

Chandra also said something, but her words were lost in the roar of the engine.

Sapana tried to be strong, but tears sprang to her eyes, she couldn't help but weep. She should have gone with Chandra, she should have gone to India, it was stupid to stay here — *what grows in these still villages but death?*

The bus rolled out of the park and turned onto the highway.

As it vanished, a sharp pain seared through Sapana. She fumbled at her neck, pulled out the chain with the key. She had no home to go back to.

The pain seared through her again. She gasped. The world was on fire. There was a bench nearby. She collapsed onto it, wailing.

"Sapana-bahini."

She heard a voice.

She couldn't stop wailing. It hurt so much inside.

"Sapana-bahini, what's wrong, Sapana-bahini?"

The voice kept talking, calling out her name, saying things.

"Sapana-bahini, what's wrong, Sapana-bahini."

The voice wouldn't leave her alone.

When, with difficulty, Sapana looked up, she saw a man hovering over her. The sun was behind him, she couldn't see who it was.

He said, "Why are you crying, Sapana-bahini?"

She squinted, shielding her eyes from the sun. It was Rudra-sir. He was wearing a blue shirt: he always wore blue shirts on Mondays. Sapana remembered this through her grief.

He sat down beside her on the bench. "Why are you crying like this, Bahini? Here, take this." He produced an embroidered handkerchief. "Your tears are staining your beauty," he said, looking at her sorrowfully with his golden-brown eyes. "Tell me what happened, Sapana-bahini. You know I've always helped you, you know I always will. It's terrible to see you so sad. What can I do to help you stop crying?" he said. "Tell me what I can do for you today."

SAPANA CRADLED THE phone in her hands, speaking into the receiver in a low, subdued tone. "What's it like, girl? Your masters' house."

"It's huge, it's as big as a palace, it's really grand, Sapana." Chandra's voice came out muffled. She didn't sound like herself on the phone. "The floors are made of white marble," Chandra said, "and the furniture's so fine I'm afraid to touch anything." She laughed. "There's a carpet in the main room, all I want to do is lie on it, it's so soft. It has a pretty pattern with flowers." She paused, then asked, "Are Muwa-Buwa all right? Have they repaired the house? Where's little Tara staying?"

"I told you, everything's fine. The wall's been patched up, little Tara's back in your old room. Don't worry about anyone here," Sapana said.

"What about your house?" Chandra asked. "Have the cracks in the wall been repaired?"

"It doesn't matter, no one lives there anyway. Tell me more about things over there."

Chandra indulged her. "The other night," she said, "the master and mistress had a party. The people who came were so sophisticated; they talked about politics, philosophy, art. Ey, did I tell you, Sapana, the government here issues ration cards?" Everything about India was new, and interesting, to Chandra. "Rich people like the masters don't need ration cards, but Surya-di has one, and everyone else has one too. It's for buying rice and sugar and kerosene: essentials. I think our government should also issue ration cards, don't you? Surya-di says she'll help me get one too."

"That's good," Sapana said. She was at the grain store, trying to hold on to her own sense of self. Only a few months had passed since Chandra left, but so much had happened. It was

276

as though the springtime earthquake had shaken up the entire reality of the world.

This part of the country had been spared by the earthquake, but the news from elsewhere was terrifying, and there were still aftershocks every other day. When the earth trembled, all of the universe's certainties seemed to tremble: and to Sapana it felt as though this changed everything, including her. When she and Chandra met next time, would things be the same between them?

"I don't like the master," Chandra went on. "He's a bit arrogant, but the mistress is all right. The children are spoiled. Ey, they bought a television the other day, it's the size of an almirah, Sapana. When everyone's out I watch the news. It's all in Hindi, I don't understand it, but it's interesting." She paused. "Have you heard from Gyanu-dai?"

"He got married."

Chandra didn't say anything about this. Neither did Sapana. There was surely so much that Chandra couldn't convey over the phone. Sapana, too, couldn't talk about everything. It just wasn't possible — there was too much.

After the earthquake, Thulo-ba and Thuli-ma began to pressure Sapana to marry. With false, overweening concern, Thuli-ma told her, "Who knows when another earthquake will take us all, Nani? We won't always be here to look out for you. Let us find you a groom before it's too late." Thulo-ba even tried to push Jeevan Bhatta on her. "He's old, but he'll take care of you, Nani." It infuriated Sapana. She hadn't told Chandra about this.

Neither had she told her about her secret rebellion.

Maybe it was wrong, maybe she shouldn't have done it. *I've always helped you, I always will.* Rudra-sir was a husband and father. Maybe she shouldn't have met him for tea, she shouldn't have gone on outings with him, she shouldn't have walked with him on the shores of the Tinau River. But when he held her hand, when he touched her and kissed her and told her how beautiful she was, Sapana felt as though she were breaking through to some fierce freedom. She didn't even know how to talk to Chandra about this.

She told her, instead, about Ava-madam's project: "It's bigger than I expected, Chandra. Ava-madam will come back to the bazaar in a month re, that's what Jeevan Bhatta told me. She's going to organize a meeting with the Department of Cooperatives."

"Will Namrata join the committee?"

"She's already paying the monthly dues. I'll be enrolled in the Plus Two by then. I can't wait for it to start. I'll escape from Thulo-ba and Thuli-ma's house, and move to a girl's hostel in the bazaar."

"And Ritu's married," Chandra said. "We've all gone our own ways, hai?"

We needn't have, Sapana wanted to say. Come back, she wanted to say. You can still come back, Chandra, we can live together for the rest of our lives. She knew it was futile to say so. Chandra was content with where she was now. The last time they spoke, she had told Sapana how good it felt to earn a monthly salary: "I'll open a bank account with it, a bank account of my own." And after the earthquake, she and Surya-di had sent money to Sapana to give to their muwa-buwa. Chandra wanted to work for a few years in India: "After that, who knows what the future holds?" she had said last time.

Now, she said, "Ey, wait hai." There was a rustling on the line, and then Chandra said, "The children are back from school, I have to go."

"I'll call you next week, Chandra."

"Call earlier in the day, we'll be able to talk for a longer time."

"I'll call an hour earlier."

"Call, hai, Sapana, call me next week for sure."

After Chandra hung up, Sapana kept the phone to her ear, listening to the silence on the line.

She wasn't sure what to do now.

She knew what Rudra-sir wanted her to do.

"Come with me," he had said this morning, at the bank. He had booked a room in a hotel at the edge of the bazaar. "I'll take care of everything," he had said. "I won't let anything bad happen to you." He had looked at her with longing, he had been sentimental, he had sighed. "You're everything to me, Sapana. You've got to believe that. You're all I have in this world."

He had told Sapana that his marriage had been arranged against his will. He didn't love his wife. Sapana wasn't stupid, she knew that married men kept girls like her off to one side, reserving the centre of their lives for their families. Yet she was tempted to go to the hotel with Rudra-sir, because if she were to ruin herself, then maybe no one would want to marry her, and she would always be free.

Reluctantly, she put down the receiver. Everything in her life felt unmade. She didn't even recognize it anymore. It was no longer what it used to be, and hadn't yet become something else; and maybe it never would. Maybe this was all there would ever be, she thought: her asking questions to the universe, and receiving no answers at all.

Nepal Gets New Charter

NEPAL NEWS SERVICE

Nepal promulgated a new constitution on Sunday amid heightened security and curfews in the southern Tarai-Madhes region, where a bandh, or general strike, has been in place. More than forty people, including eight policemen and two children, have been killed here in recent weeks.

The constitution was eight years in the drafting, following a peace process and a decade-long conflict that claimed more than nineteen thousand lives. Critics say that the new charter favours the country's high-caste political class in the demarcation of provincial boundaries and electorates. They also fault the constitution for denying equal citizenship rights to women.

The new constitution is the sixth national charter since the country's founding in 1768. It was long delayed and much anticipated. It was voted on by a majority of a 601-member Constituent Assembly and promulgated by President Ram Baran Yadav.

Celebrating outside the Assembly building, college student Bikash Woli says it's a historic day for Nepal. "Today I am proud to be Nepali," he said, though elsewhere in the country the constitution was being burned as a mark of protest.

The polarization over the new charter is set to increase in the coming days. The country is yet to recover from a devastating earthquake in April 2015, which claimed up to nine thousand lives and destroyed over eight hundred thousand homes. Over four billion dollars pledged to earthquake reconstruction by international donors remain unspent amid the ongoing unrest.

INDIRA STEPS GINGERLY on the sidewalk, her heels catching on the cobbles, her feet sore. She's determined to keep going. It's so pretty here. The air is clean, the streets tidy, the trees on the sidewalk clipped. She stops to admire a fountain in the middle of a pond, and, abutting it, a castle-like structure: the Binnenhof, parliament house.

The Hague is better than Amsterdam, she decides. In Amsterdam, when she snuck out in between sessions at the Sustainability and Gender Summit, the city felt very crowded, even grubby, perhaps because marijuana and prostitution were legal in the Netherlands. The youth looked wanton and wild-eyed. One morning, she even saw a young man asleep by a splatter of his own vomit outside a coffee shop.

There's no such disgrace in sight in The Hague. The Dutch royal family lives here, that must be why. Or maybe The Hague is just a superior city, she thinks. She walks through an arch that looks like the entrance to the Binnenhof. It opens onto an enclosed courtyard, a courtyard not unlike those in the Newari parts of Kathmandu, but, well, more European. Bigger. With big windows, big doors, and, no doubt, big rooms inside, to accommodate big Europeans.

A man in red pants rides into the courtyard on a bicycle. There's a little boy on the back seat of his bicycle. Indira walks on to the end of the courtyard. The Binnenhof is remarkably small. She wonders, in passing, how many parliamentarians the Netherlands has. It can't be many if they all fit in here.

A cool breeze sweeps through the courtyard and happiness sweeps through her. She's come to The Hague upon the insti-gation of Kadri Pütsep, who was at the summit in Amsterdam. Formidable Kadri Pütsep! It was six years since they last met, but they reconnected instantly.

"My sister Indira!" Kadri cried upon seeing her, and Indira cried back.

"My sister Kadri!"

"My sister!"

"My sister!"

Kadri is retired – so young! – but she's consulting with the Estonian government on women's rights, even though Estonian women must have equal rights? "You must come to visit me in Tallinn!" Kadri said to her. "We must have solidarity, we women."

"Of course, of course!" Indira said, though she's no longer just a woman, is she? She's WDS-Nepal's first Nepali director – who also happens to be a woman. The distinction is extremely important to her. After working on women-shwomen, gender-shender all her life, Indira has become a whole person at last.

Still, she was moved by Kadri's sisterly spirit, and when Kadri said, "You must see The Hague, it is beautiful," she took her advice and extended her trip by two days. Never before has Indira tacked a holiday onto the end of her duty travels. It didn't feel affordable till she began to earn a dollar salary. Yesterday's train ride from Amsterdam took less than an hour. She caught a taxi to her hotel in a fishing village by the North Sea, and walked on the windswept beach, and had dinner at an Italian restaurant. She has all of today to see the rest of The Hague.

Beyond the Binnenhof's courtyard, she arrives at a plaza full of open-air restaurants. A statue stands in the centre of the plaza, a statue of a king, a prince, a nobleman. Indira goes up to look at it, and notices that it has needles on top of its head.

Needles! These Europeans think of everything! Indira marvels. Someone in a government office somewhere decided that statues must be protected from birds. A consultant recommended needles – a city planner or a public works specialist.

Budgets were drawn, contracts were signed, funds were disbursed, and the needles were placed ... Tch. When will such a day come in Nepal?

No, no, no.

There's no comparing and contrasting.

Nepal is Nepal.

Indira turns away from the statue and looks around. At the open-air restaurants, people are drinking coffee, people are drinking wine. She too wants to be a person drinking coffee, a person drinking wine at an open-air restaurant in The Hague. She selects what looks like a good restaurant and takes a table beside a potted plant. The menu is printed on a paper placemat. She decides to order coffee, but when a lean, lank waiter comes to her table, she points at what a blonde woman at the next table is having. "I will have a red wine."

Why not? She deserves a glass of wine. After all, she's the boss of everyone now, everyone at work, and everyone at home too — except for Muwa. No one can ever be the boss of that old witch.

The waiter brings the wine, a swirl of ruby in an elegant stemmed glass. Indira lifts it and makes a toast to ... Nothing comes to mind. She takes a small sip. The wine is light, earthy, fragrant, not like the inky wine she had ... was that with Ava Berriden? Nowadays she goes to Ava's house every few weeks for dal-bhat and wine — expensive, high quality wine. The inky wine must have been from the wedding party. Yes, that was when she must have had it. This wine — she takes another sip — is much better than that wine. It floods her with ease.

Truly, Nepal is changing — not fast enough, of course, but things aren't as bad as they used to be, which is something. Indira takes another sip of wine. She sits back, remembering the wedding party: the swarm of guests, the clangour of a brass band, the swirl of saris — beaded, embroidered, sequined, and mirror-worked. The excitement of new beginnings. She, of course, had been at the centre of the festivities, a many-armed goddess orchestrating everything. "Have more," she said to a guest who was tucking into the biryani, enjoying it, as well as he should, for Indira had hired the caterer at no small expense. She had ordered every dish, every drink for the feast; and not just that. She had seen to the thousand finicky arrangements that went into planning a Hindu wedding. She had found a modern-minded priest to convince Muwa that there could be flexibility on caste differences in this day and age. She had drawn up the guest list herself. She had hired a brass band and a photographer too. She had even splurged on a gold-embroidered wedding sari for Durga, and on a twenty-two-carat gold necklace-earring-ring set with zirconia diamonds. The girl looked pretty as a bride. She sat on a sofa beside the groom, her head bowed, her expression demure. She couldn't smile, that would be inappropriate for a Hindu bride, but she was happy, Indira thinks. Or happy enough. Nepal isn't the developed world, after all; all we get, as Nepalis, is to be happy enough; and Durga was happy enough on her wedding day.

Hira also looked handsome as a groom, dressed in a smart white labeda sural. There were no guests from the bride's side, but the groom's side was there in force: the driver Narayan had brought Hira's entire family from the village. Everyone from WDS-Nepal was there, all the drivers and peons, all the secretaries and receptionists, everyone up the hierarchy to Chandi Shrestha and Rick Peede, only a few months before his departure from Nepal.

Rick Peede drank a whole bottle of wine by himself. "Indira!

286

Isn't this marvellous! I love Nepali weddings!" His face was red, redder, even, than his hair. "Look at my wife! Isn't she ravishing?"

Tall Misha Peede, dressed in a red bridal sari, was grinding her hips, Bollywood-style, to the din of the brass band. The guests gathered around to watch, thoroughly entertained. Ava was watching on from the side. Everyone was enjoying the spectacle.

Indira was gracious to them all, even to her now-defeated rival. "Chandi-ji, have some food, please. It's not too oily or spicy. I made sure the caterers used the very best ingredients."

"But I've already eaten, Indira-ji. It was good. The biryani was the best."

No, Chandi-ji: I am the best.

The servers served food, the guests ate, the brass band played, Misha Peede danced and the bride and groom received congratulations and gifts.

"Madam Director." John Barnett had also come to the wedding. "Madam Director," he said, holding her hands to his heart. "Please meet the love of my life."

His wife, Vidya Barnett, wasn't just beautiful, she was stunning: she glowed like a full moon in a classical love poem. She was also endlessly well-mannered. "It's inspiring to meet a successful professional woman like you," she said to Indira. "I'm just a simple housewife, I feel humbled to be in your presence."

"No, no!" Indira laughed. "No, no, no." She said, "Welcome to my home, please. John-ji, will you have wine?" She flagged down a server. "And Vidya-ji, can I get you some fruit juice?"

Vidya said, "I'll have a glass of wine too."

Of course. As a Newar, she wasn't barred from drinking, the way Indira was.

"What's a wedding without some alcohol?" John Barnett said. "Here's to weddings." He raised his glass.

His wife raised her glass.

They clearly expected Indira, too, to take a glass: the server was standing by with the tray. Indira glanced around. Muwa was out of sight. "Yes, here's to weddings," she said, picking up a glass, but as she took the first inky sip, she caught a telltale whiff of myrrh. "To the bride and groom," she said, quickly putting the glass back down.

Yes, to them, Indira thinks now, taking a sip of the light, earthy, fragrant wine in the open-air restaurant in The Hague. To the bride and groom. After the wedding, Durga and Hira moved into the newly constructed servants' quarters in the backyard, and nine months later Durga gave birth to a baby, a baby girl. Both parents were crestfallen that it wasn't a boy. Indira scolded them: "Boys and girls are equal nowadays!" They've come to accept this now, for a baby is a baby — and a life is a life. Durga has a life.

We're all resilient, we women, Indira thinks, making a silent toast. To Nepali women. She takes a sip of wine.

And to women all over the world, she thinks. They're all resilient.

To Kadri Pütsep, her dear sister Kadri, and to the entire sisterhood of global change-makers. To Abena Kwasima, to Rudo Gamble, to W. Werry, to Mei Wang, to Juana Hernández ... and to Catherine Christy and Ava Berriden too.

And to herself as well, for she, too, is resilient, isn't she? Yes, she is. She survived the darkest shadow to ever pass over her life: the shadow cast by that excrement-filth, Vishwa Bista. Despite his best effort, he failed to sully her, and Chandi Shrestha also failed. She has moved up, and they remain exactly where they were: Vishwa Bista at IDAF, Chandi Shrestha at WDS-Nepal, a mere co-director, an underling.

Indira lifts the wine glass and toasts herself: to Indira Sharma.

It's so important, she muses, not to be discouraged, no matter how challenging things become, and to move on, because what might have been is gone, but what there is now is still there, and who knows what might yet be?

The entire plaza shimmers into soft focus as Indira takes another sip. A lightness of spirit comes over her: her heart is full of wine. The sun is high up in the sky. It will stay there forever on this long, glowing summer day of the northern hemisphere.

To women, she thinks. Indira sips the wine.

To women all over the world.

To Nepali women.

To me.

IN THE JOURNEY of life, this is where Gyanu is now, in a cramped kitchen with a rickety ventilator overwhelmed by the heat rising off the stove. He wipes up around the sink, puts away the towels. The soap bottle needs refilling. He does so, and looks around to check that everything is clean. "Everything is all right, Amram?"

"Everything's all right."

"Tomorrow I will come early," Gyanu says.

"No problem, man." Amram is preparing a fresh batch of keema. Above the stove, his face glistens with sweat. "I'll stay with my brother tonight. You — you have fun," he says.

Gyanu nods in thanks.

"And don't forget: tomorrow morning's trash pickup," Amram says.

"I will take the bin out."

Gyanu leaves by the back door, the smell of hot oil trailing out behind him. The air outside is cool, and he shivers. Behind the restaurant is an empty parking lot where weeds grow in the cracks. The ventilator whirs, emitting the smell of oil as he passes the window. A squirrel darts across his path. He's still not used to squirrels. He watches it scamper across the parking lot into the back alley, and follows it out.

He draws his jacket around him. Amram teases him about wearing a jacket in the summertime, but he, acclimatized to the desert, feels a tinge of winter to even the hottest days here. The weather here surprises him.

As does the drabness of the city. Canada is a wealthy country, but it lacks the glitz of Dubai. Or maybe it's glitzy in other parts. Gyanu hasn't had a chance to look around much. After landing, he moved in with Amram, and started working at Kabob House a few days later. On his days off, he has to run errands, applying for a social insurance number, obtaining a photo card, switching to a cheaper health insurance policy. At Maleah's urging, he has enrolled in an English class for immigrants. He has yet to meet the lawyer Ava hired for him, the one who helped him with the application for express entry. The lawyer, a woman, had instructed him to obtain police clearances from Dubai, Abu Dhabi, Sharjah, and Nepal; take a health test; pass an English proficiency test. She had also transferred funds from Ava to Gyanu's bank account for the application, and transferred the funds back afterwards. Gyanu is supposed to meet the lawyer to discuss his future plans. Her office is far away, downtown. She's told him to call her in a few weeks.

At the main street, he stops and sends a message to Jairus: *I m going 2 get her.*

With its bright red façade, Kabob House stands out on the street. The rest of the buildings house small, tumbledown businesses: a dusty curio shop, an airless sports bar, a shop that sells yarn and knitting supplies. Kabob House is the only thriving business on this street, with a small but loyal following. It's just Amram and Gyanu in the kitchen. The workload is heavy, and the pay is minimum, but Gyanu is glad for the job.

His phone pings with a reply: *Now be happy, friend.*

Jairus is the one who urged him to try for Canada. In the desert, as Gyanu worked at Zafran and Maleah at the gift shop, Jairus counselled them about how to pull together a new life. Jairus first got in touch with his cousin, the chartered accountant in Australia, but the cousin was of no help. So he put Gyanu in touch with a Somali friend who used to work as a driver at his tour company, Ghedi Mahmoud. He had migrated to Canada. He now drove a taxi in Alberta. He gave Gyanu the number of an employment agency in Alberta. In the meanwhile, Jairus suggested that Gyanu talk to Ava. "Your foreigner from Nepal, she's a lawyer, na? Canada has the same kind of immigration policy as Australia, friend. Maybe you and Maleah and the boy can settle down there. Ask your foreigner for help."

Gyanu was reluctant at first. Ava had helped Chandra, and she was doing so much for Sapana and the other members of the women's committee in the village. And he knew that Ava felt like an equal, a sister rather than a patron. He didn't want to alter their friendship by acknowledging the power imbalance between them.

But he eventually overcame his reluctance; and Ava was gracious. She helped him the rest of the way. *Let me get in touch with some lawyer friends and see what they'd advise,* she emailed from Kathmandu, signing off: *xoxoA.*

Curious soul.

At the end of the block, Gyanu reaches the entrance to the subway station and takes the escalator down. This is the route he takes to work every day. The station is crowded. It's a long weekend: for what occasion, he doesn't know. He packs in against the wall beside two elderly women talking in bright, excitable tones among themselves. Beside him a young white man leans wearily against the wall. A black man in a business suit, headphones clamped over his ears, nods his head in rhythm. Three young women are talking in tones that dip and rise in a familiar cadence. Listening to them, he thinks of Maleah.

The places we come from, meri maya, the places we go.

Gyanu's journey to Canada began, in a way, on the day he invited Ava to the family home in the village. The bond they formed propelled both of them forward in their separate directions. After taking Chandra to the Sunauli border, Gyanu went on to Ava's house in Kathmandu, where she opened up her entire life to him. She installed him in a spare bedroom upstairs, and fed him a dinner of dal-bhat, offered him wine. "Stay as long as you'd like, Gyanu, I have so much space, it's great to have someone to share it with," she said, oblivious to the divides — of class, of station — that she would have been sharply aware of had she been raised in Nepal.

The following morning, she left for work early. Gyanu spent the day in the city chasing the permit paper, the visa, the air ticket. It would take weeks for everything to come through. On his way back to Ava's house, he bought white beans, bacon, lettuce, and herbs: he had noticed, on the previous night, that she didn't seem to like dal-bhat. He would cook for her as a way of repaying her kindness.

The guard, Harihar, was reluctant to let Gyanu back into the house. "How long are you staying, Bhai?" he asked at the gate.

"I don't know, Dai, a week or two, maybe more."

"There's a servants' quarters, you'd be more comfortable if you moved there with me."

The maidservant's displeasure was also evident when he went into the kitchen to cook.

"This madam, she's difficult to please," Luna said, hovering over the stove, as if staking out her territory. "The last madam was nicer. This one doesn't like our food. I have to throw out her portion from the refrigerator every day, Bhai."

"Foreigners, they're not used to our tastes, Didi."

"The thing is, even if she's hired you as her cook, Bhai, it's the landlady who pays my salary, and I'll still work here," she said.

Gyanu had to reassure her: "I'm only here for a few days, Didi."

Ava seemed oblivious to the judgments around her in the house. Only the gardener, Jaleswar, kept to himself. Harihar was always prying:. "And how did you get to know this madam?" Luna, too, loved to gossip. "Is it just the two of you tonight, or is that white man also coming? What is it re, I forget his name."

"Tomás."

"He must be this madam's boyfriend, or is he her husband?"

"I don't know, Didi."

"They have no decorum, hai, these foreigners? They do whatever they like, hai? What's her religion, Bhai? She must be Christian."

"I haven't asked, Didi."

"You must never cook beef in the house: the landlady forbids it."

Gyanu still doesn't know whether or not Tomás is Ava's boyfriend. It doesn't matter to him. He knows that Ava has divorced her husband: she told him, one evening, that she was doing so. She treated Gyanu as a confidant, talking to him about whatever was on her mind. She's unguarded and open — by character, or perhaps by culture. She's liberated: she's the most liberated person Gyanu has ever known, freer than he's ever been or will ever be. He likes that about her so much.

The train screeches into the station. The doors slide open. The crowd presses in. Gyanu keeps in step with everyone else.

In the train, all the seats are taken, so he holds onto a strap.

The announcement of the stations is like a newly learned mantra: Keele. High Park. Runnymede.

Under his breath, Gyanu murmurs: "Come to me."

He thinks: Ava must be in Canada now. She'll be north of Toronto, with her parents. She's told him where they live, and where they have a vacation home, but the names mean nothing to him. She's going to visit him at Kabob House next week.

He wonders if she's still as fragile as she was when she was in

Kathmandu. Every day after work she talked to him about her project, which was changing rapidly, almost daily, as it came together. "I'll be going back to Butwal a lot. I'm feeling really good about this, Gyanu." On his final day there, Ava came to his room looking particularly buoyant. She was going on a trek soon with Tomás, and she was excited about it. She sat on his bed and told him about their plans: "We'll drive to a place called Syabrubesi — do you know it?"

"I have not gone that side."

"We'll start our trek there — we'll go through a portion of the Tamang Heritage Trail. Have you heard of it?"

He hadn't.

They went to the kitchen. She opened a bottle of wine and poured them both a glass. He put a chicken to roast for their last dinner.

"No Tomás today?" he asked; for Tomás often dropped by.

"He might come later. You know what he's like."

As Gyanu put together a salad, Ava asked him about Dubai: what he was going to do there, what he had done before. He told her about Zafran, and about his old job at Five Spices. He talked about Jairus: what a friend he had been. He had told Ava before about Maleah. He talked about her again:

"We will marry soon."

"Here's to a happy future for you two." Ava poured them more wine. Her face grew flushed, her eyes grew bright. She was in a mood to talk and confide. She told him about her parents in Canada, and her brother and his girlfriend in America. They were expecting a baby. She wanted to know about his family too: she asked about his mother and stepfather.

"What about your real father?" she asked. "Are you still in touch with him?"

"No, I — I do not know his name."

"So does that mean you don't know your caste? How old did you say you were when your mom remarried, four or five, right? Do you remember much?"

"One-two things," he said, adding, "I do not know my background."

"Does that bother you?" she asked.

"It is not my choice."

"But if you had a choice, would you try to find out more, Gyanu?"

She was probably seeking answers to her own life in his.

He said, "I think yes. And you?"

"I guess so too." She said, "For me too, if there were a choice, I guess I'd want to know more — though actually, I'm not sure." She thought about it awhile. "I mean, it obviously matters to me a lot to have a connection to Nepal, but I feel like I'm developing it through work, and through — well. I don't have to connect with my own personal past, do I?" She looked at him. "Can you tell, Gyanu, from looking at me, what caste I was born as?"

With her sharp features, dark skin, and large, almond-shaped eyes, she could be of Newari or Dalit or Madhesi background, or, for that matter, from any number of other communities.

"It is not possible to know," he said.

"There wasn't much in my records," she said. "My name is the only thing I've got from my past." She pronounced it the Nepali way: "Abha."

"It means: when sun comes up in the morning."

"Dawn." She said, "Will you say it, Gyanu? I really like the way you pronounce it."

Ava came up to him and stood by him at the kitchen counter.

When he said her name, she reached out and put her arms around him. Unused to Western-style contact, Gyanu braced instinctively, even though her gesture was entirely chaste. She laid her head on his shoulder, and he put his arms around her uncertainly. She was small, all bones. He felt the softness of her short-cropped hair on his face and smelled her fragrance: a flowery perfume.

She stepped away. "I'm sorry," she said. "I'm not — I really needed that."

"It is all right," he said.

"You've been so good to me, Gyanu."

"It is all right, Ava."

Ava nodded. "It is all right, isn't it?" She smiled a little. "I feel like I've found a brother in you."

The train rushes on. The stations pass by. Jane. Old Mill. Royal York.

"Come to me," Gyanu whispers.

The plane will land soon. In his mind he can see Maleah walking out, as he did, to the waiting officials. He went through the same routine a month ago. He showed the officials his papers. They sent him through long, empty corridors, to the immigration desk. From there, he was sent on to a separate room to process migrants.

That room was sterile and antiseptic, and crowded. The line went all the way to the back. He stood in line for nearly an hour. Some in line were here on express entry, like him. Others had come with their permanent residency status already secured. There were whole families in that room, waiting to begin their new lives.

The train finally pulls into Kipling station and stops.

Gyanu gets off and takes the escalator up to board his usual bus. It's not crowded at this hour. He chooses a seat towards the middle of the bus. A woman at the front of the bus catches his eye. She's standing, though the seats around her are empty. Her hands are on her hips. She's dark skinned and fine boned, like Sapana. Her hair is dark, and pinned back in a braid. She turns, revealing the face of a stranger.

Regret catches Gyanu unawares nowadays. He thinks constantly of Sapana. How is she doing, how will she do? How could he have left her alone?

The low buildings of his neighbourhood roll by as they pass his stop. This neighbourhood holds most of what he's seen so far of Toronto: a wide avenue, two high-rise buildings, a traffic island, a No Frills, a convenience store.

Sapana will do all right. She has to. She will.

Maleah may get through immigration more quickly than he did, he thinks. Her case is simpler: she's coming on a temporary visitor visa. The lawyer will help her obtain permanent residency as a spouse, and for Crisanto as their son. Crisanto is almost eight years old now. They'll bring him from the fishing village as soon as possible. It might take a year, it might take two years, but they will live here as a family.

The bus turns onto the broad highway to the airport. They pass the signs for the terminals.

"Come to me," Gyanu murmurs.

He sees Maleah in church, praying. *Our Father who art in heaven.*

As the airport sweeps into view, Gyanu prays. "Come to me, meri maya, come to me."

A **WOMAN BOARDS** a bus, a plane flies overhead, elsewhere in the world people embark on journeys — in boats, in trains, in cars. Sapana takes a seat by the window and lets the wind fly through her hair. A year has passed, an age has passed. The earth keeps shuddering and shaking. Life will not be tranquil again.

The sun, the moon, the stars move in their orbits. It's night, it's day again, and the night will return. The morning is warm today, the day will be hot. After they pass Bhairahava Bazaar, the bus groans, halts, and starts up again. Is this the border? Sapana jumps off with the bus still at a roll.

Chandra, I'm here.

The other passengers who have disembarked scatter. The crowd parts. Sapana stands on the side of the road. Around her, Sunauli Bazaar is in motion: people move on foot, in cars, buses and vans, on motorcycles and horse-drawn carts. It's hot, the air smells of petrol. There's a check post, and a large gateway made out of concrete: is that the border? Some of the people who got off the bus walk towards it. Others duck into shops, hotels, restaurants. A few catch buses to other parts of the country. Sapana is the only one with nowhere to go.

She's come to the border to see what Chandra saw when she came here with Gyanu-dai a year ago on the way to India. A horse-drawn cart clatters by on the road, the passengers at the back clutching each other for balance. A middle-aged woman sails by on a bicycle, trilling the bell. Sapana has never seen a grown woman riding a bicycle. She stares. The woman's back is straight, her posture is dignified.

She's told Chandra she's coming to the border. They don't talk as frequently as they used to, but every month or so, Sapana still calls Chandra on a mobile phone she bought with money that Gyanu-dai sent. The last time they spoke, Chandra boasted about being able to speak Hindi: "I still mix in a few Nepali words by mistake, and people laugh, but they understand me. I can go to the market by myself now. And you, girl? Did you move into the hostel? What are the girls like?"

"I'm sharing a room with three girls, they're from faraway villages."

"Are you studying hard?"

"There's a lady professor, Urmila-madam, who's kind. She never loses patience: no matter how many questions you ask, she gives you the answer. But the others ... I hate the sir who teaches maths. When I pass out of the Plus Two program, Ava-madam's project might give me a scholarship to go to college." She added, "You can also get a scholarship, Chandra, if you come back."

Chandra just laughed off the suggestion.

That's how Chandra is nowadays. She's evasive, or maybe distracted. Her mind is on other matters. The important thing — Sapana has to remind herself — is that Chandra isn't unhappy. She isn't unhappy, and yet ... How can she be happy in India? Chandra never even talks about coming home any more. All she said, this time, was:

"I hope Ava-madam's project lasts long enough to put little Tara through college."

A minivan careens towards the check post at top speed.

Little Tara is no longer little. She's grown, all of a sudden, in the past year. She's almost as tall as Sapana now. She'll soon catch up with her sisters. Ava-madam's project has a component dedicated to something called capacity enhancement. That component will help girls like little Tara pass out of school, enroll in the Plus Two, and then enter college.

College. Sapana never imagined she would go to college one day. There's a commerce campus in the bazaar, she'll enroll there. Or that's what she thinks right now. She wants to study business, or maybe accounting — she hasn't decided. When she graduates, she'll find a job, or start a business of her own in the bazaar. Or maybe she'll study something else, a subject she doesn't even know about yet.

Namrata has also got a scholarship. She's back in school, studying for the final exams, but her family is looking for a boy. They say she's too old to stay at home much longer — she'll be a spinster if she waits. Ritu is living with her in-laws in the far west. Her husband's apartment in Kathmandu was destroyed in the earthquake, so they moved to his family home after the wedding. She's had a child, a son. She no longer keeps in touch with Sapana or Namrata, but they get news of her from her parents.

Sapana's stomach growls. She didn't eat before the ride, and is hungry. There's a food cart not far from where she got off the bus. She goes up to it and looks at the offerings of rotis, cooked vegetables, samosas, spiced soybeans. A woman in her twenties is minding the cart.

Sapana asks her, "How much are the samosas, Di?"

"You want a piece or a full plate?" the woman asks. Her Nepali is inflected with Maithili.

"One piece, and a cup of tea."

"It'll be twenty-five rupees." The woman pulls out a stool for her to sit on. "Are you going to the other side?"

"No, I'm only going this far."

The samosa is fresh and spicy, and the tea hot. Sapana feels better after eating. She pays the woman and then wanders around, not sure what to do next. Should she catch a bus back home? She doesn't want to, just yet. She stops to look at a clothes shop, just to pass time. All around her are signboards, billboards, hoarding boards. She walks past a row of shops and crosses the road, heading towards the gateway. What kind of threshold did Chandra cross here? What kind of threshold keeps her away now? Sapana sees minivans going through the gateway, and private cars too, and rickshaws. She watches a few people cross over on foot. She knows Chandra went over on foot. The NGO worker and she caught an Indian government bus on the other side.

Beside the gateway, men are loading a lorry with large, heavy sacks of — what? Maybe rice. Sapana watches them work.

Being here makes her feel lonely; but lonely is how she wants to feel: it's honest. She is alone in this world. She stopped seeing Rudra-sir after a few months of meeting surreptitiously at the hotel. Now that she's moved into a hostel in the bazaar, she no longer meets Thulo-ba and Thuli-ma much either. She still goes to the village to tend to the orange trees she's planted on the family fields, but it makes her sad to see the family house: the side wall, which cracked in the earthquake, has never been repaired. All the work Gyanu-dai put into restoring the house was wasted. Sapana won't ever live there again. Her brother certainly won't: he's all the way across the world now. And Chandra won't, either. The house has lost its heart, its soul.

A buffalo ambles up to Sapana. Children chase each other near the check post, squealing and laughing, playing a game of catch. The scent of petrol wafts up from the road. It's unbearably hot. Sapana wipes her brow.

At the check post, a policeman waves a van across the border. Why do so many people go to work in India, Sapana wonders. She'll never do so: there's so much to do in Nepal.

Ava-madam's project is keeping the women's committee members busy. At the start, Ava-madam spent weeks in the village just talking to them. Then she came back with a foreign expert from Kathmandu, a white sir with blue eyes and yellow hair. They organized a meeting in the bazaar, it was held in a small hotel. The expert lectured the members of the women's committee on cooperatives, and asked if they wanted to open one. The members said yes, and so Ava-madam took them all to Kathmandu, to the Department of Cooperatives, to learn more.

Sapana went on that trip. It was a thrill, an adventure — her first time in the nation's capital. They stayed in a five-storeyed hotel, they ate in restaurants, they even went to the Pashupatinath and Swayambhunath temples in their free time. There was some confusion in the women's committee about what kind of cooperative to open. Jethi-didi wanted everyone to plant oranges for an orchard, but Rama-bhauju felt that a dairy would be more profitable. After several debates and a few heated quarrels, the committee voted for oranges, because Jethi-didi already had a buyer, and the market for oranges was good. There'll be other cooperatives in the future; and in time, these cooperatives will form a federation. For now, the committee is concentrating on making the orange cooperative as profitable as possible.

It's a lot of work. There's constant training and retraining, there are scholarships and meetings and study tours. Ava-madam's project is spending so much money in the village, in the bazaar, in Kathmandu: it's astonishing. All the funding for the women's committee comes through the CBO, so Thulo-ba and Jeevan Bhatta also get a cut. They've hired half of Thulo-ba's lackeys as CBO staff. The project pleases Thulo-ba. It pleases everyone. It's a fine project. It's doing good.

Why did you leave, Chandra, when you could have stayed right here and done good?

As Sapana watches on, more and more people cross the check post: some go to India, others come over from there. At one point, there are so many vehicles coming and going, the gateway is jammed. The loneliness inside her to swell up like a bruise, tender and throbbing. Will it ever heal?

She takes a few steps forward. From where she's standing now, the lorry blocks the check post from view. The men are still loading it. The buffalo has ambled up to the front of the lorry. Sapana watches it carry on, through the gateway, to the other side.

She wants to feel what Chandra must have felt last year.

She looks around. No one's really paying attention to anyone else here. She crosses the road and sidles alongside the lorry. She reaches the gateway and her heartbeat quickens. The heat rises with each step she takes. From somewhere comes the sound of a dog barking. A minivan honks.

A man shouts from behind her: "Stop!"

She's almost in India.

She walks on.

And when she crosses through the gateway and steps onto Indian soil, she can feel Chandra: she can feel her presence again.

Here I am, Chandra.

"I told you to stop!" The man who was shouting comes running up behind her. He's a policeman. He's short. He's old. His face is contorted with the effort of catching up to her. "Didn't you hear? I've been telling you to stop!"

Sapana looks at him coolly. "Is there a problem, Police-dai?"

"You can't just go over, you have to show your papers at the post!" His voice is shrill.

"This is as far as I'm going," she says.

"You can't even do that!"

It's strange how panicky he is, though he's the authority. Sapana feels like panicking him some more.

She says, "I think I'll stay here awhile, Dai."

He glares at her, exasperated. Then he whines: "It's for your own protection, Bahini."

Her protection? Sapana is amused. "Do you know how many of us are already in India, Dai? Do you know how many of us go there, and never return? Don't worry about my protection," she says. "Go back to your check post. I'll stay here as long as I like."

Now the policeman looks upset, as though having failed to reason with her, he's failed as a man. "Don't go any further," he says. "I'll get in trouble. As will you — you'll get in trouble! It's the law!"

Sapana turns away with a small laugh.

The India side of the border isn't much different from the Nepal side. There are shops for food, clothes, pots and pans, electronics. It feels busier, though: more charged and energetic, somehow. Chandra lives amid this charge, this energy, Sapana thinks. Chandra is part of this energy now.

Something about the energy reminds Sapana of Kathmandu. There was a vibrancy to the capital city, a vibrancy that Gyanu-dai had been part of early on in his life, after leaving the village for the first time. Sapana thought about her brother a lot when she was in Kathmandu. For the duration of her visit to the capital, she felt as though she, too, were part of the vibrancy of his life.

And now, standing on Indian soil, she feels herself part of the big world, part of its charge and energy, part of the light that swirls around and the force that brings together constellations – of people, objects, circumstances – and draws them apart, making everything change, always change. Entire days pass, nowadays, without her thinking about Ba and Ma. Everything changes. She's changing too. Just as the world is Gyanu-dai's and Chandra's, it's hers too. Her life isn't small; she swirls with the whole big world.

"Come back now," the policeman whines. "It's been a hard day. You're only making it harder."

Sapana turns to him, and sees a tired man with a tired job on a tired day in a tired old world.

"I haven't got all day," he pleads.

It's childish to stand around daydreaming like this, she thinks, when she has her own life to tend to. She'll focus on that from now on: she'll think about herself, and about her own life, because you can't progress if you're always thinking about others. You must harden your heart and be selfish, Sapana thinks. Chandra has done so, Gyanu-dai has done so. She, too, will harden her heart and be selfish from now on.

She follows the policeman back across the border.

WITH A NOD to the dock manager, Ned, Ava starts the engine to the old skiff. She steers out of the dock, gliding cautiously through the marina as she passes the narrow outlet past Gord Shaw's sailboat. A red sloop at the end of the dock looks like it hasn't been out all year. Most of the other boats look well used. The Leworskis are on their weekender, unfurling the mast. "Gorgeous day!" they call out as Ava glides by.

"Isn't it?"

"The best we've had all year!"

Beyond the marina, the bay is calm, but out on the big water, the wind whips up in short, sudden gusts, rippling up cats' paws. The gnarled white pines of Franklin Island come into view as Ava rounds the bay. There's a kayak on a whaleback boulder buffeting the island. A couple is having lunch there. They watch her go by.

She's been alone at the cottage for six days. It's the first time all year that she's had a chance to be alone.

"Are you sure you want to be by yourself, honey?" Mom asked in Overwood on the way up. "Now, do you have everything you need? Don't forget, the Healies sell fresh perch from their house, and they might have frozen pickerel in stock. Oh, I really hope the Fortins aren't at their cottage. Did I tell you, they added another room, out on the western side? You can't even call it a cottage any more, it's a monster house."

"See you in a week, Mom."

"We'll bring Aunt Edie's peach pie when we come!"

A sailboat overtakes Ava as she steers west from Franklin. She watches it zipping along, propelled by the wind: soon, it's far ahead of her, a distant speck on the horizon. On the other side of the island, near the rental cottages, is a wind shadow. She steers easily along a calm, glassy stretch. This is her last day to herself. Mom and Dad will arrive in the late afternoon, with

Luke and Revolution Mary and Baby Jesus: BJ. The family will spend a week together at the cottage. Mom will get everyone to back her group that's sponsoring Syrian refugees. Dad will fish. Luke and Revolution Mary will teach BJ to swim. Dad has said that if the weather's good, he'll take Ava out on the sailboat past the outer islands.

After steering through a stretch of open water, Ava comes up to the cottage, Mom's old handmade STOP THE DROP! sign, from when the waterline was low, draped over the exposed granite. She cuts the engine and glides into the dock, avoiding the sharp rocks near the shore. She hops off, ties the boat, takes out the perch she's bought from Jane Healie.

The rest of the day follows the unhurried routine of the previous days. By noon, Ava is at the far side of the island, which is hidden from sight from the Fortins' cottage. She tosses off her clothes, and from the granite rock that juts out above the water, dives into the water, plunging into the rich blue-black depths, into life itself.

She wishes she could do this in Nepal too. How she's missed this. Georgian Bay unlocks her earliest memories of joy. Ava plunges down deep and comes up to the surface, loving the heaviness of her body in the fresh water.

From there she swims out to her favourite spot in the world, a whale rock that rises out of the lake, from where she can look out at the far end of Georgian Bay. She and Luke used to spend entire days on this rock as kids. She lies down on its hard surface, taking warmth from its sunbaked curves. The wind prickles her skin, raising goosebumps that the heat of the sun eases away.

This isn't just life itself; it is, specifically, her life, her alternative life: a life not dissimilar from her old one, but also utterly different.

After they filed for divorce, Gavin didn't communicate with her at all — till the earthquake struck. He got in touch to see if she was all right, and they've stayed in touch since, remaining amicable through all of the legal proceedings. A month ago, he emailed again, announcing that he was moving to a condo near Wychwood. He got a promotion at the bank, he wrote. *A corner office!* He added: *I'm doing okay, Ava. I didn't think it would be possible, but I'm okay.*

In Overwood, when Ava asked about Leez Anne Williker, Mom was uncharacteristically discreet. "An equity sales director — she's a bit, well, she's not you, honey, but it's good to see Gavin happy."

Gavin had written: *Your parents said you'll be here this summer. Let's meet if you have time.*

Maybe. Ava skipped Toronto on the way up, taking a rental straight up from Pearson to Overwood, but on the way back she has booked two nights at the Gladstone. Lester Prease and his wife Ruth have invited her for dinner one evening. And some of her colleagues at the firm are clamouring for a night out, though Ava also wants to go to Kabob House — perhaps with Anthony?

Anthony wrote a few days ago, saying he would fly up if she was free: *A second date might be in order, what do you think?* Anthony Watson.

I think it's a very fine idea, she wrote back. They've arranged to meet up in Toronto.

After sunning herself thoroughly, Ava gets up and plunges back into the water. There's clarity to every sensation. She can't remember, anymore, the fog she used to live in. She tumbles in the water, goes down to the depths, comes up towards the light, feels a tickle against her thigh: a hydrilla oscillating in the currents. She takes a breath and plunges back in, seeking out that plant, seeking out life. For this is life: to be here in fresh water under the sun, on a perfect summer's day. She's seen, in Nepal, how fragile life can be. It's all we have, it's all she has. A chance to be fully alive.

At mid-afternoon, she goes in for a lunch of smoked fish, then sits on the porch and reads Herman Banke's report, "Resilience: Vulnerability Index Nepal." Herman is a completely changed man. He returned from the ten-day meditation retreat at peace with the world, to everyone's surprise, including his own. And after the earthquake, he developed a new respect for his project on resilience: "The socially excluded are intensely vulnerable; only if we increase their resilience can we prevent a natural disaster from turning into a full-blown social-political-humanitarian disaster, Ava." Since then, he has persuaded IDAF headquarters to upgrade his project into a two-year program. With the promulgation of the new constitution, the peacebuilding program came to an end, and Jared Lukkinson left IDAF. Herman's resilience program is so well funded now that he's having trouble with disbursement. In their last meeting, he pleaded with Ava: "Women are so vulnerable in Nepal, the women's empowerment program must focus on increasing women's resilience, it's the only way, you have to help me, Ava."

Ava is open to it. She still wonders, some days, if there's something wrong at IDAF, especially when Vishwa behaves badly: he's struck up an antagonism with her, for some reason. But for the most part, Ava feels good about what she's getting done in Nepal.

And the earthquake changed her profoundly.

Ava was in the garden on the day the earth roared. Thrown from her chair, she couldn't understand, at first, what was happening. The trees were swaying madly above her, and she scrambled, on all fours, to a clearing. Even the sky seemed to judder and jolt. When she looked out at the city, she saw dust rising from the fallen houses. She remembers screaming.

The house suffered minor damage — a few cracks, nothing structural — but the servants' quarters were reduced to a heap of broken bricks. Harihar escaped just in time to avoid injury. Mrs. Thapa's house, next door, lost an entire front room. Ava offered Mrs. Thapa her spare rooms, but her family chose to remain in their house with the front room gaping open. Luna's family lost their rented apartment. In the first few days, she and her family — a husband and three children — lived with Harihar in a tent that they fashioned out of two pieces of tarpaulin from Ava's earthquake kit. Ava eventually moved Luna's family into the downstairs guest room. Harihar remained, out of a sense of duty — or perhaps under Mrs. Thapa's orders — in the tent. He'll move into the servants' quarters when it's rebuilt in the autumn.

Tomás's apartment was also deemed unsafe after the quake: half of the building, a late addition to the main structure, cracked apart. He moved in with Ava, and they're living together in an easy, platonic arrangement. Tomás's vow of celibacy remains unbroken. The earthquake changed him too; he passed on the job offer in Myanmar and is working in the earthquake-affected districts of Nepal. One of the areas he works in is Langtang, where he and Ava were trekking two weeks before the quake.

Ava thinks about Langtang often, and wonders how the survivors are coping. News of the area reached her late, days after the earthquake. The entire village was flattened by snow, ice sheets, loose rocks, and boulders that came crashing off the surrounding mountains. More than three hundred people – residents, lodge owners, porters, trekkers – died. The bodies were recovered slowly, over months, as the snow and ice melted. Some were never found. The village hasn't been rebuilt yet. There are plans to do so, plans that Tomás follows closely. He tells Ava about them. He's planning to return there soon. He's asked her to come too.

Ava isn't sure. For her, Langtang holds the same kind of private confusion that the orphanage does. More than a year has passed, yet the trek is still vivid, like an image etched permanently into her mind. She can't seem to shake it, she can't seem to lessen her confusion about how safe, how privileged, she is in this hard, jagged world. She's lucky – she's so very lucky – and this haunts her, because she knows that in truth, the jagged world claims her.

Ava returns to the far side of the island later in the afternoon. There's a blueberry patch beside the whale rock. She and Luke can pick them this evening, she thinks: they can make pancakes for breakfast tomorrow.

From the granite rock she dives into the water, then comes up and floats on her back. There are a few plump cumulous clouds in the sky. They form and break apart and form again at a leisurely pace. A kite, or perhaps an osprey, circles overhead. A water plane glides by. The sun dips behind a cloud and when it reappears, it dazzles.

She feels as high – or free and light in the body – as she did on the Langtang trek. She set out on that trek overburdened with work and numb from the decision to divorce. She and Tomás and two of his friends, a British expat Len and his Nepali boyfriend Bibek, were being led by a young guide named Kiran Magar.

On the first day, they took a battered old Jeep out of Kathmandu, to a road that led through high, rocky hills. The road was terrifyingly steep. At one point they had to wait for a digger to clear away a rock fall. There was a dizzying precipice on one side, with a view of high hills, terraced fields and isolated, scrabbly villages. Towards the end of the drive, they also saw snow peaks, but they vanished behind the hills as they descended into a narrow valley, to the trailhead.

They began to walk the next morning, and almost immediately, Ava's burdens began to fall away. There was something clarifying about the high-altitude air. Or perhaps it was something about walking. An unfamiliar serenity came over Ava. There was time and space enough, while walking through a narrow river gorge, to churn up emotions and to let them settle back down again. The land was vast, and everything else took its rightful place in that vastness.

By the third day, they were up at the base of the snow peaks they had seen on the drive, having meandered through several small villages perched high on the hills. There were pine forests along the trail, and rhododendron trees. A cool wind whispered through the trees. The land looked intimate but was unending. It kept unfolding into new canyons and gorges and hills, new peaks kept appearing out of nowhere. Snow glittered on the Himalayas, and every small sensation – the cawing of crows, the heat of the sun – was electrifying.

Even Tomás relaxed in the mountains. Late in the afternoon, the group would stop at a lodge for lunch, and in the evenings they would chat over dal-bhat and beer, exchanging thoughts, quips, observations from the day. In the morning they had breakfast together, but outside of meals, they were on their own for most of the day.

By the time they reached Langtang village, they were all fit and tired and exuberant. They avoided the larger lodges there, and stayed in a cozy stone house with a big, blazing fireplace. The sisters who ran the lodge told them that there was a prayer going on at a Buddhist monastery. Kiran took them to the monastery in the evening. They spent the night listening to monks chanting, beating drums, blowing trumpets, the sounds so thunderous they vibrated through the body.

That day the walk had been gruelling, and Ava fell asleep as soon as they returned to the lodge. The next morning, she awoke to a blinding white light at the window. She stumbled over and opened the curtains to see the Himalayas looming directly above her.

They were right there, within reach: all that stone, snow, light. Ava had never been spiritual — Mom and Dad had gone through a Buddhist phase, but she and Luke had always been secular — but the sight filled her with a wonder that bordered on reverence.

What a country this was.

That morning they walked on to the final village, Kyanjin Gompa, and stayed there two nights. On the second morning, after breakfast, they climbed a ridge that offered a panorama of the entire range of the Langtang Himalayas.

On the way down from the ridge, Ava came across four children bundled up in sweaters and jackets, their faces ruddy with sun. They shouted "Namaste," and Ava said namaste back, and they scampered alongside her on the narrow trail.

The eldest, a girl, asked her, "Where from?"

"Canada," Ava said. "Where are you from?"

"Nepal!" The girl giggled.

"What are your names?" Ava asked.

All of them cried out at the same time: "Pema!" "Shambhu!" "Chhakke!" "Dorje!"

Then the girl pointed at Ava and asked, "Name?"

"Ava."

"Abha!"

The others echoed her: "Abha!" "Abha!" "Abha!" Then they turned off and ran down a side trail, yelling, "Bye-bye-bye-bye-bye!"

Floating on her back in the water, Ava wonders whether the children survived the earthquake. Ava has often thought about them, measuring the value of their lives, and the value of her life, and thinking: she could have been one of them, but isn't.

She can understand, empathize, feel for or even feel like them, but she isn't one of those children at all.

She's here. She's lucky. She's safe.

She's back on the whale rock, sunning herself after a swim, when she hears the drone of an engine. She turns around and sees her parents' powerboat coursing up to the STOP THE DROP! sign. Mom's wearing an enormous pink hat, waving madly with both hands: "Darling! Ava dear! Honey!" Dad's at the steering wheel. Beside him, Revolution Mary is bundled up in a sweater, jacket, and toque. Luke has little BJ strapped into a carrier on his chest.

"Auntie Ava!" Luke lifts the baby's hand and makes him wave. "Say hello to Baby Jesus!"

"BJ, oh, my God, oh my God!" Ava cries. She scrambles to her feet, waving in excitement at seeing the newest, sweetest member of her family. "My little nephew!" she cries. "Mom, Dad, everyone! Look at how adorable he is! Oh, little BJ! I'm your Auntie Ava! Wait for me, I'll be right there! I'll be right there, wait for me!"

She dives head first into the lake to swim out to her family.

ACKNOWLEDGEMENTS

I am grateful to Kelsey Attard, Naomi Lewis, and the entire team at Freehand Books for their support through the editing and publishing of the Canadian edition of this novel. Thank you also to my first publisher, Aleph Book Company, and editor Ravi Singh, who commissioned the novel on spec. I was fortunate to have received close readings by Johanna Stoberock, Lesley Grant, Barbara Weyermann, and Wayne, Judith and Rachel Amtzis on early drafts. My deep thanks, too, to Carolyn Forde and the Westwood Creative Artists family for being calm and steady when I've been neither.

This is my first novel after moving from Kathmandu to Toronto. I couldn't have written it, or indeed continued to write at all, without the support of some key Canadian institutions. Thank you to the Canada Council for the Arts for a grant and for the Joseph S. Stauffer Prize. Thank you also to the Toronto Arts Council for a grant. I completed the first draft of this novel as a Writers' Trust Writer-in-Residence at Berton House. My time in Dawson City deepened my feel for Canada, and for this I am indebted to the Writers' Trust, and also to Dawsonites Karen Dubois, Eldo Enns, Greg and Shelley Hakonson, Dan and Laurie Sokolowski, Lulu Keating, Glenda Bolt, Dan Davidson, Kathy Webster, and Chere Wilson. I also learned much from the Dänojà Zho Cultural Centre there. In Toronto, Linda Robinson was terrifically generous in sharing the world of corporate law with me. I am also thankful to Diane Goodman, Allan Leibel, Natalie Munroe, and Mary Abbott for giving me a glimpse into Bay Street. The bulk of my research on the aid industry took place while I worked in it, sporadically and mostly peripherally, in Nepal. My sense of microfinancing was gleaned as a researcher for *Unequal Citizens: Gender, Caste and Ethnic Exclusion in Nepal* for the far-sighted Lynn Bennett. I am grateful to Jasmine Rajbhandary for offering me insight into the aid industry's more powerful and opaque echelons. In this novel I've mentioned some of the books that have influenced my thinking on the aid industry, though this novel isn't, of course, a polemic on the subject. The term PEON, or 'Permanent Establishment of Nepal,' was coined by one of Nepal's clearest thinkers, CK Lal. One need only read national newspapers to learn of the risks that Nepal's migrant workers face in the Gulf. *Registan Diary* by Devendra Bhattarai has been particularly educative for me, as have Kesang Tseten's films *The Desert Eats Us, Saving Dolma* and *In Search of the Riyal.* I've found Barbara Weyermann's views on the connections and divergences between migration and the trafficking of women very clarifying. On the earthquake of April 2015: I owe the Nepali community in Toronto, and especially Asha Toronto, a debt for supporting long-distance activism and critical engagement after the earthquake. Those involved in Rasuwa Relief and the Langtang Management and Reconstruction Committee have set an example of post-disaster relief and reconstruction. I've learned much from their work, and from the work done by other informal and non-government organizations in Nepal. Thank you to Farid Alvie and Elizabet Rhoden for allowing me to gain a first-hand sense of the UAE at the Sharjah Book Fair. The art installation I've described in the novel is *Bhumi: Where Do I Stand?* by Ashmina Ranjit. On the subject of adoption, I found *The Language of Blood* by Jane Jeong Trenka and *Lucky Girl* by Mei-Ling Hopgood very helpful. The rape at the orphanage is based on real events: a report can be found in *Nepali Times,* Issue #714, 4–10 July, 2014.

Finally, thank you to Daniel Lak for giving me Toronto and Georgian Bay; to my parents Bhekh Bahadur and Rita Thapa for giving me the world; to my siblings Bhaskar Thapa and Tejshree Thapa for blazing the trails that I, slacker youngest, follow; to Gord and Doreen Lak, Frank Thorneycroft, Sumira Thapa, Katie Parker-Lak, Brent Langille, Robert Parker-Lak, Barun Thapa, Maya Thapa Úŕaoláin, Sidhant Thapa, Alexandra Dierdre Parker-Lak Langille, and my faraway godson William Eric Hudson Schonveld and his sister Maya; and to friends far and near and also virtual. Ben Schonveld will recognize the stupor of sitting through Nepali-language meetings as an English speaker. Parag Shrestha will recognize the words "artificial intelligence," uttered in a conversation about Nepal in Parkdale. Many others will, I hope, see our times reflected in these pages. This novel came together through our interconnections, for which I am extremely grateful.

MANJUSHREE THAPA was born in Kathmandu and raised in Nepal, Canada, and the United States. She has written several books of fiction and non-fiction, and she has translated Nepali literature into English. Her essays have appeared in the *New York Times,* the *London Review of Books, Newsweek,* and the *Globe and Mail. All of Us in Our Own Lives* is the first novel she wrote after moving to Toronto. She is working on a new novel about citizenship.